Blades of
Desire

J.M. Jackie

— · —

Disclaimer

This work of fiction is a product of the author's imagination and is not based on real events, individuals, or organizations. Any resemblance to actual events or persons, living or deceased, is purely coincidental.

The views and opinions expressed within this book are those of the fictional characters and do not reflect the beliefs or values of the author. The author does not endorse or condone any of the actions, behaviors, or ideologies depicted in this work.

Readers are encouraged to approach this book with an open mind and a critical perspective. It is important to remember that the events portrayed are entirely fictional and should not be taken as representative of reality.

This book may contain mature themes, including but not limited to violence, adult language, and explicit content. Reader discretion is advised, and this book is intended for adult audiences.

The author is committed to respecting the rights and privacy of all individuals and organizations. Any unintentional use of copyrighted material is purely coincidental and will be rectified upon notification.

Thank you for choosing to read this work of fiction. Your support is greatly appreciated, and the author hopes you enjoy the story.

CONTENTS

1

BITTER ICE

CLEVELAND, OHIO 2011

Shavings of mist passed over the hills of ice as I stared out at the endless stretch of farmland in our backyard. Voices from the TV flittered to my ears, engulfing me in a familiar rush of adrenaline for the game that was about to start. *They aren't here.* My nails dug into the sofa as I checked the door for the fifteenth time.

"Ladies and gentlemen, tonight we have a clash of titans! The New York Rangers, with their storied history, will battle it out against the Boston Bruins, known for their physical style of play. It's going to be a showdown for the ages!" The commentator's voice filled the room, causing the anxiety in my chest to grow. Maybe they went drinking at a pub. Which I heard they did as a tradition every year. It seemed unlikely with the skies darkening. *Where are they? They're missing everything.* I resisted the urge to cross my arms and pout, and kept my eyes trained out the window, listening for the crack of the door and Cricket's familiar shout.

Well, not for Cricket. *For him.*

It was an itch beneath my skin, an insatiable longing to lay eyes on him. Swallowing around the blockage in my throat, I played with the threading on my old hockey Boston Bruin's jersey, not caring that it had been threadbare thin. Cricket knew what tonight meant to me, and he'd promised they'd be back soon.

My dad ruffled my hair as he passed, laughing when I swatted his arm away.

"They'll be here, buddy. Just calm down," his deep voice rumbled as he sat down on the sofa chair beside me. His long limbs splayed out in front of him as his bottle of beer fizzled when he screwed open the top.

"Still no Cricket?" my mom asked, passing me a bucket of caramel glazed popcorn, my favorite. I couldn't stomach it. She laughed when I didn't take it, brushing the flop of black hair away from my eyes before sitting down next to Dad. Her silk blouse shimmered in the lamplight, and my father curled a large arm around her shoulders, pulling her close.

I turned back to the window, a throb working low in my temple before spreading toward my eyes. Biting into my lip, I blinked back tears, knowing it was useless. *Cricket wasn't coming.*

And if Cricket didn't come, that meant *he* wouldn't come either. *What the hell was wrong with me?* Ever since that night in the bathroom, he was all I could think about. The hot press of his lips on mine while Cricket got our gear ready for a hockey game. The whole thing had happened in seconds. One minute I was tying the laces to my skates; the next I was peering up into expressive gray eyes, vast and bottomless like a stormy sea.

Grayson. A wry smile tugged at the corner of his lips, before he leaned down and pressed his cool lips to mine like it was the most natural thing in the world. Like I wasn't his best friend's brother, little brother. Then he walked out. Leaving me feeling like a huge anvil being dragged across the vault of heaven against its will, my body hissing and buzzing in all the right places, like I'd touched live-wire. It was my first kiss with a man, and I hadn't known it could feel so right.

Cricket and Grayson went to the University of Michigan. Both of them had full ride scholarships because of their talent on the ice, and I couldn't wait to join them next year. To join him. Grayson had come into my world like a tornado. My brother had brought him home one Christmas, and he never left. Every holiday he would come visit, almost as if he was our new adopted puppy. I didn't understand why. Nobody really did. Grayson was tight-lipped about those things. But he came, filling the space with his warmth and endless laughter. My brother was happier when Grayson was around.

So was I. Even if my happiness meant something different.

"The Rangers have been on a roll," one commentator chimed in. "Their offense, led by Panarin, has been red hot, and with a goaltender like Shesterkin between the pipes, they're a force to be reckoned with."

"But don't count out the Bruins just yet. They may not have the same recent championships, but their physicality and depth make them a formidable opponent. And when Rask is on his game, their defense is rock solid," the other commentator added.

My anxiety hammered like a relentless drumbeat, a fear of the unknown clouding my thoughts. It was about to start and they still weren't here. Tears stung my eyes, and I was about to flee the room when I heard the door creak open, and Duke started barking like mad.

"I'm home!" Cricket called from the entrance, and my heart leaped. I straightened, smoothing out the wrinkled jersey, a smile making my lips twitch. Duke jumped up, slobbering all over Cricket as he laughed and shrugged off his winter jacket, his face flushed from the cold. "Hey there, buddy. Miss me? I bet you did!" He kissed Duke's snout, the rottweiler's tail going wild with excitement.

"Don't get him riled up!" my dad called from his spot on the couch, but his eyes never left the TV. Running a hand through his curly black hair, Dad grabbed another beer, shrugging off the sharp look my mom gave him. "What? It's a celebration?"

"Yeah, whatever," my mom rolled her pale blue eyes, before giving me an encouraging nod. They both knew about my helpless crush on Grayson, and my face heated when another face peered past the doorway.

"Afternoon, Mr. and Mrs. Taylor. Sorry, we're late. I ran into some car trouble." Grayson's baritone voice caused shivers to erupt on my skin. He shrugged off his jacket, his shirt pulling taut against the expanse of firm muscles. I thought I'd faint when his eyes landed on mine.

A storm brewed within them, pinning me in their depths. "Jayden. Good to see you."

My tongue stuck to the roof of my mouth. I made an odd squeaking sound that caused Grayson to laugh and Cricket to stare at me with disgust. *Damn, why was I such a loser when it came to him?*

"Sup, bro." Cricket strode over to me, and I was so distracted by Grayson that I missed the twinkle of mischief in his eyes. Grabbing my head in his hand, his fingers curled into a gentle yet firm grip. I flailed, cursing that he'd gotten the drop on me before he rubbed his knuckles against the top of my head. "Nuggie!" he shouted.

I shoved him off, feeling like my face was redder than a tomato. "You're such a child!"

"So?" He nudged me over, stealing my seat near the armrest so that I was stuck in the middle, forced to make space for his six-foot-one frame. Cricket winked at me, his eyes shining like dancing evergreens. "Grayson!" he shouted, calling his friend over. "I saved you a seat right here," he said, patting the other side of me.

Fuck, Cricket. After this, I was going to kill him and hide his dead body underneath my bed. Could he make my crush any more obvious? Grayson handed my mom a single yellow flower—it was an inside joke I never bothered to look into—and then took a seat, his muscular thigh brushing up against mine.

"I like your jersey," he said, his voice vibrating next to my ear. The spicy peppermint of his breath filled my nostrils, along with the scent of soap and clean aftershave. Brown hair shrouded Grayson's eyes, and he tucked a few loose strands behind his ears.

"Thanks," I replied, leaving out the fact that I'd owned it since I was nine and refused to let my mother throw it out. "Did you guys really have car trouble?"

Grayson laughed. "Nah, your brother ate some bad burritos, so we had to stop like ten times."

"Damn," I chuckled, turning to see Cricket shift in his seat, his eyes glued to the TV. "Well, thanks for not sharing that."

"Oh, you're welcome. I'd rather not relive it."

"Will you pussies shut up?" Cricket elbowed me. "The game is about to start."

I perked up, leaning forward. This was my favorite time of the season, and I knew my team would pull through. My mom passed the popcorn over and I handed some to Grayson. Our fingers touched, grazing the large bowl. Those gray eyes snapped to mine holding a quiet intensity, like the hushed calm before a storm. I was desperate to fall into them.

Grayson. I swallowed hard and tore my gaze away.

Yet, I felt his eyes linger, like a blade pressed against my flesh.

***

"Fuck!" Cricked cursed several hours later, poised on the edge of the couch, leaning on his knees with his forearms. "What the hell was that?"

"Language!" Mom admonished, but she looked ticked as well.

The game had reached its climax, and the tension in the room was palpable. The score was tied, and the final minutes of the third period were ticking away. My heart raced as we watched the Bruins and Rangers battle it out on the ice. *Fuck, they need to win.*

"Look at McDavid go!" I yelled, my voice cracking as the player darted across the ice.

Cricket scoffed. "That's nothing! Check out Ovechkin's slapshot. It's like a cannon!"

"And Lundqvist's saves? They're like he's got a force field around the net!" Grayson chimed in, heat from his leg bleeding through the fabric of his blue jeans against mine.

As the clock wound down, the Bruins launched a furious offensive. My heart was in my throat as they passed the puck, weaving through the Rangers' defense.

"Come on, Bruins! We need that snipe!" I shouted, the pressure mounting. Then the Bruins scored. "Fuck yeah!" I leaped off my seat, dancing on the spot.

"Damn straight! Time to celly!" Cricket slapped my head and then dropped to the floor and started throwing pretend punches in an imaginary fight. His moves were as comical as they were impressive.

"You're such a loser!" I laughed along with my parents.

Grayson joined in, breaking into his own celebration dance as the game continued in overtime. He and Cricket yanked me into a strange dance that seemed to have no rhyme or flow, and then Cricket and Grayson took things up a notch and started twerking and hip-thrust-ing, their dance moves becoming more outrageous by the second. I was laughing so hard that I started snorting like a pig, tears streaming down my face. It was a full-blown belly laugh, and I couldn't catch my breath.

"I guess that's what they're teaching in college these days," Dad mumbled, shaking his head. "All right, enough before you give Duke nightmares."

"I second that," Mom said, but she laughed when Cricket dragged her in and then the TV was turned off and Michael Jackon's voice was booming through the speakers. The smooth grooves of "PYT (Pretty Young Thing)" filled the room.

"I want to love you!" Grayson screamed, sounding horrible and off key.

"PTY! Pretty Young thing!" Cricket finished, sounding like a screeching banshee.

My parents joined the fun, caught up in the infectious energy. They moved to the beat with impressive dance moves of their own, and I couldn't help but grin from ear to ear. It was clear where I got my love for music and dance.

Grayson grabbed my hand and spun me on the spot, his smile splitting his face. I laughed until I cried, and then we took our cue from MJ himself, pulling off our best moonwalks, spins, and shoulder shimmies. It didn't matter that our moves weren't quite up to par with the King of Pop; we were having an absolute blast.

In that unforgettable moment, I realized that, sometimes, the best celebrations were the ones that caught you by surprise. And as the music played on and our dance party continued, I couldn't have asked for a better way to celebrate the Bruins' victory or to spend time with my incredible family.

***

I SLIPPED INTO MY bedroom, eager to escape the lingering warmth of the living room where Grayson had just danced with me. Well, not exactly with me, but he had held me close as we moved to the rhythm of the music. The memory sent a flush rising to my cheeks, and I needed a moment to collect my thoughts and stop my dick from standing to full attention.

Fuck, I had it bad. Rummaging through my drawer, I finally found what I was looking for—a well-worn Star Trek book. Clutching it to my chest, I tried to slow my breathing and calm my racing heart.

To boldly go where no one has gone before...

I let the words wash over me, and try to get lost in the memories of my favorite book and TV show and not think about how Grayson's touch had left a lasting impression. How it was both exhilarating and overwhelming. Warmth spread like liquid gold beneath my skin, and I didn't dare go back down there until the thrumming in my pulse subsided.

Posters adorned the walls of my room, creating a colorful collage of my passions. Some depicted iconic Star Trek scenes and characters, capturing the essence of exploration and adventure. Others celebrated my beloved Boston Bruins, showcasing their fierce determination on the ice.

As I lost myself in the vibrant posters, a shout from downstairs and the sound of the front door opening and slamming reached my ears. I couldn't help but wonder what they were up to.

After the game, Mom usually enjoyed cooking dinner, and then we'd head out to the backyard hockey rink for a friendly match. It had become a cherished routine, especially since Cricket had started attending university last year. *I couldn't wait to join them on the ice.* Not that I would enjoy being away from the farm, but the city life always drew me in.

I stroked the worn spine of the book, recalling when I came out to my parents last year. Cricket already knew, but my dad and mom could be scary when they wanted to be. Dad had looked at me for several long moments and said, "I know, pass the potatoes." And that was it. Mom gave me a reassuring smile, and my heart had burst. My parents knew and didn't care, and it was way more than most kids could ask for.

A knock on my bedroom door snapped me out of my daydreaming, and I turned my attention to the present moment.

Grayson leaned against the door jamb, his chestnut curls falling in a disheveled cascade like the fallen leaves of autumn, covering his brow and framing his face. A mischievous smile graced his heart-shaped lips as he sauntered into the room, his steps exuding an effortless confidence.

My breath caught in my throat as I stared at him. He was a sight to behold—lean and muscular, with broad shoulders that hinted at his athletic prowess. He slinked onto the bed beside me, and there was an electric tension in the air. I tried to find my voice, but my thoughts were a jumbled mess. Grayson's presence was both captivating and unnerving, and I couldn't help but wonder what had brought him to my room.

"Star Trek?" He laughed, but it wasn't cruel. "Why?"

I shrugged. "Why not? It's a brilliant show and epic novel."

Grayson's mouth twitched. "Logic is the beginning of wisdom, not the end."

My eyes widened as he quoted Spock. "Do you—"

"Nah," he said, leaning his palms flat against the comforter. "My aunt used to force us to watch it and that line stuck with me. Besides, Leonard Nimoy was a total babe."

"Fuck off," I said, shoving his arm.

"What? I'm serious. Those pointy ears and stern expressions got me harder than a rocket launcher."

"Nah, for me it was always Captain Kirk."

Grayson made a disgusted noise in his throat, and I laughed.

"Come on, you've got to admit Captain Kirk was the heartthrob of the Enterprise. Those dramatic pauses and cheesy pickup lines? Pure gold!"

Grayson laughed, shaking his head. "Right, but let's not forget the fashion choices of the crew. Those boldly colored uniforms? Fashion-forward or just plain ridiculous?"

"Hey, it takes serious confidence to rock a mustard-yellow jumpsuit on a spaceship."

Grayson leaned in closer, his minty breath washing over my cheek. "And Spock's logic? Sometimes it felt like he was just trying to one-up Captain Kirk with his deadpan deliveries."

I chuckled. "True, true. And don't even get me started on the 'red shirt curse'. If you were wearing red, you were asking to be sacrificed to some alien creature."

We both burst into laughter, but the air seemed to crackle. Grayson didn't pull away, and his eyes flickered down to my lips. "Do you think your brother will kill me if I kiss you again?"

This was it. Blood roared in my ears, and heat seared my cheeks. "No, but I will if you don't—"

Lips brushed against mine, like a morning dew. My breath caught as he pressed in harder, forcing me flat on the bed. Grayson was a solid wall of muscle, and I clung to his wide shoulders, hoping against hope to be kept grounded. Nerves made me stiff. I didn't know what I was supposed to be doing.

This was my second kiss. Ever.

I lost myself to the sparks of pleasure that vaulted through me, like branches of lightning that lit up the night sky. Golden ore streaks flashed across my vision, and I could barely hear over the thunderclaps of my heart and the fizzing sound of electricity in the air.

2

— • —

PAINFUL PUCK DROP

JAYDEN TAYLOR

He swiped his tongue against my lower lip and then puffed a laugh, pulling away. "Relax."

"I—I don't know what to do." I felt shame crawl over my skin, but Grayson didn't care. He pecked my lips, slow and sweet. His cedarwood aftershave wafted toward me, enveloping my senses and reminding me of the times in summer when we ate under the shadowy groves on my family's farm.

His large hands mapped out the planes of my skin, brushing beneath the folds and pulling up my shirt to expose my taut stomach.

"Don't think. Just feel." It was so damn cliched, but I listened, allowing my body to go loose and boneless beneath his skilled hands.

"Wait," I said, breathless. "My parents—Cricket—"

"They went to the store," Grayson replied, nuzzling against my neck. "They'll be gone for a while, so the only person to put on a show for is Duke, and I doubt he's the voyeur type."

I laughed, but Grayson swallowed it, stealing the noise from my throat with a bruising, impatient kiss. His hands slid over my chest and arms, and soon he slotted between my legs, our cocks rubbing together. I gave myself to the temptation of Grayson's sinful lips, arching my back and clinging to him with all my might. Lightning flared and contorted in forks of gold behind my eyelids.

Grayson took me apart, inch by inch, leaving no part of me undiscovered. Touching the waistband of my jeans, he paused, and I peeled open my eyes, breathing hard. Gray eyes like the sky met mine. Something stirred them into a frenzy, with pockets of ash and black clouds colliding.

"I want to suck you."

I thought I'd die right there and then. "O-Okay."

Grayson's mouth curled at the edges and soon he was working his way down my body, taking the waistband of my jeans and opening them. I stared at the ceiling, trying to comprehend that this was really happening. Hot breath tickled my pubic bone, and Grayson pressed a kiss there, tonguing the hollow arch before darting out to taste it. My heart slammed against my ribcage, and my fingers dug into the comforter, trying not to blow my load right there and then.

It wouldn't take long. I was already teetering on the edge. A searing tongue lapped at my boxers, and Grayson inhaled, long and deep as if trying to memorize my scent. My brain frazzled over the sensation, and the cold air slapped against my hard cock. I panicked, looking down as the swollen head lay fat and aching against my abs. Grayson licked his dry lips before his mouth enclosed over the head. I jolted, like an explosion of lightning-flame had struck me.

"Grayson," I whined in my throat, and he grabbed my wrist, forcing me to thread my fingers through his brown hair.

I cried out when he took me deeper, hollowing out his cheeks. He started slow and the force of the suction was almost painful at first, but that gave way to blistering pleasure that covered my skin in goosebumps. My hips snapped of their own accord, my vision swimming as I fucked deeper into his mouth. Grayson didn't hesitate.

All those years at college seemed to have taught him immense stamina. I fisted his hair without realizing it, my hips coming off the bed, as he wrenched another moan from my lips.

Every slow drag of his tongue had me seeing stars. Grayson watched me, devouring my skin, as I sank deeper into the rolling clouds of thunder in his eyes. He backed off, and I yelped before he was back again, taking me from root to tip. Red rimmed his eyes, and his face flushed, his mouth stuffed like a Turkey on Christmas and it took everything not to come right there and then.

Then he sucked. So hard and so fast that I was gone.

Flung off a cliff, crashing into the stony walls and plunging head first to the ground.

"Fuck!" I shouted, hands coiling in his hair, abs trembling from the force of my orgasm.

Grayson slithered his way up my body, sealing his mouth over mine, tearing the breath from my lungs as his tongue slipped inside. I could taste myself. I could taste him.

The kiss was so wet. Brutal. Hot and hard as Grayson rutted against me, his cock singeing my flesh through the rough fabric of his jeans. "I want you. So fucking bad. I've always wanted you," he hissed the words into my mouth. Branding them into my flesh.

I want you too. But I couldn't speak. He gripped the handful of baby hairs at the base of my skull, grinding as his hips jerked and thrust. A warm tongue glided over the roof of my mouth, diving deep. I whimpered, hands curling into his shirt as I struggled for breath. He moaned, and then stilled, his hands hard and bruising against my waist. "Fuck," he whispered, taking a shuddering breath.

Kissing Grayson felt like falling, and damn, I never wanted to stop.

He sank his teeth into my earlobe, earning a sharp cry from me, and he laughed, low and rich.

"That's foul-play." I pouted, and he nibbled at my lip.

"I know," he drawled. "But don't pretend you didn't like it."

He caught me there.

I love it. Love him.

The thought felt like being doused with cold water. No. It was too soon. We had just started this thing between us, but I felt it all the same. Grayson didn't stop pressing wet, opened mouth kisses down the side of my neck. His teeth sank into my flesh, ghosting over what could only be a hickey by the way he'd been lathering it with his tongue. He found a spot that shot electric bolts down my spine and then I was curling toward him and claiming his lips. "Grayson... "

"I want to take you somewhere nice," he spoke. "Somewhere with just us, where we don't need to sneak around."

That sounded nice. I had no idea if Grayson was out, but he didn't seem like the type to care what people thought. "S-Sure," I stammer. "When are you guys coming back? Winter break?"

"Yeah, but it'll be way before that. We have a game coming up in a few weeks and I want to see you again. Be with you," Grayson said, and I melted.

"Okay."

"Okay."

Grayson's eyes pinned me, and I felt like I'd fallen into a labyrinth of phantasm-gray mist that hung over the forest floor. My brother had only been friends with Grayson for a year, so I didn't know too much about him, but what I knew was that he made every one of us better. He was like the sunlight that flittered over my palm. I wanted to grab it. To hold it close, but it always fell away. The sound of the front door opening made us jump apart. He laughed as I struggled to yank up my jeans and right my clothing. I tossed him an old pair of sweats I had lying around to hide the cum stains on his pants.

"Fuck! Fuck!" I sucked air through my teeth, running around fixing the bedding while Grayson disappeared into the bathroom.

"You guys better be decent!" Cricket called, bursting into my room, his face red from the cold. Emerald eyes surveyed the room, as if expecting to find Grayson hiding naked somewhere. "Mom says you need to help with dinner."

"Sure!" I readjust the bedding, hoping like hell my brother couldn't see the flush working its way up my cheeks.

"And..." Cricket said, stopping me in my tracks. "You better not have scarred Duke for life."

I smacked him upside the head. "Ouch!" he cried. "Mom, Jayden is being violent!"

"Jayden," my mom called. "Be nice to your older brother and come down here and help me with the groceries."

I shot Cricket a dirty look and went downstairs, but my heart was soaring like an eagle flying through the Texas sky.

***

THE OVERHEAD LIGHTS cast a bright, almost blinding glow, illuminating the ice and creating a stark contrast against the shadows along the boards. The tall, transparent boards surrounding the ice stood as silent sentinels, separating the playing area from the eager spectators. They were adorned with colorful advertisements, reflecting the commercial side of the sport, but for now, they were secondary to the main event.

Mom and dad sat beside me, wearing the Michigan Wolverines colors of blue and maize, my mom hollering at the top of her lungs and my dad palming his face.

I laughed at their antics and searched the crowd for the one person I wanted to see.

Grayson. It had been a few weeks since our last encounter, but my thoughts of him were endless. I wanted to kick myself because I didn't end up getting his number.

The scent of the ice and the faintest hint of refrigerant filled my nostrils. It's a scent that instantly sharpens my focus and heightens my senses, reminding me of the many games I had played with Cricket and Grayson. *God, I can't wait to be here with them*. In the distance, I caught glimpses of the opposing team, their sharp skates cutting lines into the ice as they warmed up. The tension in the air was palpable, like a heavy blanket draped over us all.

A man wearing a jersey with the number '52 came out first in the lineup of skaters, and my heart beat like butterfly wings when Grayson and Cricket finally came into view. They were a dynamic duo that had the crowds cheering loud. The referee's whistle pierced through the cacophony, signaling the start of the game. My heart pounded in my chest as the puck dropped, and the crowd's roar reached a fever pitch.

The game was on.

***

THE FIRST HALF OF THE game ended in victory for the Michigan Wolverines, and I couldn't have been prouder of the team. I turned to my parents and said, "I'm going to run down and say hello to the guys."

"Sure, honey," my mom said, waving me off.

Navigating through the throngs of excited fans, I made my way to the back, toward the locker room area. The air was electric with the celebration of their win. But my elation turned to concern when I spotted Grayson with his head down, his jaw clenched.

A man in a sleek blue suit crisp like a bank note towered over him, his face twisted in anger as he pointed a finger straight into Grayson's chest. He had wavy brown hair like Grayson, but it was cropped short and shaved at the sides. Something about the man set me on edge. His razor-thin lips pressed together, and he stared down at Grayson, his hawkish nose raised high. My curiosity got the better of me, and I took a step forward.

That's when it happened.

A snarl erupted from the man's throat. With his teeth bared, he backhanded Grayson across the face, sending him tumbling onto the floor. It was like the crack of thunder piercing the air. The blow was so hard and crippling that Grayson spun. He went down hard, sliding on his skates until his head slammed against the unforgiving concrete wall.

I surged forward without thinking. Anger and adrenaline coursing through me as I grabbed the man in the suit, ready to cave his face in, but before I could land a punch, Grayson grabbed my wrist, his voice urgent.

"Wait! Stop!"

I stared at him in shock, my heart pounding. "This guy just hurt you—"

"He's my dad! Let him go!"

Your dad. I stared at the bastard with disgust written all over my face. Confusion and concern swirled in my mind as I slowly released my grip on the man in the suit. He shoved me off and snorted, looking past me to Grayson. "Don't fuck this up, Grayson. You know what's at stake." Then he walked away, straightening his suit. I heard his smooth voice as he was engulfed in a sea of paparazzi that were lingering in the next hall. *What the fuck was that? Grayson's dad did that to him?*

Blood dribbled from the corner of Grayson's lip, and I moved to thumb it away, but he shrugged him off. "Don't!" He sighed. "Just—go back and wait with your parents. I'll see you later."

"Grayson—"

He walked back into the locker room, the door clicking shut behind him.

I stood there shell-shocked for several moments, trying to make sense of what I'd seen. Grayson's father beat him. No wonder he spent all of his holidays with us. Maybe Cricket knew about it and said nothing. My heart ached for him, but I could do nothing but return to the bleachers where my parents sat. The second half of the game was about to begin.

I watched with a sense of unease, my eyes fixed on Grayson as he stepped onto the ice. His head hung low, and the grip on his stick seemed almost too tight.

The crowd erupted into cheers as the puck dropped, but the jubilation soon turned to confusion and shock. In the blink of an eye, two opposing players sandwiched Cricket between them, their intentions sinister and clear. One of them reeled back and landed a brutal punch square in Cricket's face. My heart pounded in my chest as I struggled to make sense of the sudden violence. They weren't anywhere near the puck!

The scene unfolded in agonizing slow motion. Two more players closed in on Cricket, and the referee blew his whistle, desperately trying to regain control. It was chaos on the ice, and I could only watch in horror as my brother faced this brutal onslaught.

As Cricket attempted to skate away from the escalating brawl, Grayson entered the fray. I could see it unfurling before my eyes—a sickening realization that left me paralyzed with dread. Grayson's stick was held out, and Cricket, in his haste to escape the chaos, missed it entirely. He tripped over the outstretched stick, his body crashing into the unforgiving boards with a bone-chilling crunch. *No.*

The sound was sickening, and time seemed to stand still as Cricket crumpled to the ice, his femur shattered with a horrifying snap. My throat tightened, and a wave of nausea washed over me. Grayson had tripped him.

On purpose. I saw it. My mother's face was as pale as a sheet. My father stared on in shock and horror as the game came to a halt, and the paramedics ran out toward the ice. Cricket's helmet was torn off, his eyes closed, and his face was completely still.

No. No. I moved before I registered it, fighting my way through the crowds with my parents behind me. As medics rushed onto the ice, they carefully stabilized Cricket before gingerly lifting him onto a stretcher. My heart clenched as I watched them carry my brother away from the rink.

***

IN THE STERILE CONFINES of the medical room at the hospital, the true extent of the damage became painfully clear. One of the brutal punches had fractured Cricket's jaw, leaving it swollen and disfigured. The fall had been even more catastrophic as he had struck his head with devastating force against the unyielding boards, resulting in a sickening crack that would haunt my nightmares.

Hours passed like a torturous eternity, the tension in the waiting room thick and unbearable. We gathered around, waiting for the harrowing news. Even the team's heads hung low.

Grayson was nowhere to be found, and it made my blood boil.

He tripped him. *I saw it. I did.*

Hurt and rage exploded inside my heart, and I clenched my hand into a fist as I paced. Tears streaked my mother's face as she shook her head, and my father could do nothing but stand there feeling useless. What if Cricket didn't wake up? What if he was dead? Fuck, we welcomed Grayson into our home! We were there for him—I loved him, and now this? I couldn't fathom it. They would press charges. I didn't care anymore. *Grayson tried to kill him. He tried to kill my brother.* His best friend.

Nothing made sense. *Why would Grayson put his stick out like that, knowing Cricket was trying to get away from the brawl? Why didn't he just walk away? Why didn't he fucking help?* My fury felt like a storm brewing on the horizon, dark and ominous, ready to unleash its destructive force.

I want to see you again, be with you. The words were all honey-dipped lies.

My heart tightened, as if it were in a vice-grip and acid clawed up my throat when the doctor came through the doors with a grave look on his face. "Are you Mr. and Mrs. Taylor?" he asked, his kind blue eyes searching.

"Yes," my mom replied, wiping her cheeks. "That's me."

"First, I want to say I'm so sorry this happened and we're doing everything we can to help him. As for his injuries..." He paused, and I felt the weight of his words crashing down on me like fallen bricks. "The swelling in his brain was too much for his body to bear. His femur in his right leg is crushed in three places and the surgeries to rebuild the bone structure will be extensive, even so he would only retain 30% capacity of movement."

"So, what are you sayin' doc?" my dad pleaded, tears in his eyes. "A-Are you sayin' that my boy—"

"Will be crippled for the rest of his life," the doctor finished, and my mom's knees buckled. I felt like it was all a dream, if only my mom's wails didn't pierce my ears and drag me out of it.

"That's not all," the doctor pressed onward. "Like I said earlier, the swelling in his brain was too much and, unfortunately, has left him incapacitated. I'm afraid he's officially brain-dead."

At twenty, my brother was brain-dead.

The words struck like a sledgehammer, the finality of the declaration sinking in like a bitter, unbearable truth. The room seemed to close in around us, and the world outside faded into insignificance. Cricket. Whose smile and laughter could steal worlds was brain-dead.

And Grayson Hayes was responsible.

3

EMBERS OF VENGEANCE

JAYDEN TAYLOR

Darts of icy rain came spitting from the sky. They hissed and swished, shredding the farm into blankets of isolated streams. Raindrops seared the mist, ripping it apart with its stinging, silver bullets.

Gray. I hated that color. Hated the way it made everything dank and sad, hated how it made me want to curl up as if my lungs were aching. My teacher's voice droned on in the background, but all I could do was stare out the window, wishing I were somewhere else. With Cricket. The rain had washed most of the snow away, but there was still some left. Not much.

Cricket had missed the hockey season.

And he would miss the next one. Tears stung my eyes, and then the bell rang. Everyone leaped from their seats, and I packed up my books to leave as well.

"Mr. Taylor," my teacher called, and I swung my backpack over my shoulder before walking to his desk. "A word, please?"

I nodded as Mr. Andrews' frown deepened, the crescent in his eyes more pronounced.

"Sir?" I asked.

He handed me back my assignment. Lines of red covered every page, and my stomach swooped. I'd never failed before. I was his best student.

"Look, I understand. We all do. You're already admitted to Michigan University, so this won't affect your grades too much, just don't let it slip too far down."

Blood roared in my ears, and I felt heat crawl up my neck. "Yes, sir."

"How's Cricket doing?"

"Worse," I said, the lump in my throat growing. "He's not improving. Not even a little."

Mr. Andrews shook his head. "I'm so sorry, son. We all loved him."

Each word pierced my chest, but I held on strong. "Thank you."

"Look, I can get you another extension on the project, but it needs to be done. That's the best I can do, Jayden. You're smart. I know you're more than capable of getting it done."

"Thank you, sir." I nodded, and he gave me a reassuring pat, the edges of his knitted sweater vest brushing against my shirt.

"Now get out of here." Mr. Andrews mouth curved as he jerked his head, almost jostling his thick rimmed black glasses.

I failed the assignment. Mr. Andrews didn't need to tell me that if I failed another one, I'd lose my scholarship to Michigan University. Fuck, things couldn't get any worse. My parents were already stretched thin from all of Cricket's medical bills. It was so bad my dad was talking about selling the farm just to make ends meet. Life was suffocating. I wished and begged every day that God would spare us and Cricket would wake up. That this nightmare would end.

Either God hated gay people or he didn't think I was worthy enough, but I never once heard a response. I walked down the echoing halls of the school, my heart hammering in my chest like a relentless drumbeat. My footsteps felt heavy, and the weight of the stares and whispers that erupted around me was suffocating. At school, Cricket had been more than just a friend; he had been my best friend, my only friend. My shyness had made it challenging to connect with others, a trait that had persisted well into high school.

I used to follow Cricket everywhere, but now I couldn't. He wasn't here, and that realization was like a dagger through my heart. Tears threatened to burn my eyes, but I blinked them away as I reached my locker, determined to pack my things away and escape this cruel environment.

Make it so. Captain Jean-Luc Picard's voice rang in my ears. He was the commanding officer of the USS Enterprise in Star Trek. When Captain Picard said, "Make it so," he was giving an authoritative order to his crew to carry out a specific action or task. *I wished things in life could be that simple.* For so long, I believed I held the reins of my life, and if I worked hard enough, I too could "Make it so." But now I realized how foolish I'd been. Some things were beyond my reach, beyond my control.

"No way, man," one of the jocks said, his voice loud enough for me to hear. "I heard the whole thing was fake."

"Bro, what are you on?" another jock scoffed, and I slanted my eyes to stare at them in my peripheral. A sea of red and white stood around their lockers, and I remembered these guys as Cricket's old crew when he went to this high school.

"I heard the idiot tripped over his two left feet and fell into the boards," he laughed, but it was calloused. "Fuck, that shit was crazy!"

Their heartless laughter made my blood boil. Rage skittered behind my eyelids, a storm of fury exploding within my chest. How could they laugh at Cricket, who was fighting for his life?"

"Dude." someone nearby nudged the jock, his voice a hushed plea to stop. "You should shut up."

"What? I was just saying. Oh crap. Sorry, Jayden. I meant nothing by it—"

I couldn't bear to listen any longer. I slammed my locker shut with a resounding clang and stalked away from the heartless crowd. Screw these people. Striding out the dual doors, I stopped and stared up at the sky. Gray. Rolling clouds and musty air that made it difficult to breathe.

It had been one month since the accident.

Cricket's fall had been plastered all over social media and shared a billion times. There were memes too, I heard, vicious ones reenacting the most horrifying moments of my life. And yet, a strange sense of calm enveloped me. *Make it so.* I didn't have a choice in it, or else I'd succumb to the wild madness brewing inside me. Hitching my backpack higher, I went to the bus stop and stood waiting.

Plopping drops of icy rain came.

But I stayed, allowing the gray to swallow me whole.

***

THE HOSPITAL'S COLD, STERILE corridors seemed to close in on me as I approached the front desk. Rainwater dripped from my drenched clothes, forming small puddles beneath my feet. The nurse behind the desk glanced up, her eyes scanning my disheveled appearance.

"Can I help you?" she asked.

"Yeah," I replied, my voice shaky. "I'm here to see Craige Mathis Taylor Jr."

We all just called him Cricket for short.

The nurse reached for a visitor's form and handed it to me, her eyes assessing my rain-soaked attire. I took the form, and with a trembling hand, I filled it out.

The visitor's form was a stark reminder of how few names remained on the list. Just three names: Mom, Dad, and me. Others had stopped coming a long time ago. Even family members had gradually faded away as the news about Cricket's condition spread. Once they heard he was brain-dead, they didn't bother with visits anymore.

My parents and I took turns at his side, but I was the one who stayed the longest, especially after school. I would sit there, talking to Cricket, telling him about my day just like I always had. But my heart twisted each time he didn't respond. He just lay there, a tangle of tubes snaking out from his mouth and nose like a grotesque octopus.

The nurse gave me a sharp look as I signed the form, perhaps seeing the pain etched in my eyes. With the document complete, I made my way to Cricket's room.

He was hooked up to every conceivable machine; the room filled with the mechanical hum of life-support systems. Cricket's once vibrant face was now gaunt and pale, a stark contrast to the lively, adventurous spirit I had known. His shattered femur was suspended in a sling and bandaged. As I looked at him, my heart ached, and I wished for nothing more than to see a glimmer of the friend I had lost within that fragile, motionless form.

"Hey," I said through tears that I didn't realize were sliding down my cheeks. "How are you?"

The machines beeped in response.

"Good, I hope." I dropped my shit to the floor and sat down on the stiff plastic chair beside his bed, taking his boney hand in mine.

Muscle atrophy made his arms and legs slim, and his face hollow.

"Can you hear me?" I spoke again, this time lightning my tone. "If you can, say something asshole," I laughed, but it turned into a bitter sob. My eyes stung. I hated seeing him like this. I took out my homework, still trying to keep the mood light. "Mr. Andrews says it won't be long until I head to Michigan University." I took out some pen and paper. "There's a spot waiting for me on the Michigan Wolverines, they said once I get there. Your old spot."

A flash of yellow caught my eye and I turned to stare at the vase of yellow roses sitting in the corner of the room. Golden petals unfurled like rays of sunshine, brightening the space. It reminded me of the ones Grayson used to give my mom.

I assumed it was the nurse who had diligently dropped it off. Each morning, they placed it there, as if to say, "Even in the bleakest of moments, there is still a touch of brightness." Those yellow roses became a symbol of resilience for me, a beacon of comfort in the face of our unrelenting despair.

Pressing the heel of my palm to my eyes, I fought a fresh wave of tears. "You missed hockey season," I accused. "Fuck, it was an epic playoff series. The Bruins against the Leafs and I can't believe you missed it. It was Game 7, and things looked pretty grim for the Bruins. They were down 4-1 with just minutes left in the third period. But man, they never gave up. It was like a miracle."

My voice quivered with excitement as I recalled the moment. "They scored three goals in those final minutes to tie it up, and then, in overtime, Nathan Horton scored that game-winner. Man, you would have lost it. Remember how we jumped and cheered last year? That win was something else."

I paused, looking at my brother's still form, hoping that some part of Cricket could hear my words. "That series, it was a turning point for the Bruins, just like you're gonna have your own turning point. We'll get through this together, buddy. I promise. You'll wake up soon, and you'll see. I was right all along. I was right." I choked on the words.

A part of me hoped he'd open his emerald eyes and glare at me, tell me to eat shit for saying that to him, but nothing happened. Cricket lay still as if he were sleeping, and my heart shattered once again. With burning eyes, I continued to talk to him while doing my homework and the nurses would come every few minutes, shooting me pitying glances, but I didn't care.

Cricket would wake up one day.

Even if all the evidence pointed otherwise.

***

AFTER SPENDING A FEW hours at the hospital, I trudged back home, my steps heavy and laden with exhaustion. As I entered our modest house, I stared blankly out of the rain-speckled window. My mom no longer looked up when she saw me; her gaze was fixed on the bills scattered across the counter, each one adorned with red, angry words, mirroring the frustration I felt about my failing assignments.

My dad had taken on an additional job just to help cover the mounting medical bills, but it was still not enough. Our finances were spiraling out of control, and the weight of it all pressed upon us like a relentless storm.

"I'm home, Mama," I said, dropping my backpack onto the floor.

She finally looked up, her eyes rimmed red from hours of worry, and she forced a smile.

"Hi, baby," she replied, her voice wavering with a hint of fatigue. She reached out her hand, and I took it willingly, the touch offering a fragile connection amid our struggles.

I joined her at the table, my eyes lingering on the bills she had pushed aside.

"What's all this?" I asked, my curiosity tinged with a growing sense of dread.

"Nothing," she dismissed, brushing the issue away. "How was school?"

I lied to her, just as she had lied to me countless times in recent days. I told her it was great, that everything was fine. She said she made dinner, and I promised I would eat it later. We both knew I wouldn't. She held my hand with icy fingers and I clung to her, hoping that just once I could get warmth from steel. I retreated to my room, closing the door behind me, and the moment it clicked shut, tears welled up in my eyes. I stifled back a sob that clawed its way up my throat.

Cricket was gone.

And we were drowning in a sea of debt.

I hated this world, the cruelty of fate that had torn my brother away from me. I hated everything and everyone, but most of all, I hated the helplessness that had settled in my heart like an uninvited guest. Rage felt like a familiar warm embrace, slithering inside my chest like poisonous gas.

Grayson. He had caused all of this.

The legal aftermath of that fateful incident had left a bitter taste in my family's mouth. They never ended up pressing charges against Grayson. The video recordings of the incident had somehow ruled that Grayson's tripping of Cricket had been an accident. It was a ludicrous decision, especially considering the stark reality of the consequences. I wasn't there for the trial. My parents and counselor thought it would be best to skip it, since seeing everything play out again would cripple me emotionally, but I had hoped justice would be served.

It wasn't.

Grayson's father was a wealthy and influential man. He made everything disappear quietly. A hefty settlement bought my parents' silence, burdened as they were by the crushing weight of Cricket's medical bills. Even after the settlement, Cricket's hospital bills alone were enough to demolish all of it.

It had been a grim choice, but a necessary one.

As for those guys who had beaten Cricket on the ice, they received a slap on the wrist in the form of an official ban on ever playing hockey in a school setting, and six months of jail time due to having no prior criminal record. It was a grotesque joke. Cricket lay in a hospital bed, barely clinging to life, while the judge's apathetic verdict was like a brand against my skin.

Although I wasn't there to see it, my mom had relayed most of what had happened. The injustice of it all fueled the simmering anger within me, a fury that threatened to consume everything in its path.

I slammed my fist against the wall, wishing like hell I could crush them all to death.

Taking a stuttering breath, I peeled off my sodden clothes and went into the shower. After that, I finished my assignment and lay in bed, staring up at the ceiling. A memory buzzed inside my brain like the wings of a hornet, loud and insistent. Grayson's hand on my hips. His tongue in my mouth.

I want to be with you. I want you. A burn as the coarse hairs on his chin bristled against mine. Grayson's eyes were like clouds that soon blazed into the icy polar-blue sea. I didn't realize it until it was too late. Until I was caught in his snare and nobody could hear my stilted screams.

It was all in the eyes. In the gray, you see.

They melted into liquid steel like gloomy skies that were as black as the devil's heart.

***

As time went on, Cricket wasted away before my eyes, and so did my parents. My dad drank more, and my mother was distant as if she were on a raft drifting out to sea. Hate grew in my heart, wide and thick like the roots of a cypress tree. I kept my head down, black hoodie up as the days trekked on and graduation approached. While everyone was all sunshine and rainbows, I was too busy trying to survive the suffocating weight on my chest. Cricket's doctor had been asking us more and more about what we wanted to do. What our plans were. But I knew what he was really asking.

Cricket was brain-dead.

No chance of coming back.

Why keep him on life support? This wasn't a life. It was a slow, painful death. It stressed my mom out so badly; I swear her entire head turned gray overnight. My dad drank and drank, as if being in an intoxicated haze would make things better. They ignored me. Like I didn't exist.

And I welcomed it.

Mr. Andrews slapped a paper down on my desk before moving on to the next person.

I stared down at the assignment in front of me, relief and frustration warring within. I had passed, but only by a narrow margin. Mr. Andrews shot me a concerned look, but I brushed it off. All I needed to do was keep my grades up, and next year, it would be all about hockey—the game both Cricket and I loved.

"Hey, man," a voice said, and I recognized it as the same person who had mocked Cricket's injury earlier. Cal something.

I scowled at him. "What do you want?"

His smirk widened. "Nothing, but I think I have something that might help your case against that Grayson bastard."

I shot him a skeptical glance. "Who said I need your help?"

He looked affronted. "Wow, relax, bro. I was just saying, but here, check this out." He whipped out his phone and showed me a video. "You see this, right here? It's clear that Grayson tripped him."

My heart raced, and memories of that fateful night flashed before my eyes. "Turn it off," I demanded.

He laughed. "Wait, this is the best part. See, he tripped him, man. I know it."

Rage surged through me, and I couldn't control it. I knocked the phone out of his hand, and it clattered to the ground. "Hey!" he cried. "Why'd you do that? Jeez, I was providing you with evidence. You don't have to be such a pansy about it."

Pansy. The word stung, reminding me of how everyone knew about my sexuality, and I had never tried to hide it. Yet, this guy felt entitled to tear me apart by showing me my brother's demise and then insulting me for not watching.

My fist moved before I even registered it, smashing into the guy's face and crushing his nose with a sickening crunch.

4

RIVALRY ON THIN ICE

JAYDEN TAYLOR

Tension hung heavy like an impending storm. The jock, muscles rippling beneath his menacing glare, stepped forward. I tightened my fists, nerves pounding like a drumbeat.

The brawl ignited with a swift jab from the jock's massive right fist. His knuckles grazed my cheek, painting a searing line of pain across my skin. I retaliated, driving my left fist into his side with a sharp hook. He grunted, but his fury only intensified.

A right hook from him met my jaw with bone-jarring force, snapping my head to the side. I tasted copper and felt warmth trickling from my lip. It fueled the cold fury within me.

I lunged forward, landing a solid left-right combo to his abdomen. He winced but countered with a wild uppercut that grazed my chin. My head snapped back, but I remained upright.

With a swift pivot, I drove my knee into his gut. The jock staggered back, gasping for air. I seized the moment, unleashing a powerful right cross that landed square on his jaw.

The room erupted into chaos, and suddenly, I was at the center of a brawl. Despite the disorder, I couldn't help but grin; it felt like catharsis, releasing all the pent-up anger and frustration that had been building within me.

A sudden punch landed on my chin, making stars dance before my eyes, but instead of feeling pain, I grinned and retaliated with an uppercut. It connected, smashing the other guy's face wide open, blood spraying like a gruesome work of art.

A tempest of fists and fury. I couldn't have cared less about the consequences. The anger, the frustration, it all poured out.

And for the first time in a long while, I felt alive.

I wanted to fight. To hurt.

Each face transformed into Grayson's and before I could think, I was beating them all.

"Security!" Mr. Andrews bellowed and several large men came over and wrenched me off the jock, slamming me face first into the ground. Pain juddered up my spine, and my arm was yanked behind my back and held in a bruising grip. Fuck.

"That's it. You're coming with us!" They jerked me up. I looked around at the carnage before me and wanted to laugh.

***

BLOOD TRICKLED DOWN my lip, mixing with the relentless rain pelting against my skin. They had let me go, but not without a price. The threat of expulsion hung heavy in the air, and the parents of those jocks were itching to press charges. It was only Mr. Andrews' intervention that had temporarily saved me from the repercussions. But I could still see the burning fury in those jocks' eyes, promising that my reprieve would be short-lived.

I ignored the harsh glares from the hospital nurses as my wet shoes slapped against the cold tile floor. I approached the front desk to sign the visitors' form, but the nurse stopped me with an unusual expression.

"There's someone already in there. Just a reminder, only two visitors at a time."

I furrowed my brow. My dad was at work, and my mom was at home, so who could it be? Shrugging off my curiosity, I signed the form anyway and made my way to Cricket's room.

As I entered, my heart seemed to skip a beat. Broad shoulders were encased in a Michigan Wolverines varsity jacket, hands shoved deep into pockets. A cascade of brown hair framed his forehead, wispy waves clinging to his skin before he turned. Steel gray eyes locked onto mine, and my world spun out of control.

Grayson.

Deep shadows etched under protruding cheek bones, and his eyes were red, sunken pits. Grayson stepped forward, and I moved back, my heart pounding in my ears. He was here. He came.

My hands curled into fists, and I gritted my teeth so hard that a rich metallic taste filled my mouth. It was a coppery tang that clung to my taste buds, reminiscent of old coins long forgotten.

Gray pierced my flesh. Like an unholy incense, it wafted and spirited through my core, swathing everything in its vaporous path. "What the fuck are you doing here?" I spat, my teeth bared.

"Jayden," Grayson pleaded, his throat working. "I didn't do this. Please, believe me. I wouldn't—Cricket was like a brother to me—"

"Don't you dare ever speak his fucking name!" I was so angry my vision blurred like a film of plastic was covering my eyes. I hated him. Hated that he was here. Hated that my stomach somersaulted after just one glance.

I hated the guilt in his eyes. "You almost killed him! He's dead because of you!"

"No," Grayson said, shaking his head, tears brimming before falling down his eyes. "Jayden. Please. I would never. I swear."

You would. I didn't respond. Instead, I walked past him and touched Cricket's hand, threading my hand into his corpse-like fingers. I knew why he came here. It was only the guilt. The fear of people knowing who he truly was, but I knew. Grayson Hayes was a monster. The devil himself. I rued the day I ever fell for him. A glacial anger settled over me, a cold fury that held me in its unforgiving grip.

"If you ever come here again, I'll fucking kill you," I spoke low, my deep voice echoing off the tiles.

A gasp sliced open my heart, and the sound of running shoes hitting the ground and the door slamming shut punched through my ribcage. He was gone. *Good.* I never wanted to see him again.

At least, not in this lifetime.

***

THE BITCH SAID I BROKE his arm. His family pressed charges and the situation that had once seemed amusing quickly turned grim. My first-time offense led to a lenient sentence, six weeks in juvenile detention. The judge's warning about being tried as an adult after my eighteenth birthday hung heavily in the air. My mother's tears and my father's stoic silence were the backdrop to my departure. He didn't say a word but went straight to the bar, drowning his sorrow in alcohol.

As my mother dropped me off at the juvenile detention center in Ohio, I went willingly, avoiding the need for an armed escort. The formalities followed—booking, fingerprints, and the exchange of my clothes for a drab uniform. In an instant, I had become a criminal. A seething darkness welled up inside me, hot and suffocating like smoldering embers. It was all Grayson's fault, and I couldn't escape the feeling that he had brought me to this.

The other boys in the detention center stared at me with wide, leporine eyes gleaming with sinister intentions. I stood on the precipice, trapped in a pit with no way out, except to fight. And fighting was something I knew all too well.

The first night was a nightmarish symphony of screams echoing off the cold, sterile walls. The boy in the other room beside me received a merciless beating, and though he pleaded for help, I squeezed my eyes shut and ignored his desperate cries. This place was a nightmare, and as much as it horrified me, I couldn't deny that I deserved to be here. Slowly, I felt myself fading into the shadows.

Days went by, and nobody spoke to me. At first, I welcomed the silence, but eventually, I understood why they kept their distance. I had been marked. One day, as we shuffled through the lunch line, a large man with tattoos covering his neck and rippling muscles approached me. A part of me wanted to ignore him, but I couldn't.

"How are you doin', pretty?" He leered, and my heart skipped a beat at the nickname.

"Fine," I muttered.

He laughed lecherously. "Why don't you come join me and my friends later for some fun—"

"Back off, Kit," a voice cut through the air, saving me from whatever crude proposition he was about to make. "He already promised me."

Kit's nose wrinkled, but he begrudgingly backed off. "You should watch yourself," the boy warned me. "You don't want to get mixed up with Kit and his crew."

I turned to get a better look at my savior. He had tattoos running down his neck, but was slightly shorter than me, with a wiry build. "I'm Kyle, and I think we share a room."

Swallowing the lump in my throat, I nodded. "Yeah."

"Come on. Eat with me," Kyle said, and I followed him. He seemed nice enough, but I had no idea what to expect in this place. The food was awful. Brown mush that resembled eggs with bacon, accompanied by stale bread, soggy vegetables, and overripe avocado. I grimaced but ate it anyway, not wanting to skip any meals here.

Sitting across from me, Kyle's large brown eyes were perceptive "So, what are you in for? Robbery? You look like the type." The guys around the table snickered.

"Something like that," I lied, not wanting to disclose the real reason I was here.

Kyle shrugged. "This here is Ajax," he said, pointing to the guy across from him. "Six, Mase, Hammer and Dean."

I nodded to them, but kept my head low. "They don't bite none," Kyle continued, rubbing a hand across his shaven head. "Just stay away from Kit and his crew. He's been in and out of here a few years, so try not to fuck with him too much."

"All right," I said.

"And try not to go anywhere alone, too," Kyle explained. "These halls are long and some of the camera angles have blind spots, so if you're caught with Kit and his crew, you're just as good as dead in here."

A shiver rolled down my spine, but I kept my face neutral. It didn't matter anyway. Cricket was dead, and so was I. Grayson made sure of it.

"Taylor!" one guard barked, jolting me out of the dull conversation with my fellow inmates. "You have a visitor."

I hastily packed up my meager lunch tray, dumping the rest into the nearby garbage can, and then followed the guards to the visitor's area. They slapped cold, unforgiving cuffs onto my wrists and ankles before leading me to the waiting room. A thick inch of glass separated me from my mother, but I picked up the phone, my breath catching as I stared into her tear-streaked emerald eyes.

"How are you doing, baby?" she asked, her voice trembling with concern. I bit my lip, fighting back the tears threatening to spill.

"Fine," I lied, clearing my throat. "How's Cricket?"

A flicker of hope danced across her face. "I have some good news," she said, her voice quivering with excitement. "A doctor from a fancy hospital in Michigan wants to try some experimental therapy on Cricket to see if we can bring him back."

"Experimental?" I murmured, my mind racing. "What do you mean?"

She inched closer to the glass. "They say they've been developing some brain cells to help bring those who are brain-dead back to life and need a test subject to try it on. It's fully covered, and they have accepted Cricket into the program."

My emotions churned. The thought of them poking and probing at my brother turned my stomach, but a glimmer of hope ignited within me. "Can they cure him? How is it covered?"

My mother chuckled softly, her eyes still shimmering with tears. "I don't know, sweetie. They told us not to worry about it and that Cricket would be given the best care. I'm praying, baby. I'm praying to God that they'll bring him back to us."

It was the best news I'd heard in a long time, and I clung to it like a lifeline. I pressed my palm against the cold glass, my mother mirroring the gesture on her side.

***

To boldly go where no one has gone before. The opening of Star Trek sang in my ears as they led me back to my cell. Kyle was on the top bunk, humming underneath his breath while he flipped through a magazine. I took out a worn copy of Star Trek, sighing when my fingers brushed against the familiar pages. Cricket would be in Michigan. Right next to me. I could visit before and after classes once I started this fall, and who knew maybe even show him footage of my hockey games. I lay down on the cot, the wooly comforter itched my skin.

"You good, Jay?" Kyle's voice drifted from the upper bunk.

"I'm good, bro."

Kyle laughed. "You know, you never answered the question earlier today. What are you in for?"

I stilled, trying to calm the beating of my heart. Why did he want to know so badly? Then again, who wouldn't want to know in a place like this? "Assault."

"No shit, really?"

"Yeah."

"Who?"

"Some asshole who made fun of my brother," I replied, surprised by how easy it was to talk about it with someone other than my family. "What about you?"

Kyle's head appeared as he hung off the edge of the bunk bed, a slow smile slithering over his lips. "Rape."

Blood roared in my ears, and I stared into those deep, dark brown eyes. Rape. The word ricocheted deep inside my mind before landing like a balloon of burning acid singeing my flesh.

"Don't worry, bro. He wanted it. I know he did." Then he laughed; this time his serious expression broke. "I'm just fuckin' with you, man."

I breathed a sigh of relief. "Bastard."

"Nah, for real, though. I'm here for armed robbery and shit," he said, laying back down on the top bunk. "It was stupid, but I only have three more months inside this hell hole and then I'm out, bro."

"What do you plan to do?"

"I don't know." I heard him shrug. "Get a job? I'm not good for much else. Not smart enough for school, but who knows? Maybe I'll try. Those college honeys look nice. I might get me one of those."

"Yeah."

"What happened to your brother?"

"He's brain-dead. Some hockey game gone wrong."

"Fuck." Kyle whistled. "And some asshole made fun of him? Fuck, I'd have killed him too."

My lips kinked. "Right? Fucker deserved it."

"Well, stick beside me. Ain't nobody gonna fuck with you while I'm around."

I laughed, but was glad he would be there for me. It was hard to find a friend, and Kyle seemed like a good one. I turned onto my side, trying to quell the giddiness I felt. Cricket would get the treatment he deserved and maybe when I got out, things would be all right in this world. I clung to that, just like I did everything else in the world, with all my might. To boldly go where no man had gone before. *Yes, Cricket would be just fine.* My parents wouldn't be in so much debt.

Things were finally looking up.

I thanked God silently and fell into a deep sleep.

***

THE NEXT DAY, THE SCORCHING sun bore down relentlessly as we toiled in the fields, our tasks reminiscent of the farm work I had grown up doing. My parched throat signaled the need for water, and I gestured to the guards for a drink. Stepping inside, the cool rush of air conditioning washed over me as I headed toward the nearby fountain. The halls lay vacant, offering a brief respite. Suddenly, a smooth voice cut through the silence, sending a shiver down my spine.

"There you are, pretty," it purred. "Avoiding me, eh? How about some time now?"

Kit.

I looked up to find myself ensnared by his taurine eyes, glittering with hostility. They were as wild and fearsome as any bull, and panic surged within me. I bolted, my lungs burning as I turned a corner, only to collide with his waiting accomplices. They seized me, and I fought with every ounce of strength, but Kit produced a makeshift blade, his sweaty skin glistening.

"I don't enjoy having to fight for a taste, pretty," he taunted, tracing the shiv along my cheek. "This is for keeping me waiting."

He cast me a malicious grin while wielding his shiv, infused with that dark, demonic energy. A surge of battle fury ignited within me, and I slammed my forehead against his nose. An audible crack pierced the air and Kit cursed. His head flew as blood erupted from his nose. Pain throbbed like a hammer in my skull, but I would not let this fucker win.

My resolve was unyielding.

"You fuck!" Kit swung, and he plunged the shiv between my lower ribs and shoved upward. Agony coursed through me. I let out a piercing scream as he drove it deeper, twisting it.

"Hey!" a guard's voice bellowed. "What the hell are you doing over there!"

Kit ran, but more guards appeared, closing in on him. I stared at the blood oozing from my wound, its rhythmic drops staining the tiles. Dark spots danced before my vision, fading in and out.

I felt the room breathing, and the clouds shaking with rain.

Gray. So much gray.

It's the raw sensations that let you know you're dying.

Your skin feels as if it's been pierced by a thousand icy needles and scraped raw by the unforgiving texture of the floors. Your tongue cleaves to the roof of your mouth, as though it's been replaced with a parched, leathery insole relentlessly grinding away at the back of your throat. Your throat itself constricts, as if a reticulated python is determined to squeeze the life out of it.

Even your eyes seem to have liquefied and melded into the depths of your consciousness, casting an otherworldly, mirage-like veil over everything. The cold prison tiles, once simply beneath your feet, now take on new meaning—they amplify the torment, creating a relentless presence that occupies your every waking thought.

Cricket. Wait for me.

I'm coming home.

5

FIRES OF OBSESSION

JAYDEN TAYLOR

I groaned. A headache nestled in my temples, squeezing them like a vice grip, and I felt as if I were trying to contain an erupting volcano within the confines of my skull. *Fuck everything hurt.*

"You're gonna make it..."

Whispers swirled around me. Strange and elusive as I struggled to regain clarity. They danced like fireflies, illuminated by snippets of half-formed images and sentences. My throat felt raw, like sandpaper had scratched it, and it made it difficult to talk. To breathe.

Through the intermittent fog of my awakening, I perceived Cricket's fleeting presence, like a spectral figure in a disjointed dream. Distorted images flickered before my heavy eyelids, teasing me with fragments of reality until I was pulled back into the depths of unconsciousness.

The rhythmic beeping of machines served as a disorienting backdrop to my surroundings. I felt weak, vulnerable, and my body ached as if it had been through the wringer.

"Shh, don't move," a gentle voice murmured, soothing the frayed edges of my consciousness. A searing pain jabbed at my stomach, and a pained groan escaped my lips.

"Nurse!" the voice called, and moments later, blessed relief washed over me as darkness reclaimed my senses.

Time blurred, and I surfaced again, this time to a room filled with the relentless beeping of machines. Kyle sat at my bedside in his drab gray uniform, his face appearing washed out under the harsh hospital lighting.

"You okay, buddy?" he asked. "Here, drink this." He offered me a sip of water. I drank fast, sighing as the cool water soothed the back of my throat. "Slow down," he laughed and pulled it away. "They said take it slow or else I'll get in trouble."

I tentatively reached for my side, fingers grazing the throbbing wound there. "What happened?" I croaked, the haze slowly lifting from my mind.

Kyle's expressive brown eyes locked onto mine. "You narrowly escaped death, man."

Each word shot through me like a bullet. "What?"

"Yeah, bro." He ran a hand over his shaven head. "Fuck, Kit got you alone, fam. I didn't think he'd be that angry, but the fucker's got balls and he stabbed you. Shit. I knew he was crazy, but I didn't think he was that crazy. Anyway, they sent him to a real prison where ... I don't know, fam, they might seek the death penalty for everything else he's done."

Shit. Not that I cared. The bastard deserved it. "Anyway," Kyle continued. "Don't worry about it. Just focus on getting better. He's gone. Nobody will fuck with you anymore, T."

"T?" I asked.

"Yeah," Kyle laughed. "I heard your last name was Taylor, so I thought I'd give you a nickname. You can thank me later."

"I won't, but okay," I deadpanned, and he laughed harder. "Where are my parents?"

"They just left, out they'll be back. God, your mom was scary, man. I know about your brother, but she kept looking at you like you'd died or something, and your dad stank like a brewery. I thought I'd get wasted by his breath alone!"

I cringed, but there was nothing I could do. They were my parents. I'm sure hearing the news sent them both into a tailspin. I couldn't even imagine what they were thinking. I groaned again and leaned my head back against the pillow.

"Don't worry, bro," Kyle said, tapping his fist to his chest. "I got you. Relax." He placed the straw to my lips again, and I took another sip of water like it was a lifeline. Kyle pulled it away when the cup was empty and I settled back into the bed, the lumpy mattress digging into my back.

"What are you doing here, anyway?"

"Taking care of you," Kyle replied, and I kinked a brow. "Fine, they thought you might recover faster with a friend nearby so I volunteered. Besides, it beats working in the field all day, ye feel me?"

I chuckled and regretted it when my sides ached. "Yeah, I feel."

I stared at Kyle, wondering what his story was and how a guy like him ended up in a place like this. He mentioned robbery once, but he didn't seem like that type of guy. Then again, I didn't know. Things weren't always like they seemed. I learned that the hard way with Grayson. Kyle stared right back at me, and something strange flickered in his deep brown eyes. I forced myself to look away and cleared my throat. "Thanks for helping."

"No problem, T."

I nodded and then felt my eyes droop. Drifting back into slumber felt like sinking into a warm, velvety cocoon, where my thoughts unraveled like threads, and the world slipped away.

***

THE ROAD TO RECOVERY stretched before me like an endless, winding path. Pain, hot and unrelenting, flared up whenever I moved, and by the third day, I wanted to burn everything to the ground. Kyle stayed beside me most of the time, and my parents came in and out of the ward, their faces drawn with exhaustion.

My father looked even worse.

I'd never seen a man so defeated. He didn't speak. All he did was stare at me with dark hollow eyes, as if the sun would never rise again in his lifetime. *How could I do this to them? How could I have been so careless as to piss off Kit?* A part of me knew it wasn't my fault, but seeing their faces made a sickness well up inside me like a noxious, swirling vortex. Twisting my stomach into knots and leaving a foul taste in my mouth.

The following day, a doctor entered my room. "Mr. Taylor?" he began, his bright blue eyes pinned me with a blend of professionalism and empathy. "You're lucky to be alive, son. That shiv nicked one of your lungs. We did our best in surgery, but there may be occasional breathing problems. Just be cautious not to overexert yourself."

What does that mean? I looked at Kyle, whose mouth was pulled into a thin line. "W-What do you mean overexert? I play hockey. I have a full ride to university on a hockey scholarship. What do you mean, overexert?"

"That's exactly what I mean. You'll need to take it easy from now on, and hockey might need to be put on hold," he said, looking at me above the rim of his dark glasses, his brow wrinkled and his words hung in the air like a heavy verdict. My heart plummeted. No, this couldn't be happening. Hockey was my life. I had earned a scholarship to university through hockey, and if I couldn't play, I'd lose everything I had worked so hard for.

Desperation clawed at me, and I found my voice, pleading, "There has to be something more you can do, some other way to help me—something that will let me play again."

"I'm sorry. Give it time. You may build up your stamina, but your lung capacity won't be the same ever again."

An unbearable verdict crushed my hopes and dreams, shattering my world. The harsh reality sunk in: my left lung's capacity had been permanently reduced, and it would haunt me for life. Hockey, my love, was forever out of reach. The ice would never grace my feet again, nor would I witness the puck's majestic flight through the rink. Everything was gone.

Cricket brain-dead.

And my hockey skills demolished in one stroke.

As the doctor left, I felt tears welling up, their heat burning my eyes as they streamed down my cheeks. Kyle sat beside me, his head hanging low. I couldn't hold back the sobs, and I pressed my palms against my eyes, trying to block out this harsh reality.

No. No, this can't be happening. I choked on a scream, my voice heavy with anguish. Everything was falling apart, and it felt like my chest was caving in. When I tried to draw in a deep breath, the pain shot through me like a dagger, a constant reminder of my limitations.

"Slow down, man. Try to relax," Kyle urged, his hand resting on my shoulder. "You heard what he said—you can work on building up your stamina. It's not the end of the world, T."

"It is for me," I gasped out, tears drenching my face. "Hockey is everything to me! You don't understand, without it I'm nothing—Cricket got hurt for nothing if I can't play hockey!"

"That's not true," Kyle said, his voice stern. "Hockey doesn't make you, T. You'll play again, I promise. When we get out of here, I can help you. Don't worry, fam. I got you."

"You play?" I asked, eyes widening.

"Sure." He shrugged. "I ain't pro or shit, but I'm pretty decent. My older bro loves hockey and shit, forced me to watch every game since I was nine. Oh—Ah, do you know Mario Lemieux? From the Pittsburgh Penguins? I heard that motherfucker battled Hodgkin's lymphoma! Fucking cancer, but the damn bastard still played his heart out!"

I gave a wet laugh. "Yeah, man."

"And—Ah—fuck! What's his name?" Kyle snapped his fingers. "Paul Kariya! He played for the Anaheim Ducks. That dude endured several concussions and post-concussion syndrome throughout his entire career! Fam, there's so many people I could mention, but you just have to set your mind to it and commit, trust me. You'll play again."

Make it so. Captain Jean-Luc Picard's voice hummed like a finely tuned engine in my ears. *Make it so*. Hope fluttered in my heart like the wings of a butterfly. Kyle's hand curled around mine, strong and steady. I never had close friends growing up. Cricket had been my best friend and Grayson my lover, but nobody else.

Hope. Looking into those brown eyes, I latched onto it, as if it were a log drifting in the raging tides.

Friends in a place like this seemed impossible.

But that's exactly what I found.

***

I GROANED AS KYLE half pulled and half dragged me to the workout area. I was never one for lifting weights, not that I wasn't in shape, but I leaned more on the lithe side.

"What are we doing here?" I protested.

Kyle scoffed, his voice dripping with impatience. "Stop whining like a bitch," he snapped. "You've been healed for weeks, and all you've done is mope around."

He stood in front of one weight, a sly grin forming on his face. "Here," he said, picking it up. "You want to play pro hockey, right? Make it to the NHL and all that shit? Well, you gotta work for it, bro. Ain't nothing in this life handed to you, and I've got just the thing to help build your stamina."

I stared at the devious gleam in his eyes, a sense of impending doom creeping over me. "I will not like this, will I?"

Kyle let out a hearty laugh. "Nope," he admitted with a chuckle. "HIIT. Trust me, we do that shit every day, and your lung capacity will be amazing."

HIIT? Why hadn't I thought of that before? High-intensity interval training—pure genius. It was exactly what the doctor had recommended.

"You're in here for what? Two months? That's nothing," Kyle declared with confidence. "We'll get you back up to speed in no time."

I laughed and grabbed hold of the weights. "Bring it on."

***

One year later...

Rough hands fisted my Michigan Wolverines varsity jacket, as I snapped my cock deeper past a pair of warm pink lips.

"Fuck, Ian!" I growled, gripping onto the bleacher railings tighter. Ian's head bobbed, taking my cock down his throat, swirling his tongue against the tip. I threw my head back, dark spots dancing at the edges. Threading my fingers through Ian's blond curls, I grunted as his tongue flicked around the swollen head.

Ian was a fucking god when it came to sucking cock.

I grabbed onto his muscular tattooed arm, kneading the skin there and losing myself to our routine pre-game blow job. Fuck. Ian hollowed his cheeks, and pleasure erupted over my skin before I stumbled hard over the edge. I cursed as my orgasm tore through me. Spangled rays of fireworks flashed before my vision when Ian pulled off. Cold air slapped against my skin, and Ian nuzzled against my thigh before standing up, his massive frame forcing me back.

"You good?" Ian asked, adjusting his own varsity jacket.

"Yeah," I laughed, licking my dry lips. "That was amazing. Thanks."

He shrugged, his hair flopping over his brow.

"I'll see you in class later?" he asked, unable to keep the hopeful note from his voice. I nodded, leaning my head back and closing my eyes, not inclined to move just yet. Come cooled over my still twitching cock and my knees felt like jelly. "You better hurry. Coach Cornwall will kill you if you're late to class again."

"Mhmm," I replied, my voice heavy with sleep. "I'm coming."

Ian laughed, tucking my cock back into my jeans and zipping me up. "Don't wait too long."

I heard his feet swishing against the grass as he left. A cool wind invaded the seams of my jack and I shivered from the cold. Fuck, we'd have to find somewhere else to get each other off. Rolling my neck, I scrubbed a hand over my face. I toyed with my tongue ring, rolling it across my palate, its cool metal sensation dancing inside my mouth.

Ian was a good fuck. Closeted, but damn, could the guy suck a cock. What we had going was easy. Casual. I didn't need anything else to complicate my life. I shoved off from the back of the steel bleachers and stretched my limbs, groaning. I checked my phone and saw that class started in five minutes. Shit, I was going to be late and Coach was going to kill me if I failed this class.

I dashed across the Michigan University campus, my heart racing in sync with my footsteps. The early morning sun painted the surroundings in a warm, golden hue, casting long shadows on the cobblestone paths. Towering trees lined the walkways, their leaves painted with autumn's fiery palette. I couldn't help but smile as I took it all in. Fuck, this place was amazing.

After juvie, my parents were concerned about letting me go to university. But I assured them I'd be on my best behavior to keep my scholarships and not end up in that hellhole ever again. I kept my grades up the first year and earned a spot as co-captain on the team and then, finally, Coach promoted me to captain this Sophomore year. It was wild when I thought about it.

Being here, on a full-ride hockey scholarship, felt like a dream come true. The towering academic buildings, the buzz of students hurrying to class, the vibrant energy of a campus alive with possibilities—it all made me feel incredibly lucky. I had friends here. Real friends who cared about what happened to me and didn't care that I liked to suck cock. Hell, even a few guys on the team offered to blow me when they were drunk enough. I laughed it off, of course, but Ian had been serious.

Thus, our friends-with-benefits thing we had going. Coach knew and didn't give a fuck, he even once said, "I don't care if you're as flamboyant as a disco ball off the ice, but when you're on it, I expect you to be as tough as a puck to the boards."

Damn, I love that guy.

He was tough as nails, and he drove us hard, but he made me a better player.

I reached my classroom just in time and slid into a seat beside Ian, who shot me a sly look. Professor Willson glared at me, and then the lecture on chemistry began. Fuck, this shit was boring and as much as I tried to focus, I couldn't help but drift. Chemistry was my nemesis. Exercise physiology might be my major, but I couldn't care less about it. All I wanted was to be out on the ice, perfecting my skills.

Not sitting here listening about atoms and particles or whatever else.

The lecture seemed to drag on forever, my mind wandering between formulas and hockey plays. When it finally ended, I felt a mixture of relief and dread as Professor Wilson called me over.

"Mr. Taylor? A moment please," she clipped, and I knew I was done for.

"Well," Ian said, his large hand clasping my shoulder. "It was nice knowing you."

"Fuck off," I hissed, shrugging him off.

He laughed and shoved my shoulder.

"I'll save you a seat in the cafeteria," Ian said, turning to leave, a smile dancing on his lips. I braced myself for what was sure to be bad news, fearing the impact it might have on my scholarship and my future in the game I loved. *Shit. I was trying, though.* I went to all the after-school study sessions and even had Professor Wilson tutor me herself, but I still wasn't getting it.

Taking off her glasses, Professor Wilson massaged her temple, and I waited for the inevitable bad news. "Mr. Taylor—"

"I'm really trying," I interrupted her, my pulse racing. "I know you can see that. I need to pass this class, but I'm just not getting it. I'm good with the biology stuff, but chemistry it's like an alien language that I can't seem to grasp no matter what. Please. If I fail, I'll lose my scholarship and then I'll be kicked out."

Professor Wilson's mouth thinned, her dark skin smooth and ageless in the luminescent lights. Her black hair was in a French braid and piled on top of her head. "Fine."

I nearly sank in relief.

"You get one more chance," Professor Wilson said, shuffling some papers before handing me a slip. "Take this to the Academic Resource Center and they'll assign you a tutor for the remainder of the semester"—she snatched it back before I could grab it—"and I want to see significant improvement before I can pass you."

"Yes, thank you! Thank you! You're truly a godsend."

Professor Wilson rolled her eyes. "Good day, Mr. Taylor."

"You too! Say, is that a new hairstyle? You look great today, Professor Wilson!" I babbled, walking backward out of the room, hoping this wasn't a dream.

Her lip twitched, and I knew I was pushing my luck, so I fled, heart pounding. *Damn, that was close.*

6

UNMASKING GRAYSON

JAYDEN TAYLOR

I didn't know what I'd do if I lost my place here. Walking to the café, the inviting scent of freshly brewed coffee pulled me closer. Inside, students gathered in groups over textbooks, creating a lively atmosphere with the clatter of dishes and the hiss of the espresso machine. Colorful artwork adorned the walls, and through large windows I glimpsed the sprawling campus grounds.

Ian waved me over, sitting with several other guys from the team. Each was talking shit and eating, while a few hunched over their textbooks.

"You good?"

"Yeah." I grinned, and he tossed me an orange Gatorade. My heart warmed at little actions like that. Ian was always getting me stuff, always being selfless, and for the first time, I pondered why I didn't consider dating him seriously. He turned to look at me with big doe brown eyes, like two chestnuts bathed in soft candlelight. "Thanks."

Ian leaned in closer. "Do you have time later?" he asked, his hot breath brushing the shell of my ear. "You can visit my dorm room for a minute."

I bit back a groan, adjusting my cock in my jeans. "Sure, sure. I'll be there." I turned to stare deep into his eyes, feeling my heart rate increase. Damn, Ian was too attractive for his own good and it felt safe to be out among the guys and having them not care who I was sleeping with.

"Bro, did you hear?" Carson said, forcing us apart.

"Nah, what?" I asked, taking a sip of my Gatorade.

"Next week, we're going up against those bastards at Northridge University. The Frost Vipers or some shit? I heard last year they snagged our star player. Now he's going to play against us."

"Really? Who?"

"Fuck, I can't remember his name." Carson scratched his head. "Mason something, who cares? Coach Cornell wants us all on our A-game, bro. It's the first game of the season. We need to go hard."

I nodded, my head already filling with a few plays I wanted to try. I needed to run a few drills tonight, then I'd get the team ready to view some of the footage the Frost Vipers had on YouTube to see if we could figure out their strategy and help build morale for the team. "How's your right arm, Carson? Still giving you trouble?"

"Nah, I went to the doc a few days ago, and he gave me a clean bill of health. I'm set, bro," Carson said, rolling his shoulders. "Besides, I can't sit this one out just because of a bad shoulder."

I laughed. "You dislocated it in practice. I'd rather you be healthy than play with a fucked-up shoulder." Carson was a junior, but due to his skill, he'd secured a spot as the defenseman on the team.

"It's fine, Captain," he said with a wink. "Besides, my girlfriend's been itching to come to one of these games since I joined the team. I can't wait for her to see me play. Speaking of girlfriend—Yo Kayla!" he shouted, cupping his hands to his mouth.

A row of cheerleaders wearing their own varsity jackets turned their heads. Their coats, adorned with team patches, gleamed in school colors, and their spirited chatter filled the air. Kayla's head snapped up, and she placed her hands on her narrow hips. "What?"

"Come here!"

She rolled her pretty brown eyes and swaggered over, prompting several of her friends to follow. A cloud of perfume and laughter dawdled them as she jumped into Carson's lap. Another girl slid onto Ian's lap, placing a soft kiss on his cheek. I arched a brow at him, wondering if there was something he wanted to tell me. Ian laughed and patted the girl's ass.

"This is my best friend, Sarah. We go way back. This is Jayden... the guy I told you about," he said, but a blush spread down his neck and cheeks.

Sarah reached a hand over, and I shook it. "Ah, you're the handsome Jayden." She licked her bubble gum pink lips. "And I see you have my best friend wrapped around your finger. I love the tats."

"Thanks," I laughed, palming the tattoos peeking from my white V-neck t-shirt. "Sarah Simons? I think I heard about you. You're the one that runs the charity balls? I think the next one is Winter Wonderland?"

Her face lit up. "Yeah. I'm getting a degree in Humanities, but I love organizing events and shit. My mom says I should just become an event planner and be done with it."

"You should," Ian spoke, brushing her blonde hair over her shoulder. "You were made for it."

Sarah sighed. "Not in Tennessee. My dad would never go for it. Jeez, you know you've become your parents' minion when you answer their calls with 'What's your command, oh wise ones?'"

"Well, they pay for everything and money talks. But mine always says goodbye." I snorted.

"Ugh," Sarah groaned. "Being a broke ass college student is so cliche." She made a gagging noise in her throat. "The only thing that makes it worthwhile is seeing my cat Coco come running to greet me at the door at the end of the day, and then ignore me after she realizes I don't have any treats."

I laughed. "Yeah, I have a dog to provide me with unconditional love, but I also have a cat to remind me I don't deserve it. It's all about balance."

Ian and Sarah chuckled, and she leaned closer to me. "You're really hot. I might just steal you for myself if my bestie wasn't so enamored with you."

"Bros before hoes," Ian said, and then stood, nearly sending her tumbling off his lap. "Hands off." Sarah's laugh sounded like wind chimes when Ian caught her and set her on the ground. Towering over her, she looked dwarfed compared to his size. "Anyway, we need to go. We have *that* assignment, remember?"

"Assignment?" Sarah peered up at him. "Isn't that code for a blow job?"

"Goodbye, Sarah!" Ian waved her off, his face blazing as he stormed away.

We shared a look but burst out laughing, and I bumped her fist. "See you around?"

Sarah's mouth curved into a mischievous smile. "Of course you will."

***

IAN SHOVED ME ONTO the bed, and his mouth quickly swallowed my laugh. Tearing off my shirt, he pressed me deeper into the soft mattress, rolling his hips. I tasted his coffee from earlier on his lips, the scent of sweet milk invading my nostrils.

"Damn," I chuckled, breathless. "Eager much?"

Ian grunted, pulling his shirt over his head, exposing his massive chest of rippling bronze muscle. Small wisps of blond hair covered his chest and abdomen, but I was too busy raking my hands over his broad back. "I'm gonna fuck you," he growled into my mouth and I whined, canting my hips.

Fuck, this is too good.

He wrenched off my jeans and underwear in one go, and I hissed as the cool air hit my dick. Tingling. Pulsing. Aching. He would be rough. I should have noticed the signs from earlier, the pent-up arousal begging for release. Ian's hand went into his night table drawer, and he tossed condoms and lube on the bed, his gaze scorching my skin.

"Fuck, you're gorgeous," he muttered, crawling over me to tease my lips with his. "These damn tattoos get me every time."

For a split second I thought he'd show mercy, but the spark of fire in his brown eyes was as bright as the sun's first light breaking over the horizon. *Fuck me.* His lips crashed into mine, warm and soft as they parted slightly, allowing my tongue to slip inside.

Grinding his hips against mine, I groaned when he flipped me onto my stomach. His hands rough and hard as he spread my cheeks apart. We fucked regularly, so there wasn't much need for prep as I arched my back and pressed into his thick fingers. Circling my puckered rim, he eased a slick finger inside before adding another one. "Fuck me, I need you," I gasped.

"Patience, young Padawan." Ian's rich chuckle enveloped my ears.

My cock twitched, dripping pre-come all over my stomach as I pushed against him, desperately seeking release from this endless edging.

"Fuck," Ian cursed, losing the rhythm he'd built before he withdrew. "Damn, Taylor. You're gonna make me come." His hands mapped out the tattoo spanning my lower back and torso, the ink spreading all the way up to the lower half of my neck. "One day, you're going to tell me what all this gibberish means."

"Not today," I laughed, but it broke off into a moan. Breaching the ring of muscle, his cock stretched my entrance. I gritted my teeth against the burn, then finally relaxed when he sank all the way in. Ian fisted my hair, yanking my head upright, as he snapped his hips forward. I grunted, feeling his balls slap against me, filling the room with skin smacking against skin.

Blunt nails scratch at my nipples, and I clutched at his waist. Ian's hand came around my throat, hard and possessive as he drove in deeper, each plunge tearing a scream from my throat.

"Fuck, fuck," Ian hissed and spat, and I felt the pressure building in my spine. My muscles pulled tight, every tendon and ligament strung taut on a bowstring, ready for that sweet, heavenly release.

It was so close now. I could practically taste it. The headboard slammed against the wall, and the legs on the bed screeched as Ian fucked me harder into the mattress.

"Yeah, fuck me," I whined, meeting his thrust.

Wrapping a hand around my leaking cock, Ian stroked it in time with our fucking, causing my vision to fracture like shattered glass. My body barely belonged to myself. Captivated by the need to reach that release and bring Ian tumbling down with me.

Pleasure erupted within me like a dazzling fireworks display, painting my world in bursts of ecstasy. I came hard with a shout, soaking the sheets beneath us.

Ian's hips stuttered and faltered, his muscular thighs jerked, and the searing heat of his touch caused my inner walls to constrict and pulse.

"Fuck, Jayden," he whispered, plummeting off the edge. He shoved in deep one last time, choking on a cry of release as he collapsed on my back.

The rise and fall of his sleek chest made my back itch. I laughed, and it vibrated in my throat as I tried to catch my breath. Ian's sweat and musk drifted in my nose and my eyes drooped as I basked within his touch. "You're heavy, get off," I mumbled, and he rolled to the side, panting.

Ian curled his hand around the back of my head, threading his fingers through my dark curls. "Fuck, you're beautiful, Jayden."

It wasn't something guys usually said to other guys, but I was happy about the compliment. Ian had been my first. The first guy I slept with and the first guy to show me how wonderful sex could be with someone you cared about.

Licking my dry lips, I pulled away, noticing how his eyes dimmed a little. "Thanks. I really needed that."

Ian sighed through his nose and stared up at the ceiling. "So, what did Professor Wilson say?"

"She hired a tutor at the Academic Resource Center," I responded, and put my chin on my folded arms. "Fuck, I can't fail this class or I'll be screwed."

"Why don't you just change your major?"

I stiffened at the suggestion. "I can't."

"Why?" Brown eyes peered up at me, but I ignored his gaze.

This was why it was hard for me to connect with other people. Other than my brother, Ian didn't know what I had gone through just to be here like everyone else. Once Cricket was healed, I planned to help him regain his strength by studying Exercise Physiology. If I had a degree in that field, my parents wouldn't have to spend money on finding experts.

"Is it for your brother?" Ian asked, his large hand brushing away some stray curls that fell over my brow. "For Cricket?"

"Yeah," I said, my voice soft.

"Any word about his condition?"

I shook my head. Cricket's experimental treatment started last year, but so far, I hadn't heard anything. Between hockey and my classes, I wasn't able to visit much, but whenever I did, the nurse let me do some exercises to help him with his atrophied limbs. "The doctor said a few weeks ago they saw some brain activity, which was a good sign, but not much improvement since then. Gosh, my mom was so happy, but it didn't end up leading anywhere."

"And your dad?"

My jaw tightened. Growing up, we had a close relationship, but after Cricket's accident, he changed. He barely visited and when he did, he was drunk out of his mind or just staring off into space. I wanted to hate him, but found that I couldn't. Cricket had been the heart of our family and now that he was gone, it felt like there was a gaping hole punched through us.

"Well, my dad believes alcohol is a perfect solvent. It dissolves marriages, families, and careers, the whole nine yards."

Ian's face twisted, but he said nothing.

"I just wish... Ah, it doesn't matter. Things are how they are. The only way they can change is if we make it so."

"You know, after Marsha killed herself, I didn't think there was much good left in this world…" Ian said. A muscle in his cheek jumped. "Then I swore I'd live to the fullest and not let my sister's memory die with her. When we met, you helped me see that."

"When we met, I was a junior shit that thought he knew everything about hockey," I laughed, trying to lighten the mood. Marsha was Ian's best friend before she died. She'd been bullied at school and they didn't find out until it was too late. "You're the only one who saw potential in me, well, other than Coach Cornell. Hell, I started out with nothing, and I still have most of it."

Ian huffed a laugh and leaned over, kissing me firmly on the lips. "I love that about you."

"What?" I asked, breathless when he pulled away.

"You're light," Ian replied. "When I first saw you, you looked so dangerous, but who knew you were as soft and malleable as Jell-O."

"You did not just compare me to Jell-O."

"I did," Ian whispered, nibbling my bottom lip. "What are you going to do about it?"

I shoved him onto his back before straddling his hips. Ian groaned and thrust up, grabbing my narrow waist with his big hands.

"This." I propped myself over him and kissed him deeper, sliding my tongue deeper, allowing the ball of my tongue ring to run over the seam of his mouth. Ian hummed and then bit my bottom lip, hard. I yanked away and growled at his laughing form. "Ouch! What was that for?"

"There's a new restaurant called Karma. There's no menu. You get what you deserve."

"Bastard!" I hissed, and then lunged for him.

***

COACH CORNELL'S BOOMING voice echoed through the locker room, making my ears ring. His wrinkled face contorted with determination as he delivered his fiery speech.

"All right, you sacks of potatoes!" he barked, his tone demanding our full attention. "We're about to play the best game of your goddamn pathetic lives!"

"Yes, Coach!" we roared in unison, adrenaline coursing through our veins.

Coach Cornell pointed at me. "Take it away, Taylor."

"Yes, sir!" I responded, turning to face our team's eager faces.

"Listen up, Wolverines!" I shouted, channeling the power surging within me. "This is our turf. Those guys came here thinking it'd be an easy win, but we won't let them have it!"

"Wolverines!" our team chanted in response to my question, their voices a thunderous roar.

"How do we win?" I yelled, rallying their spirits.

"Smash them with our teeth and claws!" they shouted, their intensity matching mine.

I let out a triumphant howl, feeling the collective energy surge through us. "Now let's get out there and kick some ass!"

We stormed out of the locker room, ready to defend our territory and make Coach Cornell proud. Blood roared in my ears as the chanting grew louder and louder as we got into the rink. I scanned the sea of fans, the blinding bright lights obscuring my vision as the announcer boomed our names.

"Now presenting the Michigan Wolverines!" The crowd erupted in cheers as we skated onto the ice. Sweat trickled down my brow, a mix of excitement and pre-game jitters, sending shivers across my skin.

We ran circles around the ice, warming up and preparing for the first game of the season. As I skated, I spotted my mom in the stands, and to my surprise, my father was there too, holding a can of beer. A sigh escaped my lips; at least they showed up.

The deafening roar of the crowd sent my heart racing. All was going smoothly until my eyes landed on a familiar jersey number 55. My heart stopped dead in my chest.

It couldn't be.

Grayson Hayes.

Bile surged hot and thick in my throat, and I spun on my skates, momentarily blinded by the flashing lights. He was here. Playing for a different university, but the league still allowed the bastard to play, even after what he did to my brother? Impossible. There must be some kind of mistake.

Ian gave me a strange look when I stopped moving.

"Are you okay?" he shouted, but the white noise buzzing in my ears drowned his voice. I stared off into the opposite side and caught Grayson's side profile. A smile kinked his lips, and his gray eyes scanned the area before crashing into mine. Thunder crackled. The sky stirred itself into a frenzy, with pockets of gray and black clouds colliding.

It pealed and yowled with bursts of brute force, making discordant noises that shattered my eardrums.

Everything came rushing back like water filling a small cavern.

Grayson.

Cricket.

It was as if no time had passed at all. The smile adorning his lips waned before it faded entirely. Good. Rage burned hot and thick in my veins and I shoved past Ian, almost knocking him over in my haste to get in line first. Everything else was a blur.

"Ready. Set. Begin!" The puck flew and so did I, but not in the direction the puck was going.

But into him. I slammed into Grayson, using the full weight on my body to crush him against the boards. My body collided with his, the impact sending shockwaves through my bones. He crashed into the boards, a heavy thud echoing in the arena. The crowd gasped, and for that moment, all I could feel was the satisfaction of leveling the traitor. He cried out, his face wide with shock and horror as he gazed deep into my eyes.

"Remember me?" I hissed, dark and low, hatred roaring like lightning in my veins.

Luckily, the ref didn't notice. I skated away, keeping the bastard within my sights. Ian shot me a strange look and the rest of the guys were looking at me like I'd grown a second head.

I didn't care.

Because to me, this wasn't a game anymore.

This was war.

7

— • —

SECRETS BENEATH THE SURFACE

GRAYSON HAYES

We lost 5-0. My world shattered as someone tripped me, my body crashing to the cold ice. Agony erupted from my knee, a searing fire coursing through my limbs. The metallic taste of blood filled my mouth as I gasped for breath, dizziness overwhelming me. Jayden skated past me, a cruel smile dancing on his lips. *I deserved it, though.* Sprawling on the ice, I shook my battered head, feeling the aches stab like sharp needles in my back and spine.

"You all right, bro?" Devon said, helping me to my feet. "Why the fuck is that asshole targeting you?"

My tongue was cleaved to the roof of my mouth, and I said nothing, skating off to the exit. Coach Leroy caught my eye, his gaze promising vengeance, but I was far too battered to care about him or what my father would think of me acting like a pussy on the ice. Seeing Jayden again was like a lance down my spine. Those piercing emerald eyes were just the same as Cricket's.

Jayden. Whose eyes were the hue of fresh spring buds, intense and soft all at once. Fuck. My stomach roiled, and I fought wave after wave of nausea as I went to the locker rooms, peeling off my gear piece by piece. Nobody said anything as if waiting for the anvil to drop. A crushing weight made the hairs on the back of my neck bristle, and I looked up to see Coach Leroy and my father enter the room.

"So," Coach Leroy said, his thin arms were crossed over his chest, but it was his eyes that nearly ripped the breath from my lungs. "What the hell happened out there?" He wasn't loud. Never loud.

Pitch black serpentine eyes landed on me, and I looked away. *Damn it.*

"Hayes? Care to enlighten us?" he asked. His gaze was icy, stinging sharp nails that seemed to strip my skin and shrink my soul. "You seemed familiar with the guy who had it out for you all night."

"It's nothing," I replied, my voice too quick. Too dismissive.

He latched onto it with his talons. "Is that so? Well, this nothing feud you have going on just cost us the first game of the season."

A knot snarled in my throat, and I felt the weight of everyone's gaze on me. Running a hand through my sweaty brown hair, I kept my head low and nodded. "It won't happen again, sir."

"See that it doesn't," the coach spoke, then turned with my father and left.

I sank with relief, and Devon clapped me on the back. "Don't worry, man. It was shit all over. Don't let what coach said get to you."

"Why shouldn't he?" Kyle sneered. "Half the game, he was sprawled on the ice like a little bitch. And what the hell was up with the ref? Was he fucking blind or what?"

"Yeah, those fucking Michigan Wolverines play dirty!" another person chimed in.

"That guy was quick," Devon said to me. His brown eyes were wide and framed by thick black lashes. "Man, if you told me you had beef with him, I would have backed you up, bro, but having him throttle you all over the ice? Now that's fucking barbaric."

I slapped my locker door, not wanting to listen to another word. "I'll handle it. Leave it be."

Devon scoffed and went back to dressing, while I slung my bag over my shoulder and walked out, wishing to be freed from the suffocating atmosphere. I stepped outside, feeling the light rain pelt my face. A shiver rolled through me and I wished the ground would swallow me whole.

The way Jayden looked at me... well, I couldn't blame him.

He hated me. Just as much as I hated myself. I wished we could go back to that night we spent together in his house. Jayden had been so young. I never told Cricket, but the minute I laid eyes on his brother, I was gone. I waited until Jayden turned eighteen before making a move. Tears burned my eyes, and my bottom lip swelled where I had bitten into it after falling onto the ice. The skin was lightly shredded.

"Grayson," my father clipped, standing next to a sleek black limousine, hands shoved deep into his black slacks and his suit jacket unbuttoned. "Let's go."

Hitching my bag higher, I followed him into the car. I stared at the window, feeling the silence yawn and stretch, whispering a silent prayer that tonight my father would be in a good mood and let this loss slide. "You've disappointed me."

Guess not. "Sorry, sir."

"You look at me when I'm speaking, boy," he snarled, and I could feel the rage building inside him. Turning my head, I stared at my father. His brown hair was perfectly coiffed, shaved at the sides with enough on top to style. "Tonight was a fucking disgrace. I don't know how you plan to make it to the NHL when you play like a goddamn pansy. And you fucking let that Jayden boy bitch slap you all over the ice tonight. What happened? Did his family threaten you?"

"No," I replied, wishing I could end this conversation. "I just... I didn't expect to see him, that's all."

My father's jaw worked, and he nodded. "Okay. I see. Other than that, no other problems?"

I bit into my lips, tasting blood. It was now or never. "I-I want to go back to Michigan University."

"You *what*?"

"I hate it here. I have no friends. Coach Leroy is a stuck-up bastard who hates my guts for coming onto his team halfway through the year and stealing the captain's position from Devon. Everybody knows Devon deserves that position. I haven't earned it. The guys don't respect me. I want off this team—"

Pain exploded against the side of my face. I snapped back so hard, my head slammed against the glass window.

"Fuck," I hissed. Blood flooded from my mouth, salty and thick, leaving a lingering trace of iron on my palate.

"First, never disrespect me in my own goddamn car," my father snarled. "Second, after all the fucking money I paid to make that stunt you pulled two years ago disappear, you want to go back? The goddamn settlement and the medical bills I'm still paying for so that vegetable can remain on life-support?"

My breath hitched, and I turned back to him, startled.

"Oh, you think I didn't know about that?" His mouth dragged into a smirk. "It doesn't matter. The boy is as good as dead anyway. Those doctors you hired can't do shit for him." He ran a hand through his hair. "Fuck, Grayson. I don't know how you could do something so stupid—"

"It was an accident," I said, but bitter tears welled in my eyes before spilling over. "You saw the video footage. It wasn't my stick—"

"It wasn't your stick, but you were so damn close it might as well have been," he said, shaking his head. "Now you want to go back? You have it good at Northgate University. Why change? Who cares if the guys don't respect you as captain? Make them. I'm paying enough money to have you on the team. Just do what you came here to do and once you make it pro, you can spit in their faces for all I care."

"Dad," I cried, my voice cracked. I hated begging to the bastard. "I can't do it anymore. I play better at Michigan. They have better programs. I know I fucked up, but I—I just want things to go back to normal."

He scrubbed a hand over his face, his jaw tightening. "You know what? Fine. Coach Cornell did wonders for you. I'll make the arrangements tomorrow. I'll notify the housekeeper and have her get the condo ready for you near campus."

I tried not to show too much relief, but it was palpable. *God, I missed Michigan.* I didn't care if everyone hated me there; I just wanted things to go back to how they were before. My father's phone buzzed, and he whipped it out to take the call, and I knew our conversation was over.

Soon he'd leave, and I'd be alone again.

And I couldn't wait.

Looking out the window, with my face throbbing and my mouth pooling with blood, I thought of Jayden. With eyes like a fresh blade of grass covered in dew. How much he'd grown in the time I've been away. I'd make things right between us.

Just wait. Soon he'd be mine again.

***

MY FATHER MADE ALL the arrangements, and within a few hours, I had packed my stuff at the mansion and headed back to the condo I'd once wanted to share with Cricket. The valet grabbed my stuff, and my father spoke into the mouth of his phone with a harsh whisper, and I knew he'd be leaving soon. Waiting for him, I leaned against the limo, arms crossed over my chest to fend off the bitter cold.

"All right," Dad said. "Here." He handed me several brand-new credit cards. "Charge it to these accounts and I'll top you up next month. Don't go crazy with the spending like last time."

"Yes, sir." I was counting the seconds until he fucked off.

"I'm on a tour to Europe again, and I won't be back for another six months," he explained, but we both knew I didn't give a fuck. As long as he stayed gone. Checking the time again, he cursed, and then looked up to the sprawling penthouse we were standing in front of. "Call my agent if it's an emergency."

"Yes, sir."

He regarded me for several moments and then sighed. "You have a lot of potential, son. I don't want to see it wasted on nothing. Stick to your books and hockey, and I know you'll do well."

These pep talks meant nothing. Especially since he always followed them up by bashing my fucking head in. "Yes, sir. Thank you."

"Good, now get some rest. You look like shit." He jerked his head, and the valet came around to open the limo door. Watching him leave, I wished to God that his plane would crash, and he'd be burned alive inside. I turned on my heel and went upstairs with my gear slung over my shoulder. A few of the neighbors who recognized me nodded, but I kept to myself, sliding my palm down the steel railing.

I stepped into the elevator, the polished chrome doors closing behind me with a soft, futuristic whoosh. It ascended smoothly, and as the doors opened onto the penthouse floor, the opulence that had once been my mother's domain greeted me.

The condo was a symphony of chrome and glass. A lavish show of my father's success in the real estate world and becoming a tycoon in the industry. The spacious living area featured floor-to-ceiling windows that overlooked the city's skyline, offering a breathtaking view. A grand, marble-topped island dominated the open-concept kitchen, its gleaming surface reflecting the sparkling chrome appliances.

Despite the luxury, the penthouse felt empty, a stark contrast to the warmth my mother had once filled it with. Her absence echoed in the pristine emptiness.

I tossed my keys onto the granite countertop, their clatter disturbing the silence that enveloped the place. Grabbing a drink from the fridge, I wasn't surprised to see that someone had fully stocked it with a clean diet. Vegetables, fruits, diet bars and packed meats brimmed on the shelves. Even though my father had a shitty attitude, he always stressed the importance of eating clean while I was playing hockey.

I threw my bag on the floor and went into the bedroom, tossing the drink out when I passed the trash can. Turning on the lights, I sighed at the gray comforter and large panel windows. Cricket used to love to jump on my bed, and I used to laugh my ass off when he fell off.

Those were the days. I sank down at the edge of the mattress and took out my phone, thumbing through old pictures of us hiking with Jayden trailing behind, struggling to keep up. I laughed at his cute face; upturned button nose scrunched in discomfort. Tracing his face with my fingers, something hot and heavy panged in my chest.

It was all gone now.

The life. The light. I groaned, digging my palms into my eyes, and then hissed when pain jolted through the tenderness on the side of my cheek. Fuck, I was sure it looked as bad as it felt. It didn't matter.

I'd had worse. Laying down on the bed, I stared up at the ceiling. Tears stung before they spilled over, and I allowed myself a moment of weakness.

Jayden.

His eyes were filled with such hatred. *I deserved it. I know I did. I let Cricket down.* That night, so many things had happened. My father came unannounced, telling me I had to switch schools or else he'd stop paying my tuition. The brawl that literally came out of nowhere. One second, we were playing hockey and the next, these assholes looked like they wanted to kill Cricket just for looking at them the wrong way. It all happened so fast. I didn't know what was happening until I saw the guy's fist strike Cricket like a damn gauntlet. Then he was flying on the ice into the boards and when I moved forward to help him, he tripped.

On one of the guy's sticks.

We were so close together it was hard to see who was where, but when I replayed that video a thousand times, I realized then that the other guy had tripped him. That video evidence was submitted in the trial against the two bastards that attacked Cricket, and they let me off. But that didn't stop tongues from wagging. Jayden had been absent during this time, but the Taylors had let it go and I made private arrangements with them to take care of all of Cricket's medical bills and help him find experimental treatment to cure his brain injury.

Jayden had no clue and I made sure of it.

Mrs. Taylor told me when to visit to avoid Jayden and I was glad for it. The last thing I wanted was for Jayden to think I was trying to get to him through his parents. I loved Cricket. I didn't lie when I told Jayden that Cricket was like a brother to me. My chest cracked open at the memory of Cricket's face smashing against the boards, blood pouring from his lips.

I couldn't help him.

I couldn't save him.

My entire world was ripped away. Cricket had been my first friend at university. I stayed at his place, avoiding my dad at all costs around the holidays. The Taylors had become my family in such a short amount of time.

And Jayden.

He was my soul.

Green fairy-like eyes flickered in my vision. His gasp. The way his entire face dusted pink as I took him into my mouth for the first time. *Fuck, I had been so impatient.* Too pent up from wanting him and waiting until he turned eighteen. It had been my first time as well, and the only frame of reference I had was porn. Licking my bloodied lips, I sighed long and deep, my cock swelling in my dark blue Levi jeans. Jayden.

How was he now? Where did he go during the trial? Would he believe me if I told him the truth? Showed him the video? Unlikely, but I had to try.

For him.

For us.

***

ROWS OF SCARRED WOODEN lockers lined the room, each adorned with stickers and team logos. A lingering scent of sweat and old equipment hung heavy in the air. Hockey jerseys dangled from hooks, their vibrant colors contrasting the dull walls. The floor, scuffed and worn, echoed with the camaraderie of past victories. I'd spent a year of my life here and hated every second.

A large part of me couldn't wait to leave.

I packed up my stuff from my locker, taking the hockey gear I brought with me. The doors opened and closed, but I didn't stop even as Devon leaned against the lockers beside me, his black eyes drilling into my skin.

"So... are you going to even tell us what's goin' on or do we have to guess?" he asked, but he looked pissed.

"There's nothing to guess." I shoved my stuff inside with more force than necessary. "I quit. I'm a quitter. You get your position as team captain back, and I'll head to the Michigan Wolverines team where I belong."

Devon scoffed a laugh, but his face hardened. "Just like that? You run to our rival team after learning all our secret moves for a year?"

I allowed a growl around the lump in my throat. "It is what it is. You'll learn new moves." I moved to walk away, but Devon intercepted me.

"Bro, what the hell is your problem? We've been nothing but nice to you here, even considering your background. You're the best center forward we've got, and now you're just going to leave us all hanging? Some guys don't have it like you do. We can't just call daddy and switch teams whenever we want—"

"You have no idea the shit I have to go through!" I snapped at him, teeth bared. "You think I want his money? You think I wouldn't swap places with one of you for just a day, so I wouldn't have his fist raining down on me?"

Devon held his hands up in surrender. "Jeez, sorry, man—"

"Forget it. I'm gone."

Devon grabbed my arm. "Wait, fuck. That shiner, bro. He did that to you?"

I wrenched away from him, fleeing the locker room. It was all the same shit, anyway. People knew my father beat me. That Lawrence Philip Hayes Jr hated his only son. Growing up, my teachers had seen it and any that spoke up about it were swiftly removed from their position. I hated the bastard, but I needed him. The same way he needed me to fulfill some sick fantasy he had of me achieving his hockey dreams where he'd failed. I didn't need to explain my life to Devon.

I yanked out the dual doors of the university, an icy blast of wind slicing at my cheeks. Freedom. It was freedom at last.

8

SKATING ON SHADOWS

GRAYSON HAYES

P ristine snow blanketed the ground, glistening under the winter sun. Delicate frost adorned the tall trees' barren branches.

In heavy coats, students bustled about, their breath visible in the crisp air. In the winter, the Michigan University campus became a picturesque scene straight out of a snow globe. I pulled my thick jacket even closer as a gust of wind sent a flurry of snow swirling around me. The chilly air bit at my cheeks, making them rosy. I was in the midst of the semester, navigating the hassle of reclaiming my old classes after my brief hiatus.

My degree in Health Sciences demanded my full attention, and I remembered my days of tutoring on the side to earn money, reducing my reliance on my father. The threat of him cutting me off had always loomed, and since he discovered my sexuality, I knew it was only a matter of time.

I was eagerly awaiting that day as I made my way to check if my old tutoring job was available. Lost in thought, I wasn't paying attention to where I was going and collided with someone. My books and theirs scattered across the snowy ground.

"Shit, sorry," I muttered, hastily helping them gather their belongings.

"No worries," a melodic voice responded, laughing before it faltered. "Grayson? Is that you?"

My head snapped up, and I stared into Sarah's pretty brown eyes. Damn. Swallowing hard, I forced a smile. "Sarah Simons? Wow. Sorry, I'm so clumsy." I forced a laugh, but her smile waned.

"Yeah. Good to see you. How've you been?" She tucked her books away.

"Good. Good," I lied, my nervousness making my movements stiff. "Look, I owe you an apology."

Sarah looked thoughtful for a moment before nodding. "Yes, you do, but not right now. I have stuff to do."

"Then coffee later? My treat?" I suggested, my heart pounding in my chest.

She seemed to consider it before nodding. "Your number still the same?"

I had to ask, even though it made my insides cringe. "Yeah," I replied, hoping she'd agree.

"Text me. I'll meet you later," she said before walking away, leaving me with a lot to make up for. Fuck, being with Sarah during my time of confusion had been a big mistake.

I already knew I was gay, but she was there and pretty and the guys kept telling me to go for it. We only dated for a few months and I was just killing time until Jayden turned eighteen and I could pursue him, but Sarah had thought we were getting serious. I never broke things off with her properly, before everything went to hell with Cricket on the ice that night. Then I had to switch schools because the rumors were too much and I couldn't bear the videos circulating online saying that I had tried to kill my best friend.

My brother.

Sarah had been collateral then. I ghosted her and left with my tail between my legs. Scrubbing my face, I walked towards the Academic Resource Center, hoping that they still had my tutoring position available.

"Grayson?" a voice called the moment I stepped inside. "Oh, my word, is that you?" Carry gasped, placing a large hand over her chest. "You're so big! Come here and give me a hug!"

I laughed, pulling her into my arms. The scent of old perfume and crisp apple pie filled my nostrils. "Morning, Mrs. Lawson," I said, pulling away and ducking my head. She swatted at my arm.

"Call me Carry," she laughed. "Wow, you're here. Please tell me you're here for your old job back? I just had three tutors quit on me because of midterms coming up."

"Yes, ma'am," I said.

"Well, it must be my lucky day. Jamal, you'll never guess who came back!" Carry hollered.

"Who came back?" a voice asked, coming out of the office rooms. "Grayson?" Jamal's eyes widened, and he held out a massive hand. "Damn, bro, good to see you!" We clasped hands, his dark skin beautifully contrasting with mine. Jamal's hazel eyes were bright and, God, had I missed this place. "Please tell me you're coming back. Things have been crap without you here."

I laughed again. "Yeah, bro. I'm back. Officially."

"Well, that is music to my ears honey," Carry bellowed, then took out some paperwork. "Sign on the dotted line and I have a list of people right here begging for help on their Chemistry assignments. Things are different this year," Carry warned, passing me the papers. "The teachers are now asking for updates for specific students that are at risk for being put on academic probation. So, if they don't show up or they're late or not taking part in the tutoring program, we are required now to let the professors know so that they can take the next step with the guidance counselors."

"Fair enough," I replied, reading over the documents.

"Come have a seat in my office," Jamal said, waving me back. "We can catch up."

I slipped past Carry's large frame and headed into the office. The room was spacious, bathed in soft, warm lighting. Jamal sat on the opposite side of a substantial wooden table. Shelves lined with academic books framed the room. A large window offered a view of the campus courtyard. The atmosphere was professional and welcoming, making me feel at ease despite the impending conversation.

"Damn, it's good to see you. I thought for sure we'd have trouble next semester with handling the workload, but with you back I'm confident things will work out now," Jamal spoke, then reached up to boil some water on his small kitchenette. "So, what have you been up to? I heard you were playing at Northgate for the Frost Vipers?"

"Yeah, I left though. I couldn't stand it there. Plus, it was more my father's idea than mine to leave. I just wanted to wait until things died down, you know? But they just spiraled and Cricket..." I trailed off, trying not to get emotional. "Anyway, you know how it goes."

Jamal scratched his cheek, the hairs bristling. "Yeah, I tried to visit a few times, but I heard he's been moved." He sighed. "He was a great man."

I nodded, thinking back on our tutoring days together. "Yeah, anyway, what have I missed around here?"

Jamal's face lit up. "Oh, you know, same old, same old. I asked Susan to marry me."

"No shit," I laughed. "What'd she say? Judging by your smile, I guess it's a yes."

"What can I say? I've got moves," he drawled. "I told her every married person should forget their mistakes. There's no point in two people remembering the same thing."

I chuckled, then looked down at the paperwork. "When's the big day?"

"Sometime next June, but I'll let her handle all of that stuff. I really don't care, just as long as she becomes mine. That's all that matters."

"Yeah, I'll never forget when my cousin got married," I said, checking off some things on the documents. "And people she hasn't seen in years were asking why they weren't invited and how could she forget them."

"Well, you know what I always say: Where there's a will, there's a relative."

We both laughed, and I took a moment to fill out the paperwork. "All done," I said, handing it back to him. "I can be free as early as Friday. I need to head over to the arena and speak to Coach Cornell about a spot on the team."

"Do you think he'll take you back?" Jamal asked, making sure everything was filled out properly.

"I think so. We've always had a good relationship. If not, I'll sit this season out."

Jamal's brows climbed. "No way. I've seen you play. You're the best defense center they ever had. They'd be crazy to have you sit out. Then again, that Jayden character isn't bad either, but the two of you together could make waves."

I shifted in my seat, uncomfortable. Jamal didn't know we all used to practice for hours on the ice-rink at the back of the Taylor's farm. Cricket and I taught Jayden everything he knew. But that was back then. I had no idea the type of player Jayden was now.

"Okay. Everything looks good, man," Jamal said, filing the paper-work away. "I'll be in touch with the list. Should we do your usual time? Fridays 1-3 PM?"

"Yeah, that works, thanks." I stood, and we shook hands.

"Good to have you back."

It was good to be back.

***

I WAITED IN THE HALLS like a coward until the locker rooms were empty from practice. I didn't want to chance running into Jayden before I had time to mentally prepare. I knocked on Coach Cornell's door and heard him holler, "Who is it? It better be the winning lottery ticket or leave me alone!"

I entered, and Coach's grouchy expression transformed into a grin.

"Grayson? Well, well, Christmas has come early." He stood, arms open, and I embraced him tightly, fighting back tears.

"Thanks, Coach," I croaked. Coach Cornell's scent was a blend of worn leather and the lingering echoes of sweat from years of hard work on the ice. The familiar aroma wrapped around me like a warm, reas-suring blanket, evoking memories of countless practices and games. It was a comforting fragrance, a reminder of the guidance and support he had provided throughout my hockey career.

When everyone else turned their back on me.

"You're back?" He patted my shoulder, but his eyes fell on the shiner on my face. "Damn, you should've let me call the authorities back then. It's not too late, Grayson."

I took a shaky breath. "I'm fine. He's in Europe, anyway. He won't care." I sank into the empty plastic chair in his office.

"So, are you back for good or just visiting?" Coach asked, sipping his black coffee.

"Actually, I'd like to see about getting my old spot on the team back. I'll earn my position so the guys don't think you're just giving it to me for free," I replied.

Coach's smile waned, and he sighed through his nose. "You know I'd love to do that, but Jayden is the captain now, and I'm afraid he won't take kindly to having you back."

I nodded, already prepared for this. "I know. I was going to make time to speak to him first, to set the record straight. He needs to know that I wouldn't have done anything to hurt Cricket. It was an accident. A horrible one."

Coach shook his head. "That's altruistic of you, boy, but I saw the way Jayden attacked you on the ice the other night. He's out for blood. Some guys are looking to go pro, and I can't have my two best players feuding and putting everyone else's career at risk."

A wave of anxiety washed over me. I knew it wasn't as simple as coming back to my old team, but this was the only place I truly felt at home. I needed to be here, even if it meant putting up with Jayden's ire. I deserved it. I hadn't protected Cricket when he needed me the most.

"How about a trial run, then? That's the only thing I can think of. If it doesn't work, I'll quit hockey," I proposed, desperation tingeing my words.

Coach's thin brows rose, and the light dancing on his scalp made it look glossy. He leaned back in his chair, the creaking of its worn leather matching the weight of the decision at hand. He regarded me with a thoughtful expression, his fingers drumming on the coffee-stained table. After a long, contemplative silence, he finally spoke.

"A trial run, huh?" He sighed. "Grayson, I'll talk to Jayden, but I can't make any promises. The team dynamic has changed since you left, and I need to ensure that your return won't disrupt the chemistry we've built. If Jayden agrees, we'll give it a shot. But if it affects the team negatively, I won't hesitate to make the necessary decisions."

I nodded, understanding the gravity of his words. "Thank you, Coach. I appreciate the chance."

Coach Cornell's gaze softened, and he smiled. "You were always a talented player, Grayson. Give me some time to talk to Jayden, and we'll see where we stand."

I stood. "I'll be ready, Coach. Thanks again." We shook hands, and I left his office. The weight of uncertainty hung in the air. My return to the team would depend on Jayden's willingness to forgive and forget, and it was a daunting prospect. But I was determined to make amends and prove that I belonged on the ice. Jayden would see I'm not the villain here and things would change.

They had to. I had to make him see how different I was now.

I checked the time. It was after one, so I texted Sarah, hoping she'd be available to meet for a quick coffee before I headed home.

Ready for an I'm-a-piece-of-shit free coffee? I texted, waiting for a reply.

Sure, she messaged back. *As long as it comes with a side of if-you-do-that-again-I'll-break-your-nuts cookies, I'm all yours. We can meet at our usual spot. Let's say five minutes?*

I laughed, then slipped my phone into my pocket. Being back had never felt better.

***

DUSTING OFF MY JACKET, I sighed as I entered the coffee shop. The aroma of freshly brewed coffee filled my nostrils, and I spotted Sarah sitting in front of a rose gold-colored MacBook. I went to the counter and ordered her favorite coffee with a shot of espresso, along with a few triple chocolate brownie cookies, recalling her preferences.

"Hey," I said, approaching the table.

"Hey," she replied softly, her pretty brown eyes locking onto mine. "Is that for me?"

"Ah, yeah," I answered, setting the coffee and cookies on the table. My heart pounded in my chest, and I couldn't shake the feeling that Sarah could see right through me. I feared she'd discover my unfaithfulness with Jayden, but I had to come clean, even if it meant she'd hate me.

"Mmm," Sarah moaned, taking a deep whiff of the coffee. "My favorite. You remember?"

I laughed, relief washing over me. "Of course, I do."

"God," Sarah said, her eyes distant. "It feels like a lifetime ago when we were all sitting here, shooting the shit and talking about our goals and dreams. You and Cricket singing Britney Spears at the top of your lungs."

I chuckled at the memory. "Yeah, but I'm glad that I'm back. It feels better."

Sarah nodded thoughtfully. "Yeah, I met Jayden for the first time the other day. That guy is smoking hot. He looks a lot like Cricket, but those tattoos. Damn." She fanned her face, and I couldn't help but laugh again. "So..." she drawled. "Are you back for now or back for good?"

"For good. At least I hope," I replied, rubbing my shaggy hair. "Look, I owe you an apology and an explanation. Back then, shit happened so fast and I... I didn't know what to do. Suddenly, everyone said that I killed—" My throat constricted, and my breath hitched. Fuck, I needed to get through this. Get the words out. Sarah placed her small hand over mine, her delicate fingers brushing against my large thumb. "My best friend. I—I couldn't do it. Everything. I thought I'd go crazy. Cricket was my world, and then he was gone."

Sarah sighed, and tears brimmed in her eyes. "Shit. That big lug always had me cracking up." She swatted at her tears, not wanting her mascara to run. "How's he doing? Any word?"

"Same. No change." It had been like that for the past year and I was slowly losing hope.

"Miracles happen," Sarah said, her voice stern. "We just gotta pray. Have faith."

Faith? I wanted to scoff. I wished I had some of that, but I didn't want to go down that road, especially since I was supposed to be apologizing to her. "Anyway, I'm a jackass. Sorry."

"You know I never thought you were," Sarah said, then a light blush tinted her cheeks. "Well, I did, but I knew why you just left. I don't think I could handle that well, either." She reached over and touched my cheek. "And I guess your dad is still the asshole of the year."

"Yeah, but he'll be in Europe for a while. It'll give me some time to make a living for myself so that I can leave."

"That's good. Do you know how long—"

"Sarah?" a voice interrupted, causing both our heads to turn. A large man wearing a Michigan Wolverines varsity jacket stood near the coffee entrance, his knapsack piled high on his left shoulder.

"Oh, Ian!" She waved him over and my sense of uneasiness grew. "This is my friend Grayson Hayes—this is my best friend Ian Smolder."

Ian's eyes narrowed into pinpricks, his shaggy blond hair covering his brown eyes, and he held his hand for me to shake. "Pleasure."

"Yeah," I said. We shook once and then he took a seat next to Sarah.

"Where's your boy toy?" Sarah asked Ian.

"In class…" Ian's eyes flickered to me. "So, how do you two know each other?"

Sarah gave me a sly look. "Well, this is the guy who broke my heart and smashed it into a million pieces by ghosting me."

"Sarah!" I exclaimed.

"What? It's true," she laughed. "Anyway, that was in the past. All is right as rain between us, right?"

"Not if you're trying to get me killed," I muttered, avoiding eye contact with her hulking friend, who looked like he could bench press me.

"Ian? He's soft as a dove, aren't you?"

"A dove with rabies," Ian replied, and then snorted. "Nah, if she says it's cool, it's cool."

I gave a nervous chuckle, knowing that if I stepped a foot out of line, he'd be sure to crush me with his boulder-sized hands. It was good to be back… Right? Right.

Seeing Sarah's gentle smile as we patched things up made it all worth it. Now, if only I could get Jayden on my side, things would truly be perfect.

9

TANGLED LINES

GRAYSON HAYES

Strolling down the winding pathway toward her dorm room, Sarah held onto my arm, her presence bringing warmth to the chilly winter air. My breath billowed out in visible puffs, but the comfort of having her close made it all bearable. Since my return less than a week ago, things had been smooth. No awkward encounters with Jayden. I seamlessly reconnected with my old classes, and the peace and quiet of my apartment was a welcome change from the turmoil of my father's abuse. Everything seemed great, yet there was an unshakable tightness in my chest whenever thoughts of Jayden crept in—close yet impossibly distant. I needed to make amends, but how?

I didn't know the person Jayden was now.

He seemed nothing like he was in the past. Soft and gentle, like grass cresting the rolling hills. Now he was different. Carved from iron and steel, his eyes like gems. How did I get through to him?

"A penny for your thoughts?" Sarah asked, tugging at my arm playfully.

"What's your new rate for conversation now? Better start saving."

She let out a light musical laugh. "Yep, you'll have to pay up or I'm out of here." We continued down the snow-covered lane until we reached her college dorm building. Once inside, shivering from the cold, she put on a kettle and took my jacket. I settled into the compact living space, curious about her college dorm.

The room was cozy, with a few posters on the walls and a scattering of textbooks across a wooden desk. Her bed, neatly made with a colorful quilt, took up one corner, and a small window let in a glimpse of the winter landscape outside. The place was inviting, filled with the essence of her personality. I found a spot on the couch, running my fingers over the wooly knit sweater that Anita, one of the housemaids, had given me last Christmas when my dad had forgotten to buy me a gift.

Running her blood-red acrylic nails down the seams of my sweater, her brow kinked. "You look so handsome," she remarked, before plopping down onto my lap. "I love a man in a wooly knit sweater," Sarah purred, her lips brushing against mine. "You should have known that would be my weakness."

I laughed and returned her kiss, though my heart wasn't fully in it. I liked Sarah, truly, but my time at Northgate University had made me realize how much I loved Jayden. I couldn't let another moment pass without him knowing. Things were different with her. I groaned through the kiss, tasting the cream from her pumpkin spiced latte and the intoxicating scent of her shampoo. One day Sarah would make a man very happy. *Just not today.*

I gripped her shoulders and gently slid her off my lap. "We need to talk."

Her brown eyes widened. "What is it? I thought... You came back, so I thought maybe you wanted to get back together or something..."

"No," I began, clearing my throat. "I came back to tell you that... I'm gay. That's why it could never work out between us."

Sarah looked as though she'd been slapped. Fuck, I'm such an ass-hole. Guilt once again swarmed me, like termites beneath the rotting wood. I had fucked up so badly in the past, and could never escape it, but with Sarah, I knew I had to set the record straight. She deserved better than to date some closeted jerk, too afraid to come out to his father.

"It was wrong to date you before, but I thought… I mean, I thought I'd change. Like it would go away or something. It's crappy, I know, but I thought you should know."

She gave a hollow laugh and shook her head. "Wow, first my best friend and now my ex-boyfriend? Damn, for a girl from Tennessee, my gaydar is shit."

I chuckled and took her hand. "Sorry. I never meant to hurt you. I wanted to tell you the other day, but…"

"It's fine," she interrupted. "It was my mistake for thinking… Anyway, who's the lucky guy?"

"Jayden Taylor."

Sarah whistled. "Damn, well, you better get in line."

I laughed as a blush crawled up my neck. Nobody but Cricket knew the extent of my feelings for Jayden, how much I wanted him from the moment I saw him all those years ago and waited until we were ready before making a move. "He… he doesn't like me very much right now, but I'm hoping to change that."

"Grayson…" Sarah sighed.

"I know you probably think I'm crazy," I barreled through. "I feel crazy for him, though. I've tried, over the years, to make things right." Reaching into my pocket, I pulled out newspaper clippings that I kept in my wallet. "I got the judge to increase jail time for the bastards that assaulted Cricket, and then I got Cricket the best medical care in the world. He's doing some experimental treatment right now and I know in time he'll be healed. He'll wake up," I babbled, and I didn't realize I was crying until Sarah touched my cheek, her hands coming away wet. "Shit. Sorry." I sniffed and wiped the tears. "Fuck, I'm so emotional."

"As you should be, Cricket was your best friend."

"I would never hurt him," I said with pure conviction. "Jayden has to believe me. Once Cricket wakes up and explains everything, he'll understand. He'll see that I wouldn't hurt him."

"Grayson, you can't change the direction of the wind."

"I have to," I pleaded with her. "Cricket will wake up. He has to—"

"And if he doesn't?" She fixed me with firm eyes, and something inside my chest cracked open. All these years I had been hoping, praying for some kind of miracle. That Cricket would wake up and this nightmare would be over. That people would see I would never hurt him.

"Listen," Sarah said, inching forward. "Everything you've done is altruistic. You're a good man, Grayson, but I'm afraid you may need to accept that Jayden won't change his mind about letting you back into his life. You can't change the direction of the wind, but you can adjust the sails. Okay? Take it one day at a time, and I would see if Jayden comes to you first before making any moves."

Running a hand through my hair, I tried to quell the frustration clawing at my chest. I've waited years for Jayden. What was a few more months? Eventually, we would run into each other, and then I'd have my chance to explain what happened. But Sarah was right. I needed to accept whatever Jayden said and not try to change his mind. If he hated me for the rest of his life, I would accept that.

It was what I deserved, anyway.

"Thanks. For listening."

"For being your beard?" She laughed.

"That too," I chuckled, stroking her pale cheek. Why couldn't I love her? It would be so much easier than trying to win Jayden back. I shook my head and sighed. "I appreciate it."

"Whatever. The last thing I want to do is punch you, but it's still on the list."

I drew her into a tight hug. "Punch away."

"Maybe later," she sighed against the crook of my neck. "Help me study for my Humanities exam?"

"Sure," I said, getting out my textbook and remembering the drills we used to run together. Soon we lost ourselves to notes and quizzing each other on textbook passages. Studying with a friend had always been something I enjoyed here. Cricket had been a nightmare to study with. The guy couldn't sit still to save his life and more than once he'd be distracted by talking about hockey and all the new moves we wanted to try on the ice. I missed those times.

And wished desperately to go back.

But Cricket was gone as were the times we spent with him.

Leaving me to hang limp and stagnant like wet laundry hung out to dry on a cold day. There was no way out of it. I had to let things happen and accept the outcome. Jayden might continue to hate me for the rest of my life. And that had to be okay.

Because I would never stop loving him.

***

THAT NIGHT, I DREAMED of Jayden. His hands found mine, and his pale green eyes gazed up at me just like they used to. Like stars glittering in the night sky. *I love you.* I wanted to whisper into his mouth before

I kissed him. Jayden's lips met mine, and he kissed me back, his fingers tangled in my hair.

My lungs tightened as if they were being crushed. Jayden filled every muscle, every particle of my being like water flowing through a parched desert, quenching a thirst I hadn't known I had.

His touch left me withering, like a tree struck by fierce lightning. It hit me with a resounding crack. The once-mighty oak fell into two pieces, its heart torn out.

Jayden. The dream twisted and shifted, and I woke up, longing to return to that moment. Jayden had been so pliant in my arms when we were together. I cherished every sigh and gasp that escaped his lips. But now, he was different. I shook off those thoughts and headed toward the hockey arena, hoping to blow off some steam.

Dashing across the rink, my blades carved intricate patterns into the frosty surface as I thundered through a relentless series of practice drills. Coach Cornell had set a deadline for my return to the team, and I was determined to make a good impression on the guys. The ice cracked beneath my every stride, mirroring the passion in my heart. Things would be different. They had to be this time around. My father's patience was running thin and I had to make a decision this year whether or not I wanted to try and go pro or settle down with a Health Science degree.

My problem was I had no clue what I wanted to fucking do. Playing pro hockey has always been a dream, but somewhere along the line it morphed into my father's dream more than mine. I knew I was born to play, but at what capacity? What would it look like ten years down the line?

Shavings of mist passed over the ice, and I let my mind go blank. Positioned in the perfect line of fire, I unleashed a barrage of slap shots, each one finding its mark with precision. My body glistened with sweat beneath the relentless assault of training, and my gray sweater clung to me as I felt all the stress from earlier fall off my shoulders.

Coach Cornell demanded nothing less. I had to prove myself, blend in seamlessly with the Michigan Wolverines. If I faltered, my dreams of donning their jersey would vanish like fog on a summer morning. Slicing through the ice in rhythmic figure eights, I reveled in the sensation of my skates gliding effortlessly. My breath remained steady and controlled as I remembered everything the coach had taught me. This was my sanctuary, my calling, and every moment spent on the ice affirmed it. From my earliest memories, hockey had been my true passion, and now, I was ready to reclaim it as my own.

"You're good," a voice called.

Whipping my head around, I spotted a man near the board sides and my heart slammed against my chest. A flash of blond hair entered my vision, before Ian skated onto the ice, his broad frame making his dark blue sweater go taught across his shoulders. He was wearing full shoulder pads and a helmet, hence why I at first I didn't recognize him. "Ian. Fuck. You scared me."

"Sorry," he said, adjusting his stick. "Mind if I play too? Or maybe we can practice together?"

"Sure," I said, shrugging. "I was just getting warmed up."

Ian's pink lips curled. "Sure. How about we play? Best two out of three?"

"Fuck yeah. I won't go easy on you just because you're Sarah's best friend."

Ian snorted and got into position. "I never expected you to."

The ice glistened under the bright arena lights, and the air was charged with anticipation. Ian and I faced off, and I tried to keep my calm. Without warning, he flicked the puck, sending it hurtling down the area. Zipping after it, Ian put on a display of raw power, his legs churning with explosive energy. *Fuck, so that's how he wanted to play?*

He was impressive, even faster than I had expected. My competitive spirit kicked in, and adrenaline surged through me. *I couldn't let him win this easily.* My skates carved sharp lines into the ice as I pushed harder, my blood quickening, and my heart racing. I chased him, weaving and cutting in front of him so fast he didn't see me coming. I intercepted him, faking left before changing right to swipe the puck from Ian's stick when he committed to the false move.

"Fucker!" Ian hissed, his eyes flashing as my skates sliced through the ice as I raced toward his net and scored. Ian snarled and flew after me, and I laughed, the thrill of the chase fueling my desire to overtake him. We played back and forth and neared the goal once again. I saw my opportunity and seized it. With a swift maneuver, I decked left, sending Ian's defense sprawling, and I took the shot. The puck sailed through the air, and time seemed to slow as it hit the back of the net.

Victory was mine, and the taste of success was sweeter than ever.

"Fuck!" Ian cursed and shook his head as he tried to get up. I skated over to him and offered my hand, which he took. "Damn, you're fast. I didn't even see you coming."

I laughed. "Yeah, it was a trick I learned from my friend." Cricket's name was lodged in my throat, and I cleared it. "You're good too, but sloppy. You just need to work on your footwork."

Ian took off his helmet and rubbed his shaggy blond hair. "Yeah. Shit. Coach says I need to improve or else he'll force me to sit out the next game."

"Damn," I said, but I knew Coach Cornell didn't play games, especially when it came to hockey. "Sorry to hear that, bro."

Ian shrugged. "How often do you practice here? Are you joining the team?"

"Ah, yeah actually but not until next week." I thumbed my lower lip in thought. "You know what? Let's practice together. Maybe we can help each other improve faster."

Ian scoffed. "You look pretty damn good to me, man." He paused, eyeing me. "It doesn't look like you need any practice."

I chuckled. "Even the professional's practice, dude. Anyway, I want to get back into a routine, so let's say around 8AM every Thursday? I have work later today so I should get going."

We shook hands and I left smiling to myself. The thought of having a new friend thawing the ice gathered on my chest.

***

I HURRIED TO THE student resources room, anxious not to be late for my first tutoring appointment of the day. My hair was still wet from a recent shower, clinging to my scalp. I ran my fingers through it in an attempt to slick it back as I entered the room. A quick wave and greeting to Carry and Jamal, who were already there, and I began setting up my materials for the day.

"Am I late?" I panted, catching my breath as I organized my things.

"Not even a little bit," Carry reassured me from behind her desk, her voice filled with a touch of amusement.

Perfect. I could feel the residual energy coursing through my body from the hockey game earlier, making my fingertips tingle with readiness. I felt relaxed and prepared to help my new students. Taking a moment, I reviewed the profile of the student I was about to tutor. His chemistry grades had been abysmal, and I was well-acquainted with Professor. Wilson's challenging teaching style. The task ahead wouldn't be easy, but I was up for it.

I licked my dry lips, contemplating whether I had time to grab a coffee before the tutoring session. I realized I was missing a crucial page containing the student's information. Damn. I needed to print it out before he arrived. A quick check of my watch confirmed that I had just enough time to sneak in a coffee run. I informed Carry that I would be back soon and dashed to the campus coffee shop.

Ordering my coffee quickly, I rushed back to the office to print the necessary paperwork.

My heart raced as I rounded the corner. My entire body collided with something solid, sending my coffee splashing all over my blue dress shirt and black slacks. Cursing under my breath, I looked up to meet a pair of furious, flashing green eyes.

My heart froze.

Jayden.

"Watch where you're going," he snarled, his teeth bared as he walked off. All the blood rushed to my face as everyone in the hall stared at me and my clothes dripping wet. Fuck. I had a session in five minutes, and if I left to go home to change, I'd be late. Running a hand through my hair, I darted back to the Academic Resource room, my face red and panick clouding my vision.

"Bro, what happened? Your one o'clock just arrived—" Jamal said, watching me with wide eyes.

"I'm such an idiot. I spilled it—"

"No worries," Jamal laughed. "I always keep a spare, and you look to be about my size anyway. Hurry up here and get changed. I forget to give you the form regarding the student's information so I printed that off for you as well."

"Jamal, I could kiss you," I sighed, and took the shirt he pulled out of his drawer.

"Please don't," Jamal replied and closed the door behind him while I stripped. I shoved the sodden shirt in a plastic bag and tried to clean what I could off my black slacks. Since they were black none of the stains showed, and then I sprinted back out so that I wasn't late for tutoring. Jamal handed me the paper, and I grabbed it before heading into the main room where someone in a bright yellow varsity jacket was waiting for me.

"Sorry I'm late," I laughed, my eyes glued to the sheet of paper. "I had an accident in the middle of the hall and—"

My heart jammed in my throat.

10

─ · ─

THAWING HEARTS

GRAYSON HAYES

G reen eyes drilled into mine. They skewered through the sky like forked beams of lightning, narrowing to a single point aimed at my thumping heart. A shroud of eerie silence descended, wrapping its invisible cloak around us. Nothing moved. Nothing stirred. Nothing dared to breathe. *Fuck. Why did this keep happening?* A knot of barbed wire sliced through my throat, and I glanced down at the paper and winced.

Jayden Taylor. Chemistry.

I wanted to melt into the floor. Jayden said nothing, his eyes were roiling and boiling with so much hatred I thought lightning would flash from his eyes and strike me down. And a part of me prayed it did. It was what I deserved. "Jayden—"

"What the fuck are you doing here?" he growled, hands curled into fists.

"I—" My tongue was nailed to the roof of my mouth. What could I say? That I followed him here? Forgive me? I'm sorry? Everything tried to pass through at once and I ended up gaping at him like a fish on the shore.

"You son of a bitch." Jayden stood. Black hair framed his face, and steel glinted around his ears. Ink ran the length of his neck, disappearing into his white crew neck t-shirt. His muscles flexed, and although he wasn't as big as me, his slim frame from his youth was long gone. Harsh pale green eyes sparkled like sharpened diamonds, their brilliance cutting through the air like a blade. This morning's dream *felt like a nightmare.*

This man wasn't my Jayden. Not the one from a few years ago who was clean and innocent and wanted nothing more than to obsess over Star Trek and quoted the books and movies like they were his bible.

I longed for that. For him. Not this rage-filled, demented version of him. His gaze buzzed, cackled and fizzled with furious intensity. I imagined splayed tentacles of gold fire blasting forth, scorching me alive. I wanted to flee, but my feet stayed rooted to the floor, fearing that an explosion of lightning-flame would zap me. Jayden looked like he wanted to kill me and if nobody was around, he probably would have. And yet, I waited. I knew when it came to him, I was weak.

Whatever punishment he deemed fit, I'd let him carry it out.

"You fucking rat bastard. How dare you—"

"Is there a problem here?" Carry asked, her hands on her massive hips.

"Yes, there is," Jayden hissed. "I want to change tutors. There's no way I'm being tutored by this fucking guy—"

"I'll ask you not to use profanity in the Academic Resource Center, and if you do it again, I'll have you thrown out," Carry said, her gaze hard. "If you have a problem with Mr. Hayes, we can assign you another tutor. However, we are booked solid for the entire semester. You'll have to come back next year for the help—"

"You've got to be kidding me," Jayden scoffed. "I don't have until next semester. I need to pass this course now. There must be something you can do. Another tutor. Anyone—"

"I'm afraid not, Mr. Taylor," Carry replied. "If you intend to cause trouble for Mr. Hayes, then I suggest you get out now. I won't tolerate that here."

Jayden's jaw worked. He looked away and then sighed long and deep. "Fine. Sorry about earlier. I won't cause trouble."

"Good," Carry said, her eyes passing between us. "If you need anything, just holler. My office is right in there."

I gave her a silent thanks as she walked out, my blood still roaring in my ears. Jayden turned his fierce gaze at me. "You fucking planned this."

Planned what? I wanted to reply, but I didn't see a point in arguing with him. We only had an hour of tutoring before my next student arrived. "I'm sorry," I said. "It's not... ideal I know but, we'll have to make do." I sat at the desk and opened the textbook, ignoring the cold sweat dripping down my spine. "We can start on chapter one. Open your textbook and show me your homework. We'll start on a few equations that you feel stuck on."

Jayden didn't move. He didn't look at me.

I swallowed around the dagger in my throat, waiting with bated breath. Finally, he sat down at the table, but made sure to keep his body angled away from me and took out his textbook. I scribbled the date in my notebook, and reviewed some questions on the page. Balancing equations, computational chemistry, theoretical chemistry, quantum mechanics and so on. Everything I became familiar with during my first few years at university. "Okay," I said, then cleared my throat. "Where do you want to start?"

Silence.

The ticking clock echoed in the room, and I sighed. "This isn't going to work if I don't know where you are struggling."

Jayden pointed at the computational chemistry headline and then looked away. Okay. That I could work with. "Don't overthink it. Molecular dynamics involves tracking the positions and velocities of atoms in a system. By solving Newton's equations of motion for each atom, we can simulate their movements," I explained.

Jayden leaned back in his chair, his arms crossed and his expression revealing his lack of enthusiasm. He avoided eye contact and stared out of the window. I continued, undeterred, trying to break through his indifference.

"For example, we use potential energy functions to describe how atoms interact with each other. These functions account for forces like bond stretching, angle bending, and van der Waals forces."

Jayden's fingers started tapping on the table. Ignoring his annoyance, I pressed on. "Just review this passage here and—"

"I don't need a lecture from you. I'll figure it out on my own. Just give me the damn textbook and tell me what to review for the next exam."

"If you don't understand, how are you going to study for it?"

"Why don't you let that be my business?" he spat, hackles rising.

"Jayden, I'm not here to make things difficult for you. I want to help you, but I need you to work with me—"

"Just like Cricket did?" he spat, and each word was like a slap to the face. "Oh, I know all about how you try to help, Grayson. How you fucking left my brother there, beaten and bleeding on the ice while your daddy made everything go away?"

"Jayden—" I croaked.

"I know all about you," he growled. "And I want no fucking part of it." He stood, the chair scraping against the tile floors. "Fuck it. I'd rather fail this class than sit here with you another second."

I deserved that. I deserved everything he flung at me and much more. Leaving Cricket like that—I was a coward. Jayden was right. I didn't say anything when he packed up his stuff and left.

All I could do was sit there, feeling raw and aching, like a hole had been punched through my gut.

***

I WORE A STRAINED smile as Coach Cornell delivered his introductory speech.

"This here is Grayson Hayes," he boomed. "One of the best center forwards I've seen in this past decade. And we are to welcome him with open arms like the prodigal son. I mean it. I want you boys to show him so much rainbows and sunshine he'll think the sun shines out of his ass." He turned his gaze toward Jayden. "And for all the other stuff," he continued, "I don't want to hear about it. Grayson's been cleared of all charges. He didn't hurt anyone. Now, I know some of you may disagree, and that's okay. I want everyone's voices to be heard. So, we're going for a trial run, and if Grayson fits in, he'll be officially back on the team. But if there are any problems, then he's out. Same goes for those who cause problems to begin with, and I mean it! No more playing around. Some of you are looking to go pro, and I won't have the others drag you down for their own selfishness." Coach's voice carried the weight of expectation.

His stern message was met with a smattering of applause. I couldn't help but notice several of the guys glaring at me, their expressions filled

with skepticism and resentment. A few familiar faces from my previous time on the team seemed unsure, while those I didn't recognize
huddled protectively around Jayden, creating a protective barrier.

*God, I'm such an idiot. Why did I ever think getting close to Jayden
would be easy?* It was a mistake, just like coming here, but I knew I had
to see it through. The tension in the room was palpable, but I wanted
to prove myself and earn my place back on the team.

I hastily changed into my gear in the corner of the locker room. My
return was met with hostility from some and indifference from others.
I needed to stay focused on hockey and leave the personal conflicts for
another time. Jayden and I could settle this outside of the arena.

With my equipment secured, I joined the team as they skated out
onto the ice, the chilly arena air nipping at my exposed skin. Coach
Cornell wasted no time and organized a series of warm-up laps. I
pushed myself to find my rhythm, each stride feeling like a step toward
redemption.

However, just as I was bypassing another player, my legs were suddenly knocked out from under me, and I crashed onto the unforgiving
ice. Pain radiated from my covered knees, and I couldn't help but curse
under my breath. I glanced up to see Jayden gliding past me, a smirk
playing on his lips. My return wouldn't be without its challenges,
and Jayden was more than willing to make that point known. Sighing
through my nose, I pushed back onto my feet and continued onward,
keeping a sharp eye out for the next time he'd try to trip me up.

Seeing Jayden act like this was jarring.

Back then, he was never like this. Never cruel. I tried not to get
lost in the memory of his cries against my lips when I brought him
to climax, or the way his spine arched and his hips snapped when I
fucked my tongue deeper into his mouth. *Those days were long gone.*

This Jayden I didn't know, and it scared me beyond belief.

Coach split us up into two teams, and I realized with a start that I was face to face with Jayden again. Crap. His mouth slanted, and then the puck was dropped. Jayden shot out like a bat out of hell, smashing through me and nearly spending me sprawling again on the ice. I cursed, darting after him, but the bastard was faster than I thought, weaving and ducking before he scored a goal.

My heart sank, and Coach shot me a strange look but clapped his hands. "Good job, Jayden, but try passing the puck for once. Jared had a clearer shot than you did. All right, let's go! You're not figure skaters, so let's lose the twirls and start playing some real hockey!"

I got back into formation, and we went at it again.

Jayden moved like the devil.

The whistle blew and Jayden shot like a bullet on the ice, his every stride slicing through the rink with the precision of a surgeon's scalpel. How the fuck did he get so good? I asked, panting after him, my lungs cinching tighter and tighter as I struggled to keep up. Several guys blocked him, but he was way too fast, slipping past their guard and scoring another goal.

Damn. This couldn't continue.

Then it hit me. He was playing like Cricket used to. I wanted to laugh after I finally noticed that all of his moves were Cricket's old moves when we played against each other. They were bold and reckless, but there was a method to the madness. When the game was actually played, people would be too busy watching Jayden, and wouldn't notice when he passed the puck to someone else until it was too late, like Coach said. He built the momentum before sending it off to someone else for the follow through. *It was genius.*

This time I watched Jayden like a hawk, noticing his slight nod to Evanss as he barreled like a tornado down the arena and just as he closed in on the net passed the puck to Evans, who scored. It was a simple crossing pass and if I intercepted, then my team could score.

The clock ticked down and my veins surged with adrenaline, my chest pounded with each beat of my heart. *I had to prove myself. I had to win this.* Jayden and his teammates had been relentless, displaying dominance throughout the game with their remarkable skill and incredible speed. With my teammates by my side, I jerked my head at Ian signally to inch closer to the left, and then made eye contact with several more of my players, hoping they understood me when I gestured a criss-cross motion. A whistle blew, and I dashed out, intercepting Jayden's path as he sought to breach our defense. As Jayden advanced, focused on the puck, I moved in from the side like a shadow in the night. With a swift, calculated maneuver, I snatched the puck right from beneath his gaze. Gasps from the team filled the air as I sprinted towards the opposing net.

The ice stretched before me, seemingly endless, and Jayden and his teammates scrambled to close the gap. My heart raced as I approached the goal, and with a lightning-quick flick of my wrist, I passed the puck to Ian, who slammed it home.

It soared past the opposing goalie and nestled into the net.

"Now that's what I'm talking about!" Coach Cornell hollered, taking off his hat and beaming. "Damn, it's good to have you back, Grayson! Everyone not moving like Grayson and Taylor get off my ice right this second!"

Ian whooped, smacking me hard on the back, and my team laughed.

"Run it again and keep it moving! I've seen penguins move faster in a snowstorm! Pick up the pace, team!" Coach screamed, and I went back into formation, a smile dancing on my lips.

Jayden shot me a nasty look, but a large part of me didn't care.

This was hockey, after all.

And he needed to know I was playing to win.

***

EXCITED VOICES ERUPTED in the locker room as the guys chatted about the game and their fantastic practice session. The competition was heating up, and Taylor finally had some real challengers. I laughed, relishing the camaraderie in the air.

"All right, boys, you did good," Coach's voice rang out above the chatter. "You've made Daddy real proud. Now get some rest. I want everyone here bright and early at 8 AM on Saturday morning. No excuses!"

Bronze shaggy curls filled my vision as Evans approached me, wearing a stern expression. "I didn't think you'd come back." I nodded, not sure how to respond. Evans had been one of Cricket's friends and had bought into all the awful rumors circulating about me.

"Me neither," I admitted.

Evans' sea-blue eyes bore into mine. "Look, the past is the past, but you better be here to play for good. We've got six more games to get through this season, and I'm here to win."

"So am I," I replied, holding his gaze.

An unspoken understanding passed between us, and Evans nodded. "Good. By the way, I had Coach get your old jersey back. Come find me in the cafe when you're done, and I'll get it for you."

"Thanks, man," I said, grateful for the gesture, and we shook hands before Evans grabbed his gear and headed out. I hadn't realized how quickly everyone had left while we were talking, so I hurried to remove my equipment and joined them. I continued changing, waving goodbye to some guys who departed. The door clicked shut behind them, and the hairs on my neck stood on end. I turned to see Jayden leaning against the door frame, his disheveled black hair partially covering his brow, and a sinister smirk on his lips.

"I really should have known," he chuckled, but his laughter was hollow and dark. I swallowed hard, feeling a lump in my throat. I hadn't expected to be alone with him so quickly. I tugged on my clean white t-shirt and pulled on my pants, not caring about my half-dressed state.

Turning to him, I ran a hand through my damp hair. "Look, can we talk? There's something I want to tell you."

Jayden pushed off the wall and closed the distance, getting right in my face. "I don't want to hear it. Do you think that just because you've wormed your way back here, people won't see the horrible person you really are? Or that they won't know what you did to my brother? To my family?"

Each word he spoke felt like a heavy brick falling from the sky and crashing into my head. "Jayden, I'm sorry—I'm—"

"You're nothing to me," he spat, his voice dripping with disdain. "Worthless. You're a piece of shit, Grayson Hayes, and I won't rest until the world knows it." He shoved me hard, and I stumbled backward, crashing into a locker.

A piece of jagged metal pierced my hip, slicing right through my shirt and flesh. I gasped and stared back at him, stunned. Within seconds, my shirt dampened with blood, soaking through the thin cotton. Pain seared across my spine and shot up my back as he slammed the locker doors shut, trapping me inside.

I touched the spot, my hand coming away bloodied.

This was the first time Jayden hurt me.

Going as far as to draw blood.

11

LIFE OR DEATH

JAYDEN TAYLOR

The beeping and chiming of monitors echoed through the sterile hospital corridor. My heart tightened as I rounded the corner and entered Cricket's room. He lay there, seemingly at peace, if it weren't for the telltale signs of his illness. His once vibrant face now bore the marks of his suffering, with hollow cheeks and a sunken brow.

Taking a seat in the plastic chair by his bedside, I reached out and gently clasped his skeletal fingers. I couldn't help but shudder at their frailty. His skin clung to his bones, a stark reminder of how much he'd withered away. His limbs were stick-thin from atrophy. Tubes and wires connected him to various machines, a lifeline he depended on.

"Hey," I croaked, my voice barely above a whisper. "It's me, Jayden." There was no response from my brother, just the rhythmic hum of the machines.

A cool hand touched my shoulder, and I recognized the scent of my mother's sea breeze perfume. "How is he?" she asked softly.

My dad entered the room, his back to me as he stared out the window. The tension in the air was palpable, and I knew he was likely wrestling with the urge for a drink to numb the pain that seemed to hang over us all.

The doctor came into the room. He was a short young man with brown hair, kind brown eyes, and tanned skin. "Mr. and Mrs. Taylor?" he asked and my dad turned on the spot, his eyes bloodshot.

"Yeah," he responded, his voice gruff and deep.

The doctor nodded. "My name is Mohammed Amar. First, I want to say I'm so sorry you had to go through this. It must be a very challenging time for you and your family." He paused, letting his words sink in. "I wish I had better news, but the experimental treatment doesn't seem to have much effect on Cricket. We've done all we can, and I can say the initial diagnosis of brain death still stands. We can continue to keep Cricket on life support, but he'll need to be moved to a regular hospital. Unfortunately, this program is in high demand and the waiting list is very long. We pulled a lot of strings to get Cricket on the list, but the treatment now seems ineffective."

Ineffective.

The words snaked in my mind like a missile before exploding. *Ineffective.* So, they were just going to toss him out like trash? Forget about everything they said they would do? Rage tore through me, shredding my insides like a meteor.

"What are you saying? That it's over? That we either keep Cricket on life support or kill him? Is that what you're asking us to do?" I snarled, teeth bared. *This doctor was a quack!* We'd go to someone else. Cricket didn't need to be subjected to this craziness. He'd wake up. He had to. He'd wake up and look at me and smile.

The doctor faced my enraged outburst with a steady composure, his eyes filled with understanding. "I know this is incredibly difficult for all of you, but the experimental treatment has not shown the expected results. We can continue life support, but that might only prolong his current state. Quality of life must be a consideration, too. We're not asking you to decide lightly, but we have to discuss the options available."

"Doc, can't you try something else? Another procedure, another doctor, anything?" My father's voice broke, desperation creeping into his every word.

"I understand your frustration, Mr. Taylor. We can certainly transfer Craige to another facility, get a second opinion, but I need to be candid. The chances of a different outcome are slim. We're dealing with a very rare and complex condition. We can keep exploring options if you wish, but I want to prepare you for the harsh reality we face."

The room fell into a heavy silence, broken only by the rhythmic beeping of the monitors.

"So... he's gone," my mother's voice pierced it and she placed a trembling hand over her mouth and turned away. If I wasn't already sitting, my knees would have buckled. Cricket wasn't gone. He couldn't be gone. It just wasn't possible. I clenched my fists, refusing to accept defeat. *No. I won't give up on my brother. We'll explore every option, every possibility. Cricket deserves that much.* I couldn't bear the thought of losing him without a fight.

"I think..." my dad croaked, and then coughed to clear his throat. "We need a minute."

"I understand, and I'll support you in any way I can. When you're ready to discuss the next steps, I can gather all the information you need to make a decision about Craige's future. The social worker will be in later on to discuss anything you'd like and things the hospital can do to support you in the future." He gave another curt nod before leaving the room.

"He's gone," my mom repeated, and I wanted to scream at her and tell her to stop saying that. "My baby's gone." Then her knees buckled.

Luckily my father was there to catch her. Blood roared in my ears and everything behind my eyelids throbbed. Cricket couldn't be gone.

This treatment had to work. He'd wake up. Call me dumbass. Sing Michael Jackson. Laugh with me. Talk hockey with me. He'd be there like an older brother should be. Something splintered and fractured in my chest, like a log being hacked with an ax. My dad and I locked eyes. Seconds ticked by, and then twenty and thirty, and finally the pain pulled back and then rushed in all at once like the tide. I was striding over to them before I even registered it and my dad was pulling me into a brusque hug so tight it rattled my bones.

"He's gone," my mom wailed.

My head throbbed and sharp hot needles pierced my eyes, and tears drenched my father's shirt as we all held each other tight, like trying to seal the cracks of a crumbling dam.

***

THERE IS A WAY OUT of every box, a solution to every puzzle. It's just a matter of finding it. Captain Jean-Luc Picard words chimed in my ears and I stood outside letting the rain pelt against my cheeks. What if there wasn't? Smoke curled around my nostrils as I breathed out and stared up at the cloudy sky, swollen and bellowing in the distance. My parents were still inside talking to the social worker about their next steps, and I stepped out for a moment to think.

To breathe.

Cricket wasn't gone. I refuse to believe it. He'd come back. I just had to study hard enough. I'm sure if I looked into it, there might be untapped theories or methods that could help someone wake up. But fuck, I didn't have time. Hockey training made it impossible to do anything and that paired with school meant my schedule was jam-packed. It didn't matter. This was life and death. I could do some research on the side and figure things out. Cricket had to make it.

"Hey," my father's baritone voice snapped me out of my musing. "Can I bum a smoke?"

I handed him a cigarette, trying to cover my shock at hearing him speaking to me. *God, I don't know how long it's been since we talked.* We stood in silence for several moments, listening to the rain that was quickly turning into snow trickle above our heads. "I hate your tattoos," he spoke. "I hate that you smoke now."

I stared at him, not sure what he wanted me to say.

"I hate your piercings," my dad continued, then his voice cracked. "But damn, do I love you, Jayden. I love you so much and I'm sorry I haven't been there. I'm shit at this. Cricket was—he was the light. The sunshine we all tried to hold, no matter how much it kept slipping through our fingertips. He's gone, and I—I can accept it."

I shook my head manically. "No. You can, but I refuse. He'll wake up. He'll wake up and you'll all see—"

"Buddy," my dad said, his eyes red and voice hollow. "He's gone. God took him that day on the ice. We just need to let it all go now."

A blistering red haze filled my vision. "So, you're just gonna quit? Give up?"

My dad turned his face away, and it took everything in me to stop myself from shaking him. To tell him that things would work out and that what they said wasn't true. Cricket would be fine. They just needed to figure something else out, that was all. Bringing his arms around me, I didn't fight him. I just allowed his chin to rest on mine, feeling the vibrations of his voice as he spoke. "Do you remember that game night we used to have, just the three of us?"

I nodded, my heart aching at the mention of those cherished memories.

"We'd go to see a hockey game, remember? The Detroit Red Wings against the Chicago Blackhawks. Cricket was so excited he couldn't sit still. And then, during the match, he had to pee so badly that he refused to miss even a second of the game. He held it in until he couldn't anymore, and he wet his pants right there, in the stadium, just so he wouldn't miss a goal."

I chuckled through my tears, remembering that hilarious and embarrassing moment from our childhood. "Yeah, Dad, I remember."

"And what about the time you twisted your ankle in the backyard, trying to copy Wayne Gretzky's famous slapshot move? You were determined to master it. Cricket was so worried, he ran inside to get the first aid kit, but you just laughed through the pain."

Tears fell from my eyes as I nodded, those memories of our carefree days feeling both distant and precious.

"Those memories, son, they keep Cricket alive in our hearts. We have to hold on to them, and we have to hold on to hope."

My throat constricted. Pressing my palms to my eyelids, I sighed, my soul feeling wafer thin. A tremble rolled through me as the cold nipped at my skin through my sodden clothes. This nightmare had no end, and it kept going on and on. I knew their decision before they spoke it aloud. They had given up. After a year of no improvement, to them Cricket was as good as dead.

"I'm gonna head back to school," I lied, unable to bear the weight of our sorrow any longer. "Give me some time."

My dad understood the unspoken words in my heart. "Yeah, we won't do anything until... until we're sure."

I pulled away from the hug and made my way out of the room, each step a painful reminder that this nightmare needed to end, and

Cricket had to wake up. I strode to my car and got in. Hate moved like doom-black clouds that churned and roiled, looking as vaporous as mist and as fleecy as black wool. I sat there for several moments, trying to make sense of everything that had happened today, but I couldn't. All I felt was a blinding fury that tore my insides to shreds.

Grayson should have been the one to get hurt.

Grayson should have been the one on life support.

Not Cricket. A frigid rage gripped my heart, its frosty tendrils spreading like a winter's chill, all while my thoughts fixated on Grayson. The bastard who laughed and smiled, taking my brother's spot on the team and relishing in the victory.

He was responsible for everything, and I'd do everything to make him fucking pay.

***

I STOOD ACROSS THE locker room, my arms tightly folded, a storm brewing inside me. Ian's voice, though nearby, seemed distant as my focus zeroed in on Grayson. It gnawed at me to see him here, knowing my brother's life hung in the balance. Grayson didn't belong here, not now.

Not with my brother being so close to being cut from life support.

I wanted him gone from my sight. In a few days, we'd have our tutoring session, but I couldn't wait until then. I needed to do something now. Grayson Hayes couldn't stay here. I wouldn't let him. I watched as he went to put on his hockey gear, chatting with Evans. His being back here had been a slap to the face. Coach said it was only a trail run, but I'd make his time here so horrible Grayson would run back to Northgate with his tail between his legs. I watched with a giddy fury as he went to put his gloves on, only to cry out in disgust when his hand came away covered in shaving cream.

Laughter erupted from the others, and someone nudged my shoulders. I met Grayson's gaze, and a wicked smirk crept onto my lips. He knew it was me, and he knew I wasn't done. I caught Grayson's gray eyes and winked. Then I turned to get dressed. He didn't say anything, but everyone knew how Coach was strict with punctuality and it would take Grayson several minutes to wash all the gunk off and be ready on the ice.

"Did you do that?" Ian asked, his expression troubled.

I offered a one shoulder shrug and finished getting dressed. Soon I was on the ice, the wind against my face and playing the game I loved. The ice was cold beneath my skates, and the familiar sound of blades slicing through the frozen surface echoed in my ears. I lost myself in the game.

The world outside the rink ceased to exist.

It was just me, my teammates, and the pursuit of victory.

Fuck the world and everyone in it. Right now, I was flying.

***

FIRM LIPS PRESSED against my neck, and I groaned as skilled hands roamed my pecs and biceps, and then landed on my narrow waist. The locker room was empty as Ian and I rutted against each other, gasping loud and hard, as his kiss took my breath away. I had a tutoring session with Grayson soon, and I'd be late if I didn't pull away, but Ian felt so good in my arms. Yet, my heart wasn't in it. Thoughts of Cricket plagued me, and I didn't know what my parents planned to do next.

"You feel good, baby," Ian whispered against my lips, thumbing the waistband of my gym shorts. "Fuck, if I didn't have class, I'd take you right here."

I laughed, but it sounded strained. "Yeah, maybe next time."

Ian pulled back, and then cupped my chin, pulling my face up to his. "Everything okay? You seem... distant. Something happened with Cricket?"

I yanked out of his hold and went about packing up my things. I didn't want to talk about it, fearing I'd break down again. "We got some bad news, that's all. I'm fine."

"Bad news?" Ian's brow furrowed. "No improvement or—"

"I'll see you after class," I dismissed, slinging my duffle bag over my shoulder and walking out.

Putting my stuff away in my car, I changed into regular clothes, some jeans and my varsity jacket, before making it to the Academic Resource Center in a nick of time. Grayson was already waiting for me, dressed in black slacks and a crisp button-up shirt that made him look older and not at all like a twenty-three-year-old college student. I slumped down in the chair, not bothering with pleasantries, and started pulling out my textbook. Exams were coming up and if I didn't pass this stupid class, I'd be fucked.

"So, what would you like to work on today?" Grayson asked, his deep voice causing me to suppress a shudder.

I hated how much he made me feel. How sensitive I was to him.

I gritted my teeth and slid over the practice test we had the other day. Angry red marks appeared all over the page, and I scowled. "Looks like your tutoring isn't helping."

"Did you do the homework I asked?" Grayson asked, and my scowl deepened.

Who the fuck could do homework at a time like this? I was barely holding on. The chill of my anger ran deeper than frostbite, an icy tempest that threatened to consume me whole. "No. I've been busy. My brother is in the hospital, or have you forgotten already?"

Grayson flinched, and a vicious delight curled through me. Stormy clouds of gray met mine, and I saw his cheek jump. He was pissed. *Good. I wanted to see him unravel beneath my fingertips.* Long ago, I had been meek and submissive to him, allowing him to do whatever he wanted. Grayson and Cricket were like gods to me. I worshiped them until everything shattered beneath my fingertips.

"I can't help you if you don't do the homework, Jayden," Grayson reasoned, and I hated the way he said my name, the way it rolled beneath his tongue as if he were tasting it like a rich delicacy.

I want to be with you. I want you. Filthy fucking lies. He wanted to fuck me and take my brother's place. A smile tugged on my lips before I spoke. "I'll do better next time... By the way, how did you like my shaving cream surprise?"

Grayson examined the test, his expression bored. "Tasteless. You're supposed to mix the shaving cream with itching cream. That would have made the prank better."

Shit. I knew I was forgetting something. Damn. Grayson turned back to me. "Childish too. Since when do you behave like a five-year-old?"

The fizzing sound of electricity crackled in the air between us. I realized now that I had poked a sleeping bear that was now snarling, its lips pulling back to expose razor-sharp teeth.

My bleak smile grew.

12

The Shattered Glass Beneath

Jayden Taylor

"Since now." I shrugged, knowing my blasé attitude would piss him off. "Don't worry. The next one will be better."

"I won't hold my breath," Grayson muttered. "Now, let's get back to the test. We can go over the answers and how we arrive at them in order to break down where you went wrong—"

"Did it hurt when you left my brother fending for himself and bleeding on the ice?" I interrupted, not done with the conversation. "Because it didn't look like it. In fact, it looked like you couldn't get out of there fast enough when he was being taken to the hospital."

"I'm not discussing this with you."

My lip twitched. "Why? You said you wanted to talk. To explain—"

"Not here," Grayson gritted out. "I thought you were serious about your studies, but if you're not, I can pack my shit and walk out right now, and you'll be on your own until the end of the semester."

"*Motherfucker*—" I cursed, but Grayson glared at me like darts of icy rain spitting from the sky.

He had all the power, and he knew it. *Fine. I'd get him back some other way.* Grayson wrenched open his notebook and threw the test paper back in my face. "Now, if you're done wasting your own time, let's begin."

My anger was like a blizzard, swirling within me, chilling my veins, and clouding my judgment.

Fuck him. He'd pay for that.

***

THE NEXT TIME I showed up I didn't say a fucking word.

Ignored everything the bastard said and attempted to do the work on my own. I hated anyone having power over me, least of all Grayson fucking Hayes. The bastard didn't deserve it. Grayson had given up trying to talk to me, and instead, we sat in stony silence for over an hour each week. The semester dragged on, and we had a game coming up in a few weeks that I couldn't wait to play. Smashing guys into the ice would be almost therapeutic at this point. Ian had gotten busy with studying and finals and so had I, but Professor Wilson's class would literally be the death of me. I failed another quiz, and I could see she was getting antsy. Fuck, I thought, glaring at the red scratches all over my paper. Who the hell understood chemistry, anyway? This shit was like another language! I snarled and stood from my desk, storming over to her and waiting until she finished with the student she was talking to. *I can't fail this class. I can't.*

Maybe if I explained that to her, she would see things in a new light. Finally, the student walked away with a giddy smile on their face and then it was just me and Professor Wilson. She looked up at me beneath her dark-rimmed glasses. "Mr. Taylor. Can I help you?"

I held up the quiz. "You failed me. Again."

Her lip curled, and she raised a brow, waiting for me to ask a question. I huffed through my nose, hitching my backpack higher. "Look, I'm trying. I really am. I need to pass this class. My scholarships depend on it—"

"Mr. Taylor, you know the Academic Resource Center reports back the progress the students are having and from Mr. Hayes report, you don't participate in the tutoring session."

I felt like I'd been doused with cold water. What? Grayson was reporting the shit that went on there back to her? The ground moved from beneath my feet and the world spun. Anger welled up within me like a violent tempest, a churning maelstrom of emotions. *What the fuck?* I wanted to kill him. *First, he destroys my life and now this? Was the bastard trying to get me kicked out of school?* I stood there gaping at her like a fish, and then she looked away.

"Look, you have one more chance at the final exam, but if you don't pass, I'm afraid I'll have to fail you for this semester, Mr. Taylor. You can visit your guidance counselor if you need further financial assistance, but aside from that, my hands are tied."

I swallowed around the dagger in my throat. *This was it.* She went back to reviewing papers, dismissing me entirely, and I wanted to scream. My parents were deciding whether or not to kill my brother and now I was close to being kicked out of school.

Storming through the lecture hall, I threw open the door, rage boiling beneath my skin.

Fuck Grayson. The bastard was dead to me.

I considered finding him and smashing his fucking face into the ground. I went to my dorm room, throwing my backpack at the wall, a scream clawing its way up my throat. Screw Grayson. Why was he doing this to me? Pain flared in my chest. I loved him. I had loved the bastard so much and now it was all gone. Now all he did was seek to ruin me and my family. Perfect Grayson. Who had a billionaire father and more money than God. *But his father beats him.* A voice whispered to me, but I was too engrossed in my turmoil to care. Fury surged within me like molten lava, scalding every fiber of my being. I ran to my laptop, searching the files on my computer before landing on the video I never dared to click open. It was the security footage of that night.

Of what happened to Cricket on the ice.

Ice crept down my spine, and my heart hammered as I clicked it up and then closed it shut. I couldn't watch it again. I couldn't see it. Cricket's final moments were forever burned into my retina.

Grayson had tripped him. I saw it and I didn't give a damn what anyone said. Scrolling through the source file, I opened my YouTube channel, my pulse pounding in my throat.

Grayson Hayes was a depraved monster.

And it was about time I started reminding people of that.

***

BODY-CHECKING GRAYSON into the boards, I snarled and then raced after Carl, who had the puck. My team gave me a wide berth, wondering what in the hell had possessed me to attack someone on the same side. I didn't care. I played like a man possessed, channeling all the rage and aggression coiled in my gut.

"All right, guys! Let's call it quits," Coach Cornell shouted, his gaze piercing mine. "Taylor, come with me!"

I ripped off my helmet, my face flushed and eyes blazing as Evans helped Grayson stand. There was a single cut above his brow, but otherwise, he seemed unscathed. I skated over to where the coach was standing, my anger radiating like a dark cloud.

"What is it? Can we make this quick? I need to get home and study—"

"Oh, yeah, let's make it real quick," Coach Cornell interrupted, his teeth bared. "If you ever, in your life, assault one of my players again, I'll kick you off this team so fast and so hard it'll make your damn head spin."

I was taken aback, feeling like I'd been slapped. "What? Grayson—"

"Is your teammate," Coach roared. "And you will treat all teammates with courtesy and respect! I won't tolerate any form of bullying on this team, Taylor. Got it?"

I slammed my helmet onto the ice, a sickening crunch resonating as it cracked down the center. But I was beyond caring. "Do you know what he did?" I screamed in his face. "He killed my brother! My brother is dead because of him! Because of what he did!"

My knees buckled, but Coach caught me in his arms and held me up. Tears streamed down my face as I sobbed into my hands. "They're going to take him off life support! He's dead! He's dead!"

"I'm so sorry, son," Coach whispered in my ear. "But Grayson didn't do this. Believe me on that."

A wail ripped through me, and I could barely see past the blur of tears as I felt Ian's hands come around my waist to help Coach lift me up. Several guys came out of the locker rooms to see what the commotion was, but everything was crashing down around me. Nobody wanted to see the truth, that Grayson had destroyed my life and taken everything from me. Ian hugged me, cupping the back of my neck. "It's all right. It's all right now. I'll get him inside," Ian said.

"Everyone, go back in!" Coach yelled. "There's nothing to see here!"

Someone else came to help me get off the ice and onto the bench. I buried my face into my hands, feeling my lungs cinch tighter and tighter. There was no way out of this hell. Cricket was dead. All the shit I was studying in university to help him get better meant nothing now. He would never see me play a winning game or make it to the NHL. He'd die at twenty-one, forever frozen in time. That knowledge was a visceral agony, an unbearable mountain that crushed my heart and left me gasping for air. Coach knelt in front of me, tears sliding down his hollowed cheeks.

"There are no words I could say that can comfort you, son. Just know that you are not alone. We will help you carry this burden, because that's what teams do. We help each other. Cricket was one of us, and he always will be."

I broke down again, clutching my chest as if to keep my soul from fracturing. Everything had gone to shit and the worst part of it was I knew there was no way out. Cricket's life was gone.

And I had to live in the shadows of what that meant. More guys come out of the locker room, ignoring what Coach had said. Peeling my hands from my chest, I looked up and fell into two gray storm clouds.

***

"YOU'RE ALL RIGHT, BABY," Ian whispered against my temple, his body holding me close.

Our legs were intertwined on his single bed, which was so cramped that he was pushed against the wall. These beds weren't meant for two full-grown men. He pressed a kiss to my cheek, rubbing slow circles on my lower back and shoulders.

It was after we left the arena and got back to Ian's place that everything poured out of me like a dam bursting. Grayson. Cricket being taken off life support. My parents. My failing class. I told Ian everything, and all he did was hold me, wrapping me up in his powerful arms and cradling me to his chest. If there was anyone who understood what I was going through, it was him.

"I'm so sorry, baby," he murmured. "I wish I could do more to ease your pain."

I laughed because he was doing more than enough. Checking the time, I realized I had to go if I didn't want to be late for the tutoring session with Grayson.

"I gotta go." I tried to squirm from his arms, but he held on tighter. If I didn't show up, Grayson would tell Professor Wilson, and that would make things worse for me.

"Wait," Ian said. "Look, whatever happens with Cricket, I'm here for you. But this thing with Grayson... it's got to end. It's affecting the entire team. I understand what he did and why you hate him, but I really think it was an accident, Jayden. I've spoken to him, and he doesn't seem like the type to—"

"You don't know him," I cut in. "None of you do."

Ian's face pinched. "I know enough. Just try to let it go for now. Focus on school and other things. Okay? Promise me you won't go after him again like you did before."

My jaw worked. "Why shouldn't I?"

Ian's brow furrowed. "You know how my sister died, right? They bullied her so badly she took her own life. I can't sit back and watch someone go through that."

Betrayal ripped through me. "And I can? I can watch my brother die? My best friend?" I spat and then shoved him away, getting off the bed.

"No, I didn't mean it like that—"

"Yes, you did," I growled, tossing my bag over my shoulder. "Stay the fuck out of it, Ian."

Ian's mouth thinned into a hard line and he said nothing as I packed my shit and went out the door, slamming it shut behind me. Trudging through the harsh winds and snow, I finally made it to the Academic Resource Center, my face throbbing from the cold. Grayson wasn't there, and I hurried to the printing room to print off my assignment so that we could go over it together. The machine was tirelessly working to churn out the stack of documents I needed. Its mechanical symphony filled the air, a rhythmic dance of whirs, clicks, and shushes. Each page emerged with a soft thud into the output tray.

The soft click of the door closing behind me made my head turn.

Grayson.

Two gray clouds collided with mine, and my heart quickened when he stepped forward. His tight shirt clung to his muscular frame, but his eyes held a strange spark of determination, like no matter what, he was going to get through to me. "Are you okay? I saw what happened on the ice—"

"I'm fine," I lied, but I knew I looked like shit. "Don't worry about it."

"I worry about you."

I cocked my head to the side, a cruel laugh bubbling from my chest. "Why? Just so you can have someone to continuously fuck over? I heard you told Professor Wilson I wasn't participating. Well, that's just fucking great. She might even fail me earlier now, thanks to you."

Grayson had the decency to look away. "I'm required to send her updates. You know that—"

"All I know is that every time I turn my back on you, I find another fucking knife in it," I spat.

"Jayden." Grayson's throat bobbed as he stepped forward. "Please. I'm not that guy. You know me. I would never hurt you intentionally, or Cricket."

"And yet here we are, hurt by you," I sneered. "Stay the fuck away from me. If it isn't about tutoring or stuff to do with the team, I don't want to hear it."

Lightning fury flashed in his eyes. "You think I haven't tried? That I don't want to forget. I can't. I see it every fucking day, Jayden. Every time I close my eyes, I see it happening in slow motion. The fight. My inaction. I feel the weight of it like a boulder on my chest every single day. I loved Cricket. He was my brother."

"He was *my* brother," I hissed, teeth bared. "You're nothing to me. Take your damn apologies and shove them up your ass."

Grayson's charcoal eyes became a wispy silver. Heat burned my cheeks, and my blood pounded in my veins as he inched closer, his long legs eating up the space between us.

"Grayson—what—"

He yanked me close, his body enfolding against mine in a hug so tight I thought my rib cage would crack. Grayson's hot breath tickled my neck, and heat crawled over my face as my cock stirred in my jeans. "Fuck, what are you doing?"

"I'm sorry."

Those words were like a blade that pierced my heart. *Sorry*. Tears burned my eyes, and I froze, shock rippling through me. Grayson felt guilty. As he should.

He moved again, closer, holding my waist, nearly nuzzling against me. Rock hard pecs brushed against my sensitive nipples, and I remembered what it was like to be held down by him. To be owned by Grayson Hayes.

God, I still wanted him. I breathed in the scent of cedarwood, his aftershave intoxicating my senses and making my cock twitch and pulse in my jeans. His eyes locked with mine.

Two eyes like the rolling clouds of thunder. There was a madness there. Vast and infinite like the sky that tethered me to him. Grayson would not let this go and if I was honest with myself, I didn't want him to. My gaze darted to his lips. Pink and pale, slightly parted.

Grayson's mouth hovered over mine, waiting. A wave of dizziness came over me, my chest rising and falling as I fought to see reason. To come back to myself, but the truth was I wanted him.

I wanted him now, just like I wanted him back then.

Grayson's lips claimed mine in a brutal kiss, the force of it sending us both stumbling against the printing machines. I gasped, crying out as it dug into my lower back, but Grayson covered my mouth again, slipping his tongue between my lips, stifling my cries.

Fuck. Grayson attacked my mouth, taking me apart as if he were a man dying of thirst and I was a moist fruit. White heat scorched my skin, and I fisted his button-up shirt deepening the kiss. Losing myself to the taste and feel of him. *Of home.*

I hated him. God, I did, but my body screamed otherwise. My soul cried out for him. Yet, I wanted to make him pay for everything he had done to me and my family, yet I couldn't stop.

Madness, I thought, dragging him closer. Moaning as he licked and sucked on my lower lip, dragging his tongue through the wet cavern of my mouth and pulling me under into ecstasy. I thought I'd die in his arms like that. With this man devouring my soul inch by inch. My dick was so hard it was bursting through the zipper on my jeans. I wanted him to take me there and then split me open with his cock. Fill my lungs with brazen fire.

Salty tears invaded my mouth, and I didn't know if they were mine or his.

Grayson pulled away, his eyes rimmed red, cheeks burning. My lungs were heaving. The papers I had printed earlier were strewn all over the floor as we stared at each other. Fuck. I touched my chin, feeling where his facial hair had chafed against my skin. Shock rippled across Grayson's face as if he finally registered the magnitude of his actions.

He took one last look at me, then fled.

13

NOW OR NEVER

GRAYSON HAYES

Crap. What the hell did I just do? Heat singed my cheeks as I fled the printing area, my heart slamming against my ribcage. Did I just kiss Jayden?

Fuck. Scrubbing my face, I packed up my stuff, ignoring the strange look Carry was giving me before I ran from the room. *What was I thinking? Jayden hated me. Right?*

And yet... I thought back to the feel of his lips on mine and realized with shrinking horror that he'd kissed me back. With equal fervor. I groaned aloud and kept walking, too embarrassed to do anything else. I had kissed one of my students in broad daylight in the tutoring center. If that didn't get me fired, I didn't know what would.

Jumping into my sleek black Volkswagen, I sped out of the parking lot. I got home twenty minutes later, my eyes stinging as I dumped my stuff on the floor of my apartment before I started pacing the hardwood floors. Damn. How could I do that? It would make him hate me even more. *Why did I kiss him? What possessed me to do such a thing?* I couldn't fathom it. Panic surged through me, and I ran a trembling hand through my hair. The room seemed to close in on me as I continued to pace, grappling with the consequences of my actions.

"Fuck," I hissed, sucking in air through my teeth. This would be a total fucking mess. What could I do to fix it? Reaching into my pocket, I pulled out my phone to call someone, but who? I didn't really have any friends anymore because of what had happened with Cricket. My thumb hovered on Sarah's number and I dialed it, hoping she'd pick up and cursing when it went to voicemail.

Okay. Try to calm down. It was just a kiss. Jayden wouldn't try to kill you over it. I shivered at the thought. Maybe he would, but it wasn't like he hadn't wanted it. I saw his eyes dart to my mouth and his pupils dilate and all it did was take me back to that night. The first time I took his cock down my throat.

Teasing the head with my tongue, running it along the seams of his swollen head, lapping at the slit and tasting his spend. I dug my palms into my eyelids, wishing the memory would go away. Black tousled hair filled my vision, and the feeling of his tongue ring invading my mouth made my cock pulse in my jeans. Fuck. I sighed long and hard through my nose and then reached down to palm my jeans.

I sat on the couch. Wrenching my zipper open and pulling down the waistband of my Calvin Kline underwear. My hard cock sprang free. Closing my eyes, I imagined how things would have gone had Jayden let me fuck him in his old bedroom. A shudder rolled through me, and I snapped my fist into my aching cock imagining his sweet expression.

"Jayden," I whispered, my voice tight as I thought about mapping out each tattoo with my mouth and tongue, licking long, clean wet stripes down his pale chest, circling around his nipple. Then I'd spread him wide on the bed, take his puckered hole into my mouth. He'd moan, back arching off the bed, his thick cock slapping against his stomach, while the head jerked and spilled milky liquid onto his abs. Rubbing my thick thumb across Jayden's hole, I'd press in gently, not enough for pleasure, but enough to elicit a soft gasp from his lips. Fuck, then I'd dip down and taste his crack, run my tongue along the patch of dark hair covering his puckered dark brown hole and balls. Taking each one into my mouth, I'd suck and roll them beneath my tongue and teeth, yanking several cries from Jayden.

Then I'd spit down his crack and enter him with my finger in one clean thrust. Jayden would cry out, tears brimming from his eyes as he snapped his hips in time with my fingers.

"Ah—fuck—" Pleasure jolted through me. More come erupted from the head of my cock as I stroked furiously to the images flashing before my eyes. Jayden would shout and scream curses, canting his hips blindly chasing his release until I curled my fingers and struck his prostate.

I'd flip him over then, watch him bounce onto his stomach and have his perky ass right in my fucking face where I'd nuzzle deep inside him. Then I'd spread his fucking cheeks, and force my hard rod through his tight, white heat.

A cry ripped through me, and I plunged over the edge, my cock erupting in my hand as come splattered over my shirt and chest. Blood roared in my ears as waves upon waves of pleasure blasted through me, and I groaned, snapping my hips into my fist, chasing the images and more of my release.

Damn. I sighed when I came down, my cock still twitching in my hand. Panting, I reached over to grab some Kleenexes and wiped the come from my chest. My bones felt like jelly and my shirt was ruined, but I was home, so it didn't matter. *Fuck, what the hell was wrong with me? Why was having him so close affecting me so badly?* I thought back to the last time I had sex and realized that Jayden was the last person I'd been intimate with.

Since I had first laid eyes on Jayden, I'd wanted him to be my first.

My phone beeped, and I picked it up, only to see Sarah's name flicker across the screen.

In class. Everything okay? I can come over later. Her text message read.

And see me like this? Hell no. I thought, typing out a quick response. *Yeah, it's fine. I just was seeing what you were up to.*

Okay! She responded. *Evans is having a party tonight. Want to come? Just a few friends.*

Alcohol and conversations? Why not? It would give me a chance to meet more people, instead of being stuck in my head all the time. Plus, the holidays were coming up, and I really hated being alone during this time. Dad never remembered, and it wasn't like I wanted to spend another minute with that bastard.

Sure. I texted back, getting up and heading to the shower. *What time?*

***

COMBING MY HANDS through my still slick, wet hair, I arrived at Evans' house, which was bursting at the seams with students. The crisp wind slapped against my cheek, but the warmth radiating from the house made my smile grow. Christmas lights adorned the front porch, and students stood around, sipping from their red plastic cups. Weaving my way inside, I spotted Sarah immediately. She was dressed in a comfy white, thigh-length cashmere sweater, engaged in conversation with Ian, her face flushed from alcohol.

I walked over to her, until I could peck her on the cheek. She laughed and spun around, her big brown eyes staring up at me. "You came!" she exclaimed, wrapping her arms around me.

"Of course. You invited me," I chuckled, and Ian handed me a drink. I downed it, ignoring the burn, and shrugged off my jacket, revealing a gray sweatshirt that hugged my body in all the right places.

Sarah ran her hand along my bicep. "You clean up nicely, Hayes," she purred. "Anyway, you won't believe the crazy day I had."

I listened to Sarah's amusing story about a flying goose attempting to steal her homework before pooping on her head. Ian and I burst into laughter. As I scanned the room, my gaze landed on a pair of piercing emerald eyes. I choked on my drink.

Jayden.

He was here.

My throat went dry when he strode over wearing all black, his ink standing stark in the room, causing several heads to turn in his direction. Jayden's eyes were trained on me, but I knew something was wrong. A slow cruel smile caused his lips to hook into his cheek, and his shirt was a size too small so that it rode up exposing his sharp pubic bones. Blood rushed to my head, and my tongue felt cleaved to the roof of my mouth as he came closer, his cheeks flushed from the cold.

"Hey," he spoke, his voice rough and deep.

My eyes flew down to his lips, remembering that I had sucked and teased the skin there earlier today. I was just about to respond when Ian leaned over and claimed Jayden's lips.

I felt like I'd been doused with cold water. My vision fractured like shattered glass, and it felt like hot needles were pricking at my chest. Jayden's eyes were wide open, watching me as he kissed Ian.

My heart jammed into my throat, catching those glittering gems turning into wicked slits when Ian deepened the kiss. *Fuck.* I tore my gaze away, my hand trembling.

"Get a room," Sarah said, nose wrinkling as she swayed on her feet.

Ian laughed, pulling away, his lips still moist. "Maybe later."

Sarah made a gagging noise in her throat, but Jayden's eyes never left mine. I gritted my teeth, now understanding why he did that. *Fine. Message received.* Jayden probably only kissed me back because I had taken him by surprise, but if Ian was really his boyfriend, then clearly, he wanted me to fuck off. Pain stabbed at my heart, and I tried to will away the burning behind my eyes, but the party was already ruined for me. *God, I was such a fool.*

Of course, he despised me.

After everything I did to Cricket and his family, why wouldn't he? I drank long and deep, before walking to the kitchen to get another one. When I came back, Jayden and Ian were gone, but my body buzzed and twitched, feeling eyes on me. Looking around the room, I spotted them again. This time Ian had Jayden backed into a corner, their bodies pressed tight together and Ian was kissing a wet trail down Jayden's naked throat. Large thumbs dug into Jayden's pubic bones and all the air rushed from my lungs. They were practically fucking out in the open. Didn't anyone care?

Drake's latest song blared through the speakers, and everyone else was too drunk to care.

"I love this song!" Sarah cried, dragging me onto the dance floor. I swallowed around the blockage in my throat, and I forced a laugh, trying to dance. Sarah swung her hips seductively and several guys in the room stopped to watch her move, but I felt the pull of Jayden's gaze across the room.

Damnit! Focus.

I spun Sarah around before dragging her close, making sure her hips were flushed to mine as we gyrated on the dance floor. Hip-hop music pumped like live wire in my veins, and the alcohol made my limbs loose. My eyes snapped up to Jayden's finding his heated gaze on mine as Ian continued to kiss down his neck and chin, Ian's large hands splayed over his chest, thumbing his nipple through the thin cotton of his black shirt, before moving down to the thick bulge in his jeans.

Arousal shot through me, stealing the breath from my lungs. Ian thumbed Jayden's sharp pubic bones, fingers teasing the waistband of his jeans before he whispered something in Jayden's ear that made a heavy blush spread down his neck.

Jayden laughed. His thick Adam's apple bobbing before his gaze found mine once again. Liquid heat spread through my core, and before I registered it, I was practically grinding my dick against Sarah's backside.

Fuck, I was hard as steel. Aching to the point of pain. Disco lights flashed across the room as they dimmed the lights and the party really started. Jayden pushed off the wall like a sleek panther, ignoring Ian's puzzled look as he made a beeline to us and fucking joined in.

Jayden grabbed Sarah's hips, laughing when she swung them in time with the beat against his crotch. My rhythm faltered when he stepped into my space, and I inhaled his sea breeze cologne that instantly reminded me of Cricket.

"Do you mind?" Jayden asked, his voice a deep rumble in my ear.

"By all means." I swallowed and allowed him to take Sarah off my hands. Smiling and dancing with her, while I stood there like a fucking loser. Running a hand over my face, I walked back into the kitchen to grab another drink, well on my way to becoming shit faced for the night.

Jayden was fucking with me.

Every touch, every whisper, was a fucking taunt. Telling me I could fucking look but never touch. *And God I was a fool for it.* I wanted him so badly it made my chest crack open. Evans was near the keg, pouring a cup of beer, when he spotted me. "Hey man, you made it!"

"Yeah," I said, bumping his fist.

"Sarah said you'd be here," Evans said, then grabbed a bottle of vodka and some red bull. "This still your poison?"

I laughed. "Am I that predictable?"

"A little," Evans replied, then stepped closer to me. "But I wanted to say your playing has improved tenfold. I'll tell you, several of the guys and I are really impressed, man. Are you looking to go pro after this?"

I sipped my drink. "Not sure, man. I think so, but you remember how fucked up my dad was. Him having more control over my life wouldn't make things good for me."

"Yeah, I hear yah," he said, nodding. "My best friend Alex is the same fucking way, bro. Families can be shit, but I think you should really look into it. Aside from that, Coach is considering you to be the new captain."

I nearly spat out my drink. "What?"

"Oh, he didn't tell you?" Evans asked, brows climbing. "Shit man, I hope it wasn't a secret. I'm shit at keeping those."

"No, he didn't say anything, but I thought—isn't Jayden your captain?"

Evans scoffed. "Yeah, but he's hot-headed. You seem a bit more strategical than him. Not that he's bad or anything. I mean, I respect the guy and shit, but he's still a rookie. You'll be graduating next year and he's still got a lot to learn. It's fine. Don't think too deeply into it."

How the fuck could I not? Jayden would hate me if I took his spot on the team after I'd only been here a few weeks. *Fuck, this was bad.* Scrubbing a hand over my face, a tiny girl with russet skin and waist length hair ran into Evans' arms, throwing her arms around his neck. Her eyes were a swirl of autumn leaves, greens and bright hazels. "Baby, you're missing the music!" she slurred, and Evans looked at me and shrugged.

"Duty calls. I'll catch you later, man!" he called as he was dragged off and swallowed by the sea of dancers. The music pounded in my ears, but I felt like I'd been carved open.

Jayden. Hockey. The kiss.

Everything was crashing down, and I needed to get out of there fast. Grabbing my jacket, I left. Just in time to see Jayden climb the stairs with Ian in tow.

Tears stung my eyes, but I kept walking, bursting out the front door, the icy winds slapping against my face. I circled the block for a long time, allowing the heaviness to weigh on my chest. Jayden didn't want me. *That was fine.* I should have prepared for this, yet it hurt more than anything I'd ever felt in my life. Sarah said he might not go for it and to prepare myself for what happened next.

Looking up at the sky, I saw the bright moon illuminate the dark streets, and the trees frozen like twisted metal. A tear slipped free, and I sighed. *It was fine.*

Having Jayden once, for that one kiss was more than I deserved.

***

STRIDING INTO THE hospital, I clutched my yellow flowers tighter to my chest. A few of the nurses who knew me nodded, while others shot strange frowns. I ignored them and made my way to Cricket's room. The beeping of the ventilator filled my ears as I sat down at my usual spot, taking my best friend's hand in mine.

"How are they treating you here, buddy?" I said, smiling. It had been at least a few weeks since I visited, and I silently promised myself to come more often. "Good, I hope. Listen, let me talk to the doctor really quick, and I'll be back—"

"Oh, I thought I saw you come in," Doctor Mohamed Ahmed said, smiling as we shook hands.

I settled into my seat. "How's everything going with Cricket? I noticed the regular payment didn't come this month, so I thought—"

"Yeah, that's what I wanted to speak to you about," the doctor said. "Look, we appreciate all you've done to get Cricket into the program, but I think you should know that there has been no improvement in at least a year. So, we've decided to no longer continue with the treatment."

I felt like the breath had been punched out of me. "What? You aren't going to continue?" I asked, feeling dumb.

"No, Mr. Hayes. I'm sorry. Cricket's condition is complex, and even though we did everything we could, I'll have to stick with the official prognosis. Mr. Taylor is brain-dead. I've told the family to make the arrangements, whether that means cutting the cord for good or keeping him on life support—"

"He's still alive!" I seethed, rage filling my core. "He's moving and breathing—"

"Without that machine, he'd be dead, Mr. Hayes. I'm sorry, but I've urged the family to prepare for the worst and so should you. There's no rush, of course. This is a big decision, but please understand that we've done all we could to bring him back."

Bile surged hot and thick in my throat. We've done all we could. Doctor Mohamed patted my arm, and then I heard footsteps coming down the hall. My brow furrowed, but there was no time to brace myself because Mrs. Taylor rounded the corner and walked right into the room.

14

TRUTH OR DARE

GRAYSON HAYES

All the blood drained from my face as we locked eyes and I wanted the ground to swallow me whole. "Good to see you, Mrs. Taylor. We were just wrapping up. If you have questions, you can come visit me in my office," the doctor said, completely oblivious to the horror skirting over her face.

"I'm sorry—I should go—" Shit. Shit. If Jayden found out I was here, he'd kill me. I felt a sinking feeling in the pit of my stomach. I knew she probably hated me for what happened to her son Cricket. The air in the room seemed to thicken as we both grappled with the weight of the situation.

"Wait—" Mrs. Taylor said, holding out a hand to stop me, then she cleared her throat. "Stay a while? I just got here."

What? I stared at her like she'd grown a second head and started juggling it. The doctor nodded and excused himself and Mrs. Taylor took a seat on the opposite side of Cricket, near the window. I sat down gingerly, trying to make myself small while my heart wanted to flee my chest.

"Look, I'm sorry—"

"How have you been?" We both said and she laughed, tucking a black strand of hair behind her ears. She had Jayden's wide eyes. "Sorry. It's good to see you again, Grayson."

A lump formed in my throat, and I looked away. "You don't have to be polite to me. I know what I did."

She smiled sadly. "What did you do, Grayson? Because from where I'm sitting, I should do a lot more than just be polite to you."

My gaze snapped to hers. "You knew?"

"Of course I did," she said. "This is America. Miracles happen, but not some experimental treatment that takes years of being on the waiting list just having an empty spot. I knew something was up and besides, don't you remember? You always brought me yellow flowers."

I broke then, cracking into a million tiny pieces as sobs tore from my body.

Mrs. Taylor was on her feet and coming over to me, but I tried to hide my face, wishing like hell I could disappear. Tears slid down my cheeks as I stared at Cricket's hollowed face and thin, stick-like arms. Pale skin clung to his bones, and his once handsome face was sunken. He was dead. I refused to accept it. We all did. Warm arms came around my neck, and I allowed myself to cry in her arms, my heart cracking down the middle like ice.

"Shh, it's not your fault."

"It was—" I huffed. "Had I been stronger, faster, they wouldn't have—I was just so shocked and I—I didn't know what to do. What could I do? They came out of nowhere to attack him."

"I know, and we're going to get to the bottom of that soon. Trust me," she replied, her voice stern. "But you can't keep beating yourself up. I saw the video, Grayson. You didn't trip him. Yes, you were close by, but that wasn't you."

Scrubbing my face, I nodded, but I couldn't believe her. Everyone thought it was me and even though a select few people knew it wasn't, I couldn't help but feel guilty. I was Cricket's best friend. I should have been there to take the fall for him, or at least back him up when those guys started attacking him. But I had just been punched by my dad, and it was like my limbs had locked up and I couldn't move.

I took several calming breaths and she pulled away, patting my back. Mrs. Taylor sat back down and sighed long and deep. "I come here every day, you know? Just to see how my baby is doing and maybe, just maybe, he'll wake up and look at me." She laughed, but tears filled her eyes. "Maybe he'll say," she cleared her throat, deepening her voice to intimate Cricket's. "Mom, did you know King Henrik is one of the greatest goaltenders in NHL history? He's also named—"

"King of New York City." we both said at the same time, chuckling. "Yeah, Cricket loved pointing out useless facts."

We lapsed into silence for a moment, and then she sighed again. "I think my husband is right, though. Keeping him like this... it's barbaric. Why not let him pass on? Find warmth in the bosom of God."

I never believed in God. If there was one, why did he let such a horrible thing happen? Then I stared down at Cricket and realized that it didn't matter if I believed or not. Cricket was gone, and he wasn't coming back, and it was comforting to think he was in a better place, happy and full of life and gladness. Mrs. Taylor's hand touched mine, her eyes red rimmed with tears. "Cricket said once that you loved Jayden."

My breath caught, but I nodded, my own tears burning down my cheeks.

"Keep loving him. Please," she begged. "He needs you. Now more than ever. Don't let him push you away. Okay? Don't let him."

We sat there in silence for a long time. Both of our hands joined, and after I left with the sun dipping past the skyline, I knew that the decision to take Cricket off life support had already been made.

A brisk chill crept beneath my coat, but I didn't care. I walked outside the hospital building, feeling numb. My face throbbed, and a headache threatened to split my skull, but none of that mattered. An ache cracked my chest open as I took several more steps before my legs buckled and my hands scrambled against the rough brick of the side wall to prevent me from tumbling over.

A scream clawed its way up my throat, but I fought to suppress it. Tears blurred my vision, making everything throb and strobe in and out. Cricket was gone—my best friend, my soul friend. In one night, all our dreams had been shattered. I crumbled in the mud, feeling the slush seep through my jeans and soak my underwear.

Bitter tears blazed down my cheeks. Jayden should never forgive me for this, because I would never forgive myself. My phone buzzed in my pocket. Taking it out, I saw Sarah's face flash on the screen. I pressed "ignore," only for it to ring again, accompanied by several urgent texts.

I opened it, and my heart stopped.

***

A SCORCHING ANGER, fierce and unrelenting, coursed through my veins, turning my vision red with fury. I was on my feet in seconds, sprinting towards my car and tearing out the hospital parking lot like my life depended on it, tires squealing as I tore down the freeway.

Fucking bastard! I wanted to scream, smashing my fist against the steering wheel. How the hell could Jayden do something like this? To me? To Cricket? What the fuck was he thinking? It was as if an unquenchable wildfire of rage had engulfed me, consuming me from the inside out. The very thought of Jayden sharing that video again stoked the flames to unbearable heights.

I stormed into the locker room, slamming the door open, causing several of the guys changing to jump.

"Where's Jayden?" I barked, nostrils flaring. The guys stared at me in shock before one of them took a shaky finger and pointed it at the showers. Ripping open the door, I carved a warpath through the showers, ignoring the strange looks I received because I was still fully clothed. Jayden was in the furthest stall, whistling while he lathered himself up.

"Get the fuck out!" I screamed at everyone, and all the guys jumped, fleeing the room. I locked the door behind them. Jayden's eyes widened when I tore off the shower curtain, a blast of cold air hitting his skin and causing goosebumps to rise all over his flesh.

"*What the—*"

I slammed him against the wall, my hand curling around his neck as he clawed at my wrist. "What the fuck is wrong with you?" I shouted in his face. Not caring that the spray of water was soaking my shirt and jacket. "How could you leak that video? Do you know what you've done? What my father has done to keep that video hidden—"

"What? Scared people are going to find out what you did?" Jayden rasped, his face going red, and he laughed. "Fuck you! You killed my brother and now you want me to keep quiet about it? No fucking way—"

My throat constricted. "I didn't kill anyone—I—Jayden, I would never hurt you or Cricket—"

"You're hurting me now!" Jayden snarled, his eyes flashing. "Look at you, you've fucking deceived yourself so much you actually think you're the good guy. That you did nothing wrong, but I see right through you, Grayson," Jayden hissed, inching closer. "I know *exactly* who you are."

No. I shook my head, desperately trying to fight the thick syrupy fog trying to drag me under. *No. I wasn't a monster. It was an accident.* Everything that happened was an accident. Jayden's eyes were lit with brazen fire, a giddy fury that raised the hairs on my arm. The air crackled between us as if a single vein of lightning had struck me. Jayden's green eyes were deep and fathomless, hooded as they stared into my soul as if daring me to make a move.

The fucking fiend hooked his leg over my hip and I gasped when I looked down and saw his cock was hard. Swollen even, flushed and resting on his stomach, begging for attention. My eyes snapped back to his and a smile curled his lips.

"This is what you want, right? What you told Cricket you wanted when he left you alone in my house that day? Here's your chance. Take it."

My lungs cinched tighter and tighter. Black spots edged around my vision as I struggled to make sense of what he was saying. Jayden gave an impatient snort, then he moved in, lips hovering over mine while droplets of water trailed down his inked flesh. "I'm yours. Take me."

I growled low and deep in my throat. What a mockery! I hated him for saying those words to me. If we were together, it would have made my heart soar. But now that I knew that all of this was just a fucking joke to him? Then fine. *I'd take him.*

And damn myself to hell and back.

Jayden's mouth descended on mine with a resounding crack. I gasped, when he claimed my lips in a brutal kiss. An unholy clash of teeth and lips, as I grunted taking hold of those deliciously narrow hips and hooked both of his strong thighs around my waist.

With a mighty crash that shook the ground, I shoved him against the tile wall. Jayden cried out, and I kissed him harder, fisting his hair and swallowing his cries in a vicious kiss that rattled my bones. *Fucking hell.* I sucked air through my teeth, rutting against his hot body. Steam made it impossible to breathe. The thick fog covering the room forced me to peel off my winter jacket and shirt. Throwing it all on the floor where it made a loud wet flop.

"Fuck, yeah—" Jayden hissed when I hiked him up higher, attacking his neck. Sinking my teeth into his flesh as he cried out harder, grabbing my shoulders and clinging to me. I growled in my throat, sucking on his collarbone before working down to those perked nipples. Nibbling around the head, I bit down hard on one of them, watching Jayden moan and shudder.

It was fast and dirty.

And everything I hated about meaningless sex.

The slut bitched and moaned beneath me, and I dropped him back to his feet before I spun him around hard, pressing his face against the tile wall. Wrenching my fly open, my aching cock sprang free, and I lined it up with his hot puckered entrance. Water beat down on my back, my face stung with tears and my throat burned with bile. As I cupped his neck, forcing him to turn to me while I captured his mouth. My tongue slipped into his wet cavern, tasting the glint of steel on his tongue.

"Jayden," I rasped, this would be my first time. I didn't want to tell him that. I couldn't bear the mocking shimmer in his eyes. Jayden pushed back against my cock, back arching.

"Fuck me," he groaned, low and deep, and I could do nothing but comply. I wanted him. I loved him. Grabbing the base of my cock, I swirled the head around his hole, but the water made him slick and gaping. I shoved it in. No lube.

No protection.

Raw and hard, like silk over steel.

Jayden moaned long and low, his breath hitching. My vision stuttered before fracturing into a thousand million pieces and white-hot heat engulfed my shaft. "Fuck," I cried out, trying not to thrust deeper and chase my release "Jayden—are you okay? Did I hurt you?" I asked, not sure what else to do.

"Fuck me!" he barked, pushing back against me.

I nodded and gave a few shallow thrusts, and then Jayden leaned back, his head falling on my shoulder as he gripped my lower back. "Yes! Fuck yeah, harder baby—fuck me harder—"

I groaned, relishing the hard demands before pistoning my hips. Skin slapping against skin filled the air. My balls drew up high and taut against my body. I could feel the rapid rise and fall of Jayden's chest as he cried and grunted, and I kissed and sucked on his neck. Losing myself to the heat made my head spin. Reaching down, I clasped his thick shaft, stroking him in time with my brutal thrusts.

Burning desire pulsed through my veins. I never knew it could feel like this. That Jayden would ever allow me to have this with him. A part of me worried about Ian, but I was far too gone to care right now. Jayden was meeting my thrusts, his voice growing louder and louder. I slapped a hand over his mouth to stifle his cries, plunging my cock to the hilt before pulling out all the way and slamming forward.

Jayden was a fucking mess.

Water mixed with drool dribbled down his mouth, his face flushed and beaten raw. His blunt nails dug into my hip and then he was coming in milky white spurts on my hand and all over the tile wall. I growled in my throat; I grabbed his neck to apply just the right amount of pressure. Stardust burst before my eyelids and then I was coming in searing spurts deep in his perky ass. I choked on a sob, driving my cock home and pressing him harder into the tile wall.

Another harsh thrust made him cry out, instinctively clenching his body tight. A half-stilted yell tore from his throat and he was coming again, his body shuddering so hard I thought he'd pass out. Pulling out, I spun him around, kissing him so hard and fast he went limp beneath me. I love you. I sobbed against his mouth, feeling my chest ache with insurmountable pain.

Jayden didn't see it, though.

His bones were limp, and a laugh bubbled up from his mouth. "Fuck, Hayes. You fuck just as good as you play hockey."

It was all a joke to him.

My first time.

Exposing that video for the world to see. All of it.

I stepped away with a shrinking horror filling my chest. Jayden looked blissful and fucked out, come cooling on his stomach and his skin red with marks. What had I done? I played right into his hands. I hurried to zip up my pants, then I grabbed my jacket from the floor and sped out of there. Jayden called my name several times, but I kept walking. Luckily it was late, so everyone had left the locker rooms, but shame crawled all over my face.

Fuck. What the hell was I thinking? Taking Jayden like that in public! Anyone could have walked in and saw us together! Running to my car, I opened the door and sped home, trying to make sense of what happened today.

Cricket would be taken off life support.

Jayden and I fucked for the first time.

My head spun in a whirlwind. Too much shit was happening, and I could barely get a grip. I came back to my apartment soaking wet, clothes drenched from falling in the mud and the involuntary shower

I took earlier. Shedding my clothes, I took another quick shower, washing the scent of sea breeze off me, and went to my bedroom to sleep. It was a long fucking day, and it wasn't even over yet.

Laying on the plush mattress, I stared off into space.

I couldn't do this anymore. Not with Jayden. After today I'd end things. Jayden had a boyfriend and I needed to move on with my life. We fucked. So what? I could get over it. Jayden could move on too once Cricket was officially gone. And yet, Mrs. Taylor's words rang in my ear.

Don't let him push you away. Okay? Don't let him. I scoffed.

She had no idea what her son was doing to me. Teasing me past the point of insanity and all I could do was let him. Jayden was so different. So callous and cold. I knew he hated me, but did I really deserve this? To be treated so badly by the person I loved? A thick lump formed in my throat, but I didn't cry. By now, I had no more tears left.

15

DATES AND DECISIONS

JAYDEN TAYLOR

Throwing my arm over my face, I tried to quell the pounding in my chest. My skin felt raw. Aching from every touch and images of our fuck in the shower replayed on a loop in my mind. A mistake. One that I'd probably make again a thousand times over.

Fuck. I thumbed my stinging lips, relishing the taste of Grayson. His sharp cedarwood cologne. Those massive arms crowding me into the wall. Gray eyes wild and mad as a raging bull. The minute he stepped into the shower my breath hitched, pulse throbbing with a furious delight when his eyes raked over my naked body. Then those hands went around my neck and I was hard instantly.

Fucking Grayson. Peeling my arm away, I stared up at the ceiling, wishing like hell I'd made it last longer. The feel of him. The weight of him. *God, it ignited something inside my chest.* Like water in pipes solidifying into ice, swelling until it burst. Now that I had a taste, I wanted more.

I hated Grayson. Yet, all the feelings from the past came rushing back.

That night at the party, I kissed Ian, made love to Ian, but all I fucking thought about was Grayson. Slamming my fist against the bed, I growled, feeling angry and frustrated with myself. *Was I sick for wanting him?* After everything he's done to my family? He murdered Cricket, and all I could think about was getting fucked by him. The enemy. *What the hell was wrong with me?*

A swift knock on the door brought me out of my thoughts, and my brow furrowed, wondering who it might be at this hour. My skin was still chafing from the shower with Grayson, and my asshole stung something fierce. Throwing on a thick gray sweater, I opened the door, only to be stunned when Ian stood there. *Fuck, this day couldn't get any worse.* "Ian—I—"

He shouldered past me and walked into the room, his large winter coat hugging his massive frame. Opening the doors to my bathroom and closet, his eyes darted around the room as if he were looking for something. Or someone. Blond hair flopped over his brow and he sighed, before sitting down at the edge of my bed.

"What are you doing here?" I asked, finally finding my voice.

"They said Grayson was yelling at you," Ian replied, and then laughed. "I thought... anyway. What happened? Are you okay?"

I swallowed around the lump in my throat. "I'm fine, just tired. We can talk tomorrow—"

Ian stared at me, not moving an inch. "Did he hurt you?"

Shit. Shit. Blood roared in my ears as I stared at his too calm expression. I wasn't sure I could stomach telling Ian what happened afterward. We weren't a couple. Ian was my friend, but sometimes, like now, I always felt like he wanted something more. Most of my fear stemmed from what he would think of me. Or what everyone else would think of me. Falling for the man who killed my brother. *It was disgraceful. Sick. Wrong.*

No. I couldn't tell Ian or anyone else. My hand went to my throat, thumbing the swollen skin there, and my mouth tugged into a smirk. "I got him worse. Don't worry about it. We're good."

Ian stood and sighed, cupping my face. His calloused fingers brushed my cheek, but his lips pulled into a frown before his eyes snapped to mine.

A minute passed before he pulled away.

"Okay. Yeah. I'll see you later."

"Wait—" I said, but he was already closing the door shut behind him. Closing my eyes, I sighed through my nose and went to turn off the lights in the bathroom. However, before I did, I caught my reflection in the mirror. *Fuck. Fuck.* Blistering red hand prints littered my skin, but just below my cheek was a hickey the size of a damn golf ball. There was no way in hell Ian missed that.

I groaned, feeling like a bus had hit me. Shit. I'd have to find him to explain things, but knowing Ian, he'd shut down immediately. We never talked about being more, but I could tell he wanted to. Now everything had gone to shit.

Because of fucking Grayson.

Damn him! My hand balled into a fist, but I knew he wasn't entirely to blame. I was the one who was sleeping with Ian anyway. I should have told him no. Forced him away after that first kiss, but I couldn't seem to stop myself.

And something kept telling me this hailstorm of shit was just beginning.

***

STROLLING THROUGH THE hospital, I scrubbed my face. Last night I didn't sleep a wink. Exhaustion made my limbs heavy and my feet drag, but I was determined to see Cricket today. My mom texted me, saying she was already there but dad was at work. She said she wanted to talk to me about something and the thought made my stomach clench. I knew they had decided about Cricket, but I wouldn't let him go. Cricket was alive dammit! I would not let them cut off his life support. He'd wake up. Once I graduated and made it to the NHL, I'd fly him all over the world to get him the best treatment. Cricket would come back. They'll see.

I grumbled under my breath and walked into the room. A flash of yellow in the corner caught my attention, and I snorted, wondering who the hell was bringing those hideous flowers. My mom got up from her seat and gave me a tight hug and a kiss, and I sat down opposite her.

"What happened to your face? Are you okay?" she asked, alarm in her voice.

"Fine. Stupid fight. I'm good, though."

"Are you sure? Let me have a look at it." She reached for me, but I jerked away.

"I'm fine, Mom, just a bit sore. It'll heal." I turned to glance at Cricket. He was worse. Skin ashen, dark circles beneath his eyes. He was wasting away. "Can't they feed him more or something?"

She shook her head. "It seems his body isn't ugh... taking the food. The doctor says it's only a matter of time now." What the hell was that supposed to mean?

"Well, then we need a new doctor. We can go back to the other hospital. I'm sure we can get a second opinion."

My mother's face pinched. "I don't want a second opinion."

My eyes narrowed. "What? What the hell are you talking about? Cricket just needs some exercise, and then he'll be better. Trust me. I read about it in my class—"

"Jayden, honey. You know what I'm going to say next."

Rage burst through me, and I wanted to grab the nearest object and throw it. Why the hell was nobody listening to me? He was alive. Why couldn't they see that? Why couldn't they wait?

"What kind of mother are you—"

Pain skittered from my cheek as a resounding slap rang out. I stared at my mother in shock, noticing the furious tears that trailed down her cheeks.

"How dare you speak to me like that!" she shrilled. "Is this how you talk to your mother? Your father? Grayson?"

"Grayson?" I spat. "What the hell does he have to do with this?"

"Who the hell do you think paid for all this shit?"

I was stunned into silence. Suddenly, it all made sense. Yellow flowers. Experimental treatment. *Fuck, I should have known.* It was all him the entire time, watching over us. Tears stung my eyes and I let them fall, staring down at her.

"Haven't I been through enough?"

Shame crawled across my skin like a thousand ants. How could I say something so cruel to her? What was I thinking? "I'm sorry. That was wrong. I didn't mean it."

My mother's shoulders slumped, and she sat back down in her chair, wiping the tears from her cheeks. The room was heavy with a painful silence. The weight of everything we'd been through pressed down on both of us.

She finally spoke, her voice softer. "I know you're hurting, Jayden. We all are. But I need you to understand, we've consulted the best doctors. We've tried everything, and it's just... it's just not working. Cricket's been suffering for too long, and it's time to let him go."

Tears welled up in my eyes as I looked back at my best friend, still and lifeless in the hospital bed. I choked on my sorrow and nodded, unable to speak.

My mother reached out, taking my hand in hers. "We're all in this together, Jayden. You don't have to carry the weight of the world on your shoulders. We love Cricket, and we're going to make the best decision for him. I know it's hard, but sometimes letting go is the most compassionate thing we can do."

I squeezed her hand, the anger replaced by a deep sadness. She was right, but that didn't make it hurt any less. Cricket was my brother, my best friend, and I couldn't bear the thought of losing him.

Together, we sat in silence, the unspoken understanding that we were facing an unimaginable decision, and it was tearing our family apart.

***

LEAVING THE HOSPITAL, I wandered around the block for what felt like an eternity. Snow fell gently from the sky, creating a tranquil white blanket, but my heart was heavy. Cricket was gone, and the world felt a little less bright without him in it. How could I go on without my brother, my best friend?

And then there was Grayson. Where did he fit into all of this? I had never mustered the courage to watch the video. I couldn't bear to see the horrific incident again. But if Grayson was truly innocent, and I had unjustly accused him by sharing that video, then wasn't I the real bully in this story?

The one in the wrong.

For a long time, it had been easier to blame Grayson, to believe that he was responsible for what happened. It felt more comforting than facing the possibility that it had been a freak accident. Cricket was not clumsy, and he wouldn't have just fallen on the ice like that. Someone had tripped him, but who and why? We had never found answers, and the mystery gnawed at me.

Nothing was making sense, and my head throbbed with pain. As I returned to my dorm room, I retrieved my chemistry textbook. Opening it up, I examined the notes Grayson had written in his elegant handwriting. There were pages of them. Cheat sheets. Study notes. And I wondered when the hell Grayson had time to slip all of this shit between the pages of my textbook.

Fuck. It was probably during all those times I ignored him whenever he tried speaking to me. Running a hand through my thick black hair, I sighed. *Was I really that much of a bastard?* Yes. Probably.

I thought back to Kit and my horrible time at juvie. Could I really blame Grayson for all of that? Back then, yes, but now I wasn't so sure. It all seemed stupid and unbelievably petty, especially since my mom seems to think he did nothing wrong.

I got a few hours of studying in, reviewing the notes and cheat sheets Grayson made without my knowledge, and then finished up the rest of my assignments. I only had a few months left before the end of the semester, and I couldn't waste them. I knew Professor Wilson would fail me, and then what? Closing my books, I checked the time and realized it was well after midnight. I rummaged through my backpack and took out the t-shirt Grayson had left on the floor. I hurried to wash it and throw it in the dryer. I'd give it to him tomorrow.

That was if he'd let me. *God, I was a bastard to him.*

And a large part of me wasn't even sure if I was sorry about it.

***

LIGHT SLICED ACROSS my vision as I walked through the halls of the Academic Resource Center. The sun filtered through the large panel windows as I took my usual seat near the front. Taking out my textbooks, my heart slammed against my ribcage and my knee bounced as I waited for Grayson to come. What was I going to say to him? Sorry? Thanks for paying my brother's hospital bills? It felt like a thistle was lodged in my throat. Sorry for being an ass to you now and all those years ago?

I wasn't even sure if I wanted to apologize to him just yet. Yes, what he did was amazing, but why didn't he say anything? Why did he lead me to believe he was a jackass? Then again, would I have let him explain? Probably not.

Jamal came into the room, his mouth pressed into a hard line. "Grayson won't be in today, so let's get started. Take out your textbook to page 184 and we can start there." Not in today? I felt the breath get punched from my lungs. Why not? Something happened? Or was he avoiding me? Jamal refused to meet my eyes, and it seemed like that was the case. I deserved that, I guess.

The tutoring session went on with little fanfare, but after it was over, I went to find Grayson. Even though he was avoiding me, we still needed to talk. About what? I wasn't sure, but I knew after everything my mom said, I owed it to him to at least say thank you for doing what he did for Cricket and apologize for acting like a complete tool most of the time. Rounding the corner, I saw Grayson at his locker, talking to Sarah. His thick black sweater stretched across his muscular frame, and I remembered what it felt like to be pinned down by his massive bulk. My cock thickened from the memory, and adjusted it as I walked over to them.

"Hey," I said, but my voice sounded rough, so I cleared my throat.

Sarah shot me a sunny smile. "Hey there, what happened to you? You look like you got run over by a bulldozer."

I slung my arm around Grayson's shoulders, watching him tense. "You should see the other guy."

Sarah's eyes widened and flickered between the two of us, noticing the cut above Grayson's eye. The one I'd given him during practice a few days prior. Grayson shrugged my arm off, his expression stony. "I have class. Sarah, I'll talk to you later."

"Sure…" she said, but concern was flashing in her eyes. "Call me if you need anything."

I watched her walk away and gave an encouraging nod because she kept stopping and looking back at us, as if she wasn't sure she should have left us alone.

Gray eyes collided with mine, and it was almost like the sky was stirring itself into a frenzy. His glare was dark and thick, like black rolling clouds of thunder. "What the hell do you want?"

Each word felt like a dagger to my chest. I knew he was pissed, and I deserved it after yesterday. "Look, about yesterday—"

"Nothing happened yesterday," Grayson hissed. "Now you've got ten seconds to get the fuck out of my face."

Woah. Where was all this hostility coming from? I knew I was an ass, but did I really go too far last night? Frustration warred within me. It was hard enough for me to stand in front of the bastard and feel like I owed him everything, and now he was being a total dick. "Grayson," I replied. "I'm sorry. I—what I did was stupid and I—look, can we talk somewhere?" I asked, the noise in the hallways making it hard to get my point across.

"There's nothing left to say," Grayson said through gritted teeth. "Jamal will be your tutor going forward. So, unless it's about the team, we have nothing to talk to each other about."

Fuck. Things were going south quickly. "Okay. I deserve that." And everything else. "But I really am sorry. If you'll just give me a second to explain—"

"There is nothing to explain," Grayson snapped. "Everything that happened—it was an error in judgment on my end, and trust me, it won't be happening ever again."

Now that stung. What the fucking hell did he mean by an error in judgment? "What? So, your dick in my ass was an error in judgment?" I flung the words back at him, causing several heads to turn.

"Yes," Grayson spat, looking at me like I was filth, and I felt the words like I'd been slapped. Who the hell did he think he was, treating me like this? After all the pain and suffering he'd caused? After everything he'd done? I slammed him against his locker, arm posed around his throat with my teeth bared.

"You self-righteous piece of shit—"

"Jayden." Ian's voice filled my ears, and I turned to see him standing there with Sarah, his face clouded with fury. "Let him go."

I dropped my arm and Grayson shoved me off, grabbing his stuff from his locker and walking away with Sarah running after him. Everyone in the hall was staring at me. Ian's gaze pierced my skin, and I sighed, running a hand through my hair. "It's not what it looks like—"

"It's exactly what it fucking looks like, Jayden," Grayson snarled. "Since the day he got here, you've been bullying him nonstop. Well, I won't fucking stand for it. We're done."

Done? What? Ian moved, but I grabbed his bicep hard, yanking him back. "Ian—what?"

"You're not who I thought you were," he hissed. "Jesus Christ, my sister died because of people like you. People who pick on other people for no reason other than your own damn selfishness!" He pushed me back hard. "I said nothing because I was scared of losing you, but then I realized I never had you to fucking begin with." Then he was gone, swallowed up by the crowd and leaving me there, staring after him in shock.

Fuck. My hands balled into fists, but there was nothing I could do. I had fucked up. Ian was right. Grayson was right. *I was a mess. Toxic waste.* It was so bad I even justified it as me being the good guy. That bullying Grayson and making him feel like shit was in Cricket's best interest.

God, I was such a fool, and I just lost the two people I care about the most because of it.

16

BREAKING THE ICE

JAYDEN TAYLOR

S hoving my gear into my bag, I kept stealing glances at Ian, hoping that he had found my "I puck-ed up" apology note taped to his stick earlier. The locker room was relatively quiet, everyone lost in their own thoughts, until they began filing out one by one. Grayson was the first to leave, his expression fierce as he stormed out of the room. I swallowed hard, hoping to resolve one thing at a time.

As the room emptied, Ian slowly put his stuff away until he and I were the last ones there. "Hey," I called out to him. "Can we talk?"

His blond hair covered his brow as he gave a short, stiff nod. I walked over to him and slumped against the wooden doors with a sigh.

"I'm an asshole. I know it. Slap me," I said.

Ian eyed me wearily. "Don't tempt me. I might get my glove and do just that."

I laughed, but it died down as I noticed he wasn't laughing too.

"Things are complicated with Grayson. I... for a long time, I hated him. I still do, for everything that's happened. But you're right. Treating him like that was wrong, and I barely recognize myself when he's around, and I—"

"What am I to you?" Ian's question cut through my explanation.

My stomach swooped at the sudden change of subject. "What? What do you mean?"

"I see the way you look at him," Ian continued. "You never looked at me like that. Even at the party, you stared at him the whole time. Are you fucking him?"

All the air was punched out of my lungs. I never wanted Ian to find out, especially not like this. Heat crawled up my neck, and a knot swelled in my throat. "Ian..."

"Oh," he laughed, but it sounded bitter. "So, I'm the idiot, hoping one day we'd be together."

"It happened once, and it was a mistake—"

"Yeah," Ian interrupted, slamming his locker shut. "I've heard that one before."

Then he walked away, and I let him go. Cursing under my breath, I couldn't help but wonder how things had gotten so bad. A part of me knew Ian wanted more, but I thought he'd get over it some day. I never saw Ian like that, but I wasn't willing to give up the sex we were having to clarify exactly what I wanted.

Scrubbing my face, I groaned. This was really turning into a shit week.

***

THE ROLLING HILLS WERE covered in a pristine layer of snow as I sped down the freeway. The Christmas holidays arrived faster than I had expected, and before I knew it, I was packing up my stuff to head back to my hometown in Cleveland, Ohio. Listening to "Jingle Bells" on repeat was enough to make me want to blow my brains out, but it was a nice distraction from the thoughts bouncing around in my head.

Ian was still ignoring my calls, and Grayson... God, I didn't even want to think about him just yet. Too much had happened between us. I couldn't wrap my head around everything he'd done for Cricket, and I felt lingering resentment toward him for not saying anything. My heart and head were a mess, but I knew I had to start making things right. I didn't want to be that kind of person anymore. I wasn't like Kit. I didn't want to mindlessly hurt people and destroy their lives because of my selfishness.

I arrived home late in the evening, and Duke ran out to meet me. I laughed when he jumped into my arms, barking like mad. "There's a good boy!" I kissed his snout and rubbed his ears as my dad came out to help me with the rest of my luggage.

"Good to see you," my dad said and hugged me.

I pulled back and stared deep into his eyes. My dad was sober for the first time in years. "You too." I hugged him back tighter. "Where's Mom?" I asked.

My dad's mouth pulled into a smirk. "Inside cooking."

The smell of freshly baked cookies and crisp apple pie filled my nostrils. The cozy warmth of our home embraced me as I walked inside. My mother, flushed with happiness, bustled in the kitchen, her cheeks rosy from the heat of the oven. Her joy and the aroma of her cooking filled the house. It was the warmth that was so familiar, so comforting. We hugged, and I saw the table was set for three.

I felt a pang in my chest. The absence of Cricket's presence loomed large. His laughter, his quirks, his essence were missing from our home, and it was impossible to ignore. Heading to my room, I gazed at the old Star Trek posters on my walls. The familiar scenes and quotes provided a sense of nostalgia.

Flopping face first onto my bed, my thoughts wandered back to Grayson and the kiss we had shared here. His lips on mine had been urgent and yet gentle, filled with unspoken emotions. The way he held me, the sincerity in his eyes—there was no malice there, only love.

Grayson loved me, and I had been a fool not to see it.

Rolling onto my stomach, my thumb hovered over his phone number. I wanted to call him, to clear the air, but I hesitated. What if he rejected me? What if he told me to go to hell? But the pain of the unknown was becoming unbearable.

Summoning the courage, I dialed his number. It rang several times before he picked up. "Grayson."

"Don't hang up," I said, my voice quick and breathless.

There was a long silence on the other end, and I checked to make sure he was still on the line before I pushed forward. "I'm an idiot."

"Jayden—"

"I'm a bastard and I'm—" I said in a hurry. "I'm so fucking sorry. You aren't the monster I was making you to be—"

"What if I am?" Grayson responded, but his voice sounded off. Slurred. "What if I am a monster?"

Tears stung my eyes. "You aren't. You didn't hurt Cricket. I should have known you wouldn't have done something like that—"

"I did hurt him. More than you'll ever know. I killed him. It was all my fault."

Shaking my head, I got up. "Grayson, what are you talking about? Where are you?"

"It's too late," Grayson said, but his voice sounded further and further away. "I'm already dead."

The call ended and my heart jammed into my throat. I tried dialing his number again, but it went straight to voicemail. Fuck. I got up from the bed and grabbed my keys. I shouted to my parents I was going out before slamming the door shut and racing to my car. It was the holiday season. Grayson never spent time with his family and if his bastard father was nearby, no wonder he was probably getting shit faced. Cricket had mentioned a pub they used to drink at during the holidays close by. I'd try my luck there and, if not, I'd make the long journey back to Michigan to see if I could find Grayson's apartment.

Loud shouts and jeers pricked my ears as I entered the pub. The place was alive with people engrossed in the game playing on the TV screens. Normally, I'd be up to date with the hockey season, but I'd been so engrossed with school and other matters that I'd missed half of it already.

Surveying the bar, the dim lighting and the crowd made it challenging to spot anyone familiar. But then, my gaze locked onto a mop of brown hair and gray eyes amidst the crowd. Grayson sat alone, nursing a beer, his body slumped and turned away from the screens.

Grayson's eyes, like the Arctic-blue and corpse-cold sea, held an intense and chilling allure. They seemed to carry the weight of impending storms, a tempestuous darkness lurking within their depths. His gaze pierced through me, just like the lightning that slashes through the ominous sky before a tempest. *Fuck what the hell happened to him?*

I marched over to him just as he was about to take another swig and took the beer from his hand. "Are you finished?"

His eyes, once sharp and determined, now looked weary. They were rimmed with red and sagging. He looked awful, like he hadn't slept in days. "Where did you park? I'll take you home."

Grayson's jaw tightened, and he snatched the drink back. "Nowhere to go."

My eyes scanned the room again. "You can't stay here. Come home with me."

Grayson scoffed, but there was a hint of resignation in his expression. "No thanks. I don't think the bed will be big enough, especially if Ian is already in it."

His words stung, but I knew there was no point in arguing with a drunk man. "Come on, let's go. My parents are expecting you."

I managed to get him off the stool and into his winter jacket. It was evident he was in no condition to drive, so I decided to pick up his car in the morning.

The ride back to my house was quiet. Grayson leaned his forehead against the window, and I couldn't help but sigh. When we pulled into the driveway, we got out of the car and made our way inside.

"Jayden? Where did you go? Dinner is almost ready—oh!" My mom stopped in the doorway. "Grayson? Are you staying?" Her face lit up. "Well, that's great. The more, the merrier!" She laughed, and my dad stepped out of the living room. "Want to catch the rest of the game? I think it's in the third period now."

I shrugged off my jacket and guided Grayson into the house. "Who's winning?"

On one screen, the Calgary Flames were battling the Chicago Blackhawks. "It's 5-0 with the Blackhawks in the lead."

Ten minutes in, Grayson and I were perched at the edge of our seats, both of us hooting and hollering in support of our chosen teams. "Come on! They're practically handing him the puck!" I yelled at the TVs. "Who taught these guys how to skate? The zoo?"

Grayson and my father couldn't help but laugh at my animated commentary. "I know, right?" Grayson joined in. "This is painful to watch."

"Well, it's not like the Predators are doing much better in their match against the Capitals," my dad pointed out.

Grayson chuckled. "Yeah, but at least we're not serving turnovers like it's a buffet, unlike your Flames."

I raised an eyebrow. "Oh, really? Coming from a Capitals fan, that's rich."

"All right! Dinner's ready!" my mom shouted from the kitchen. I shut off the TV not sure my eyes could take anymore of the humiliating loss the Calgary Flames were facing against the Chicago Blackhawks. What a joke! When I made it to the league, they'd never see me coming.

As we walked into the kitchen, the table was adorned with the finest Christmas dinner spread. In the center, a lavish roasted turkey sat like a crowned jewel, its skin glistening with a perfect sheen. The tantalizing scent of sage and rosemary filled the air, and the meat was tender and succulent.

Beside the turkey, dishes of creamy mashed potatoes and savory stuffing beckoned. Steamed vegetables glistened with a buttery glaze, and cranberry sauce added a burst of color to the ensemble. There was a bowl of rich gravy, perfect for smothering everything on your plate.

"Damn," I whispered, reaching out to touch, but mom smacked my hand away. "Ouch!"

"Grace," she admonished, and we all sat down, linking our hands together.

"Father, please bless this food, Amen," my dad said, and we all dug in.

"Thanks for having me, Mrs. Taylor," Grayson spoke, helping himself to the food.

"Of course," my mother replied, but there was a twinkle in her eyes. "I'm glad to see Jayden finally got his foot out of his ass to ask you to dinner."

The food nearly dropped out of my mouth as heat flared across my cheeks. "Mom!"

"What?" She gave me a coy smile. "I'm down with the cool kids. Don't worry, Jayden. I left some lube in your top drawer."

"Please stop talking."

"I second that," my dad replied, his nose wrinkled. "How did you know where to buy the lube from, anyway?"

"I have my ways." My mom winked. "Maybe you'll find out later tonight."

"And I'm officially scarred for life."

Grayson laughed, his entire face lighting up and thankfully Duke changed the subject by demanding the turkey bones from my plate with a loud bark.

***

GRAYSON'S THUMB DRAGGED along the old posters in my room, his lips curling into a smile. Laying on my back with my arms behind my head, I watched him with hooded eyes. That same black sweater stretched across his broad chest, his jeans hung low, exposing a small sliver of skin on his taut abdomen.

Fuck, he looked delicious just standing there, and all the memories of the past came rushing back to me. Heat seeped into my skin as he sauntered toward me and sat on the edge of the bed. "Feels weird being back here," he spoke, his deep voice sending shivers down my spine.

"Yeah."

Grayson stared off into space. "Why did you bring me here?"

I froze, not sure what I should say to that. *Because I wanted to apologize.* The words were on the tip of my tongue, but I swallowed them back. "I don't know."

Grayson nodded once; his face turned away. "You still hate me."

"I don't know," I said again. This time I realized how stupid that sounded. "No. Yes. I don't fucking know."

"I tried to stay out of your way, Jayden," Grayson said, but his jaw was clenched. "I wouldn't have—bothered you or your family at all—"

If I hadn't gone after him first. Made his life hell first. "Fuck—I know. I'm sorry—"

"So, what do you want from me?" He turned to me then, his gray eyes lit like fire. "You have a boyfriend. What we did to Ian—it was so beyond the realm of fucked up and I don't want to hurt anyone ever again—"

"Ian isn't my boyfriend," I blurted out.

Grayson stilled; his breath caught. "What?"

"We fuck, but we aren't together. I'll talk to him. It's my fault. I fucked up with him, but we aren't together so you aren't a... homewrecker..." I said, feeling lame.

Grayson's gaze turned skeptical. "Oh, but he seemed upset the last time...?"

"Because I'm a fucking tool," I sighed. "I told you before, it was my mistake. I'll clear things up with him later, I promise, but I don't want you to think we're something we're not. Ian and I are friends."

Grayson nodded, but he still looked doubtful. We lapsed into silence, and I struggled to gather my thoughts before he spoke again. "So... your mom told you?"

I nodded and kept my gaze down. "But—my apology was long overdue."

Grayson's mouth thinned into a hard line. "Fine. I accept. Good-night."

"Wait—" I reached out to touch him, but he recoiled. My heart lurched, but I stamped it down quickly. "I—I want you to stay here for the holidays. Don't go back to your apartment."

Grayson's eyes narrowed. "Why?"

Heat burned my cheeks as my thoughts whirled. How could I explain what I was thinking? Or what I wanted? Ever since that day we spent in the showers, I felt all those old feelings come rushing back and I realized, like a bolt of lightning that I had never stopped loving Grayson. I always had and I always would. But too much time had passed between us. I had no clue about the man Grayson was today, and Grayson didn't trust me. It would take time to rebuild all of that.

Our eyes met and as I looked into those frigid depths, I felt as if I were standing at the edge of a turbulent sea, on the cusp of a tempest. His eyes mirrored the roiling waters, their underbelly heaving with untamed emotions.

Just like the sea's mighty waves, Grayson's gaze surged and boiled, dragging me into a tumultuous current of uncertainty. It was a billow-ing and surging force, one that I found both captivating and daunting, much like the unforgiving breakers that cascaded toward the unfor-giving land. *God, I felt myself falling all over again.*

Grayson always had this effect on me, as if he could hold me captive just by a single glance.

"Because..." I cleared my throat. "Cricket would want me to."

Grayson's mouth slowly fell open, and he turned his face away. "Is this some kind of fucking joke to you—"

"No—" I reached for him again. "I—I know he would, and I do too. You meant a lot to us and to—shit, why am I fucking this up so badly? Just stay, damn it!"

Grayson's mouth twitched, as if he were fighting a smile, and he nodded. "Fine. I'll stay in the guest room. I'll need to pick up my car tomorrow, and I don't have any clothes—"

"We can pick some up at your place too," I offered. "You can stay the rest of the holidays."

Grayson nodded, then got to his feet. "Fine. Goodnight then."

"Night." The door clicked shut, and I flopped back on my bed, breathing a sigh of relief. Fuck, that was painful, but despite that my lips tugged into a smile. *But it was a start.*

17

RECKONING ON THE RINK

GRAYSON HAYES

Light inched across the wooden floors toward the bedpost. I groaned, attempting to shield my face, and my alarm clock beeped with a shrill, jolting sound.

"Damn it," I muttered, checking my phone, only to realize it was already past ten in the morning. Blinking away the remnants of sleep, I surveyed the unfamiliar surroundings.

Oh, right. I was at Cricket's house. My throat felt dry and scratchy, likely the result of that Irish coffee mixed with tequila from last night. Ugh. I rubbed my hands against my eyelids, hoping to ease the pounding in my head before I lost my breakfast. Memories of the previous night rushed back to me—the fight, Jayden, Jayden, Jayden. Crap.

A throbbing headache intensified as I remembered Jayden's face when he saw me drinking at the bar. His pink lips slightly parted, his green eyes wide with fear. I didn't want to care about him, I reminded myself as my hand involuntarily curled into a fist. But despite my best efforts, it seemed like that was all I did. I left with him last night, and I couldn't get him out of my mind.

I hated the holidays. My bastard father never remembered them and I spent most of them in a drunken haze. That was until Cricket found me one night and forced me to come home with him. Checking my phone, I saw that all my text messages to Sarah had gone unanswered. Rightfully so. I had slept with her best friend's boyfriend? Fuck buddy? Whatever. Who the hell could keep track of where Jayden stuck his cock? Bottom line was it was all a fucking mess and I couldn't do anything feeling sorry for myself sitting in this room. Several pictures on the wall caught my attention, and I realized with a shrinking horror that this wasn't the guest room, and that I had accidentally fallen asleep in Cricket's old room. "Shit," I hissed. Throwing off the covers, I hurried to get dressed.

I can't stay here another minute. Not with Jayden and his attitude that was giving me whiplash, and not with the memories of the past threatening to engulf me whole. Tip-toeing down my hall, my feet creaked on the floorboards as I tried not to wake anyone in my haste to leave. If I left now, I could make it back to my apartment in Michigan before nightfall. Stepping outside on a wintry day felt like plunging into an icy embrace. The brisk air seized my breath, and my lungs tightened in response to the frigid touch. Clutching my coat tighter, I walked several feet and then stopped.

"Fuck!" I didn't bring my car. I left it at the bar last night.

A loud bark made me jump, and I turned to see Duke rolling around in the snowbank and Mr. Taylor giving me a strange look. "Morning, Grayson," he said gruffly.

Heat flared across my face, and I cleared my throat. "Morning, Mr. Taylor—eh—well—"

"Why don't you come in the garage for a moment?" he said, wiping some snow off his bright red gray goose jacket. "I want to show you something."

Since I had no ride and no way of getting home, I really didn't have a choice. Following him inside the garage, I coughed at the musty smell that invaded my nostrils. Boxes were piled high, most of them filled with old hockey gear, but some of them contained clothes and various other items. Mr. Taylor took out a stick and grinned, running his palm over the ends and the white tape.

"Remember this?" Images of Cricket playing with his lucky stick until it broke flashed before my eyes, and I laughed. "Yeah. Damn. Did you fix it?" I marveled at the once-splintered wood, now smoothed and polished.

"Yeah. A few weeks ago. Jayden just got back, so I'll give it to him," Mr. Taylor said, running a hand through his long, dark hair. "Here. There's something for you, too." He picked up Cricket's old tape and a few of his gloves that were still in good condition.

"No—I can't take this—"

"Why not?" Mr. Taylor asked. "He'd want you to have them."

I shook my head, feeling my throat close. I couldn'tn't take them. I didn't deserve them. Being here. Mr. Taylor's kindness. None of it. I wasn't worthy enough for any of it.

"Did Jayden ever tell you why he loved those Star Trek shows and movies so much?" Mr. Taylor asked, changing the subject.

"No."

"There was an accident on the ice when he was young. There's a lake out back, and Cricket and Jayden were playing there late one day, and then the ice gave way and Jayden fell through. My soul nearly left my body when Cricket and Duke ran to get me, barking and screaming like mad." He laughed mirthlessly. "Luckily, it wasn't deep, and Jayden washed up on shore several feet down the pond. Pale as a ghost. The only thing he kept repeating was 'Resistance is futile,' you know, from that stupid Borg thingie."

I chuckled at his strange gesturing.

"Anyway," he continued. "That's when his obsession started. Something about never giving up. That boy is so stubborn like his mother sometimes, and for those of us caught in their orbit, we can't do anything but go along with it." Mr. Taylor sighed. "You know, after they told me Cricket was gone, I felt... peace. For the first time. That we can let him go, because he's not really dead. As long as we remember him." He nudged my shoulder. "Now that I got from Star Trek." I chuckled, and he handed me more of Cricket's gear. "This way, we can take a piece of him with us everywhere we go."

How could he say that to me? I was the reason Cricket was in the hospital. It was all my fault. "Mr. Taylor—"

He waved me off. "Cricket told us about your family. My father had taurine eyes that were as wild and fearsome as any bull. Some people don't need a reason to be violent."

They knew. The whole time. The realization unfolded within me, spreading like wildfire, as if my chest were a dry forest suddenly ignited with the searing knowledge of truth. No wonder they hadn't bothered to ask questions like why I never stayed at home for the holidays. Mrs. Taylor accepted my yellow flowers and flimsy excuses, all the while knowing what was happening behind the scenes.

Tears stung my eyes, and I bit into my bottom lip while Mr. Taylor slapped my shoulder. "Let's get something to eat. I'm famished. Plus, it's so cold outside my balls might freeze off."

I gave a wet laugh, and he handed me more of Cricket's things.

Things I would cherish forever.

***

I WENT INSIDE TO WASH up before breakfast. Shrugging off my coat in Cricket's room, I realized then that I had nothing to wear. I was just about to go out and ask Mr. Taylor for some clothes when Jayden's form filled the doorway. Leaning against the frame, his mouth curled into a smirk, and my heart hammered as piercing emerald eyes found mine. Jayden looked lean and taut, muscles bulging in his black sweater, his tattoos standing out on his wintry pale moon skin.

"Trying to escape?" he asked, brow lifted.

I turned away. "Maybe."

"Well, you can't leave. Not if I have anything to say about it." He tossed a pair of jeans and a wooly sweatshirt on the bed. "These should fit. We need to pick up your car, and then I want to go to the market later."

I gritted my teeth. It wasn't like I wanted to leave, but I knew staying would complicate things between us. "I should head home. It's late—"

Jayden was already walking away. "I wasn't asking, Hayes."

Damn. I yanked off my shirt and then went to the shower. Stupid Jayden. I had no choice but to go with it until I got my car back, but I knew I'd stay. Those green eyes were hypnotic, dragging me under like the undertow in the sea.

***

AFTER OUR HEARTY BREAKFAST, Jayden and I embarked on the brief journey to the pub to retrieve my car. The drive was mostly silent, filled only by the soft hum of the radio playing in the background. It was a strange mix of comfort and tension. I couldn't help but notice the lingering scent of Jayden's soap and sea breeze aftershave, which permeated the car. Inhaling it, I savored the familiar aroma.

The dryness in my throat wasn't solely due to the hangover, but also the memory of our shared moments in the shower. The sensation of Jayden's lips on mine, the heat of his skin, and the firm grip of his rough hands on my hips played on a loop in my mind.

As we approached the pub, I couldn't help but wonder for the hundredth time why Jayden had brought me here. Was it pity? Did he feel responsible for my situation, and was he merely trying to make amends? The thought twisted inside me like a sharp knife, and I couldn't bear the idea that Jayden's intentions might be driven by pity. I would rather have him hate me for my role in Cricket's life.

Anxiety tightened my chest as I parked the car in the pub's lot. I swiftly got out, eager to put some distance between Jayden and me. But he followed closely, catching up to me before I could escape.

"Wait," Jayden said, pulling out his phone. "Let me give you the address of the Christmas festival. We can meet there."

I gritted my teeth, frustration bubbling up. "I'm not going there with you."

Jayden's emerald eyes narrowed into pinpricks, his patience evidently waning. "Not this shit again. We're spending the holidays together, whether or not you like it."

His determination stunned me into silence. "Why? Just a few days ago, you hated my guts. Now you won't let me out of your sight. Did you suddenly grow a heart? Or are you just looking for a new boy toy for the holidays?"

My words hit their mark, and I watched Jayden wince, his expression briefly faltering. "No—I just—"

"What? Ever since I came back, you made it your mission to make my life shit at every chance. Now you want to act like we're friends? Like you give a shit what I've been going through the past year? Or did

I just fuck you so good you forgot all about the past and your shitty attitude?"

Jayden's jaw worked. "Don't flatter yourself. Besides, it wasn't that good."

"It wasn't?" I scoffed. "Then why the hell are you here now, following me?"

"To apologize!" Jayden exploded in my face. "You're such a bastard! I'm here to apologize! I know my attitude was crap, okay? I'm sorry. I thought—it doesn't matter anymore you didn't do what I thought you did to Cricket. I misunderstood. I'm a bastard and I want to make things right."

"Why?" I demanded, swallowing around the knot in my throat. "You apologized before, and I accept it. There's no need to—"

"Because I can't do this alone!" Jayden snapped, but his voice broke. Tears brimmed in his eyes before he cursed, turning his face away.

All the air whooshed out of my lungs as I stared at him, trying to understand what the hell he was saying. Do what alone? He had his parents. His family. I had nobody. What exactly was he doing alone?

"They're going to pull the plug," Jayden croaked. "A part of me wants them to do it and another part wants to fucking tear them to shreds for even thinking about it. He's alive. He's fucking alive. One day he'll wake up and look at me and ask me why I didn't fucking wait—" Jayden's words choked off into a sob. "I need you. You're the only person in the world who knew him better than me. You're the only person who understands what I'm going through."

My arms went around his waist, hugging his body close to my chest. Fuck. Cries wracked his entire frame, and he clutched his face, sobbing into his palms. Anguish bit at my heels, but I forced it back, wanting to be there for Jayden. The holidays were a nightmare for me, but I couldn't even imagine what it would be like for him and his family.

Pressing my lips to the nape of his neck, I sighed, wishing I could take all the horrible words I said back.

Jayden's chest rose and fell in time with mine and we stood there in the parking lot, ignoring the eyes on us. I held him firm. Hoping against hope to stop his entire body from cracking into pieces and falling all over the pavement. Eventually, Jayden turned in my arms. His eyes rimmed red.

He looked so young then, and I felt my heart lurch.

"I meant what I said. I want you here. We all do," Jayden spoke. "I don't think I'll be able to get through this holiday without you."

My thumb brushed over his cheek. "You did before... I don't see why now things are so different."

Black lashes stuttered the moment my thumb touched his skin. Jayden sighed long and deep. "I know, that's because now I realized I don't have to."

Because now I don't have to. His words landed on my ears like a soothing melody, instantly melting my defenses. There had been so much hate and rage in his eyes the moment he saw me again, and I knew things weren't as simple as saying 'I forgive you', but deep in my heart, I felt maybe Jayden was beginning to.

Pulling my thumb away, I licked my dry lips and nodded. "Okay."

It was a good place to start.

I had no idea where this path would lead, but the way Jayden was looking at me made something crack inside my chest. He didn't hate me. Why, I had no clue. I could never be Cricket's replacement, and judging where his parents and the doctors wanted to go, Cricket would be officially dead before the end of the year. How would Jayden cope then? Would we be using each other as a crutch? What did it mean after everything was over? I could barely wrap my head around what we were now. "Let's just enjoy what's left of the day," Jayden proposed, and I was inclined to agree.

I wanted to say no. To turn around and flee from these strange emotions bubbling deep within my chest. But I could feel myself drowning in those evergreen eyes, completely lost in the uncharted territory as if I had stumbled upon a hidden paradise.

There was no going back. The only way forward was to go through. I had already gone through the fire for this man once. Was I willing to do so again?

Jayden ducked his head. Those dark lashes fluttered in the sunlight and I knew for a fact the answer would always be yes.

***

AMID THE TWINKLING LIGHTS and the sweet aroma of roasting chestnuts, Jayden and I wandered through the Christmas market. The festive ambiance filled the air, and our breaths turned to mist as we strolled along, sipping on steaming cups of hot cocoa.

"Can you believe the size of that tree?" Jayden exclaimed, pointing toward a towering Christmas tree bedecked with ornaments that were larger than life. "I feel like it's going to steal Santa's thunder."

I chuckled, feeling the warmth of the cocoa spread through me. "They definitely went all out on that one. Maybe Santa's reevaluating his career options."

We both laughed, the sound blending with the cheerful carolers and the chatter of fellow market-goers. "Shit, I know I am after Professor Wilson's class," he mumbled.

My mouth curved into a smile. "Why are you failing her class, anyway?"

"Fuck if I know. She hates me."

"Nah," I said. "You're just overthinking everything. I saw your notes. You aren't horrible. You just second guess yourself when you already know the right answer. Chemistry really isn't that hard."

"Yeah, says the fucking Health Science major," Jayden muttered. "Seriously, I really feel like I'm going to fucking fail that class and my life will be over. I can't afford school without my hockey scholarships, and if I get kicked off the team then I'll be fucked and not at all in the way I like."

I laughed. "Think of chemistry equations like decorating a Christmas tree. You've got your reactants, which are the ornaments you choose for the tree."

"All right, so what's that arrow for?"

"That's like the string of lights on your tree. It connects the reactants to the products, just like lights bring out the beauty of the ornaments."

"And the products?"

"Those are like the final look of your decorated tree. They represent what you get after the reaction, just as your tree's appearance is what you aimed for."

Jayden chewed it over for a moment and then shook his head. "Nope. I still don't get it. I'm too stupid to understand."

"How the hell did you even get into university?" I grumbled, and Jayden nudged my arm.

We stopped at a candy cane vendor, and I couldn't resist the temptation. I picked up a massive, swirled candy cane in my hand, and Jayden raised an eyebrow. "You planning to eat that whole thing?"

I grinned and broke off a piece. "What can I say? I have a sweet tooth."

As I savored the candy cane, Jayden's gaze lingered on me, his eyes half-lidded with a mysterious depth. Licking the head, I swirled my tongue and laughed when his face heated.

"That shit you're doing with a candy cane should be illegal."

We locked eyes and the heat spread to my groin.

18

---·---

FROZEN HEARTS, THAWING SOULS

GRAYSON HAYES

I laughed as we continued to walk through the crowds. Our fingers brushed, sending a jolt of electricity through me. Jayden cleared his throat, shifting the conversation. "So, Health Sciences, huh? What do you see yourself doing if hockey doesn't pan out?"

I shrugged, watching the twinkling lights dance in his eyes. "Teaching, probably. I've always wanted to help others. What about you, Mr. Exercise Physiology?"

He chuckled, his breath forming little clouds in the cold air. "Well, I'd love to work with athletes, helping them reach their full potential. But hey, I could always become a personal trainer for you."

"No thanks. Considering how many times you've body-checked me on the ice, I have a feeling you'd cripple me just to put me back together again."

"Kinky," Jayden whispered in my ear and I gave him a playful nudge, and the mood between us turned light and easy. "But seriously, have you ever considered the possibility that hockey might not work out?"

"Yes," I replied, tossing my candy cane wrapper into the trash. "To be honest, hockey was more of my father's dream. I love the game and the thought of going pro gets me just as excited as the next guy, but... if I really had a choice, I think I'd teach hockey or play it leisurely. What about you?"

"There are no other options for me," Jayden said, staring off into the distance. "I thought I'd study Exercise Physiology for Cricket, but now that the plan's been shot to hell, I just want to focus on the thing I've always been good at. The one thing I know will make Cricket feel proud."

"I think he'd be proud no matter what you do, Jayden," I spoke, my voice soft.

"Yeah." Jayden stared up into the sky, his eyes twinkling like the stars. "Maybe."

***

AFTER WE RETURNED HOME, Mrs. Taylor prepared a delicious dinner for us. Emotionally drained from the day, I headed to bed early. Collapsing onto Cricket's old bed, I stared up at the ceiling, my hand resting behind my head. Today had been good, even great. Jayden and I weren't exactly friends, but I sensed his heart thawing toward me. Maybe in the future, we could be something more.

I pondered everything that had happened, wondering how my life would be with Jayden in it. *Did he want me as much as I wanted him? Would he still care about me if he knew what a coward I was? What caused his change of heart?*

I was too weak for this. For Jayden. Everything he said had me second guessing myself and thinking twice about my next move. Maybe I should have left when I had the chance. Staying here just complicated everything. I checked my phone again and saw no new messages from

Sarah. I sighed, hoping she would give me a chance to explain. It wasn't like I didn't know Jayden and just fucked him. We had history together. A past that went far beyond Ian. No matter what, Jayden and I would always be intertwined. Sleeping with him while he was with Ian had been wrong. I wouldn't fault Ian for hating me for that, but if I could just explain what happened, perhaps things would be better.

"Fuck," I muttered. If I didn't, I knew Coach would have my fucking balls at the next game.

Our team needed to work well together and with all this growing discord, I feared he'd find a reason to kick me off. Shit. Or even worse, tell my fucking father. The bastard has been MIA since I went back to Michigan University and I hoped it stayed that way.

The last thing I needed was him breathing down my neck and asking questions I didn't have the answers to. Sleep slowly took over, and I closed my eyes. A few hours later, I awoke to the door creaking open. Jayden crept into the room and slid onto the bed beside me.

"Jayden..." I gasped, but his lips found mine, claiming my mouth in a passionate kiss. This was such a bad idea, but I couldn't seem to stop as his tongue slipped into my mouth and I moaned. "Fuck—what are you doing?" I hissed, watching him peel off his sweater and crawl down the length of my body before settling on my hard chest.

"Living out my fantasies," he whispered, kissing me again.

Damn it. I growled into the kiss, tasting ice-cream on his lips, licking into his moist mouth and nibbling on his bottom lip. Jayden gasped, then gave a throaty chuckle as he slowly rolled his hips against mine. Our crotches met. His thick cock pressed against the zipper of his jeans. Pleasure sparked through me like lightning, and I felt breathless and dizzier than ever before. Jayden tugged off his crisp white shirt and threw it to the floor. It dropped with a solid thud along with his jeans and underwear.

My throat went dry when he leaned back on his heels. Skin pale as the wintry moon, tattoos spreading down his naked chest like vines. Mapping them out with my hands, I groaned as my hands roamed all over his smooth skin. I touched a spot near his stomach and he flinched, his body going rigid. The skin was raised, ridged beneath my fingertip. "What's that?"

Jayden's smile grew. "I got stabbed at juvie," he replied, pressing down on me, his swollen cock nudging against my stomach. "Some fucker thought it would be funny to see how far he could push me."

My heart throbbed, and I fisted his hair. "You went to juvie? What the fuck? When did this happen?"

"I'll tell you another time. Do you want to talk or do you want to fuck?" Jayden whispered against my lips.

"Why can't we do both?" I asked, chuckling when his hands rucked up my shirt.

"I'm not that good at multitasking," Jayden murmured. "Besides, I'd like to give your cock the attention it deserves." Jayden's dark eyes flashed with intent, rippling gems in the dark when he kissed me again, slow and deep, tasting every inch of me. "Fuck, I used to dream about this."

I made a noise in my throat, taking him deeper. Slotting over me, Jayden rocked into my body at a languid pace, sighing at the rolling heat from his body and hands. I could feel his hot erection stabbing into my own. The contact sent jolts down my spine as I thrust up to meet him. Jayden broke the kiss, gasping for breath, his eyes nearly pitch black with pleasure .

A haze of lust wrapped around me like a warm, velvety cocoon, soft and inviting, cradling me in a world of exquisite sensation. "Fuck, Jayden—" My chest burned with a fierce intensity.

For a moment, he stilled, gazing deep into my eyes, his mouth wide open.

His mouth kinked as he hooked his thumbs into the waistband of my jeans and boxers, tugging them down in one go. Lifting my hips, my erection bobbed free, slapping against my stomach, the sound echoing in the room. Jayden's hand curled around the base. He pressed his mouth to mine, swallowing my sighs and moans with each heated kiss.

"Fuck—" I hissed, thrusting in his hand, nearly crying out when his thumb circled the head. "Shit—I'm gonna come—"

Jayden paused, shock skittering over his features. "Already? We just got started."

I almost choked on the knot forming in my throat. Heat blossomed on my cheeks and I wondered if I should tell him that I had very few sexual experiences. This and the time we fucked being one of the few. "I—It's my first time."

"What?" Jayden jerked back; his eyes widened. "Shit. You're a fucking virgin—"

"I was," I interrupted. "Before we had sex in the shower."

"Jesus fuck, Grayson. Why didn't you say anything?" Jayden snapped, running a hand through his hair.

There wasn't anything to say. I wanted it and so did he. It worked out well for us now. "It's fine... you can make up for it now."

Jayden eyed me wearily, then sighed. "I guess I'm the world's biggest asshole."

"You will be if you leave me hanging like this," I whispered, tugging him back to my chest.

"I had no idea how someone who looks like you could be..." Jayden's words died in his throat as he stared at my angry cock. "Never mind. I'll shut up now." He leaned down, taking my cock into his mouth like I did to him so many years ago. I grunted, fisting his thick, unruly black hair, groaning low in my throat as he bobbed his head. Closing my eyes, I resisted the urge to buck into the searing heat as my balls drew up tight. Fuck, Jayden was an expert at this.

Licking and swirling his tongue over the head, he hollowed his cheeks, and I saw fucking stars. The wet warmth of Jayden's mouth was unexpected, yet not unwelcome. Blood rushed so fast to my cock it swelled to the point of bursting. Pink lips teased the head, flicking the slit and I jerked my hips, losing myself to the rhythmic slurps and sounds Jayden was making.

Jayden took me deeper. Sending a zing of pleasure through my body, it bristled over my flesh, causing it to raise in goosebumps. "Jayden—" I gasped through gritted teeth. "I'm gonna come—fuck—"

Jayden yanked off my cock, and I almost sobbed, but his mouth covered mine. "I want you to come inside me. I want you to fuck me." He moved to straddle my hips, and my back arched as I grabbed a handful of his ample tight ass, spreading his cheeks apart. *It was so beyond perfect*. Dipping my fingers inside his hole, I found it already slick and wet. I circled the rim, shuddering at the hair that bristled against my skin there before sinking my finger in right to the knuckle.

"Grayson—" Jayden grunted, rubbing his cock against my abs. "Please. I need you."

With my other hand fisting Jayden's hair, I pushed it away from his face, my fingertips scratching his scalp before tightening. Fuck, he belonged to me. Jayden's hands were braced against my hips while I thrust my finger in and out of his wet hole, watching him writhe and moan on top of me.

I captured his lips, drinking in each sound in a brutal kiss that left him breathless and rutting against me. An encouraging hum left Jayden's throat, the vibration thrumming through my body again and

again, hips bucking as pre-come leaked from his cock. Blunt fingernails dug into the meat of my shoulder and I cursed, adding two more
fingers, stretching Jayden wide open.

I know I'm much thicker than the other guys I've seen in the locker
room, larger even than Jayden.

Fuck, I was so close to the edge. I knew the minute I got inside him
I'd come and it would be over way too soon. My lips clamped around
Jayden's throat, sucking a bruise into his skin and watching his hips
stutter before losing their rhythm.

"Fuck—yes—" he cried out.

As I reached down, I took hold of his aching cock, stroking it in
time with my fingers thrusting. Jayden lurched. His lips bit down hard
on mine. Hard enough to draw blood.

"I want you inside me," Jayden murmured. Then he leaned back,
forcing my fingers to slip free. Taking out a condom from its wrapper,
Jayden rolled it onto my swollen dick. I held the base, trying not to
come right there and then watching him. Jayden's body was a work of
art.

Black ink spread down his heaving chest that was slick with sweat,
his hips were narrow and jutted, while his ass looked plump. I smacked
it hard when he got into position over my cock, and it took everything
in me not to force him down and slam home. "Christ—baby—" I
moaned.

Jayden stared down at me like he wanted to devour me whole. It
was almost too much. My heart hammered in my ears. I felt like I was
filled to bursting when he sank down inch by inch.

The sight of Jayden's flushed cock standing proud against his stomach, and his flushed cheeks as he was impaled to the root on my cock
nearly sent me over the edge. Jayden rocked his hips, and I held onto
his ample ass for dear life, hoping that I wouldn't come too soon.

But fuck, it felt so good. Jayden's ass was like a vise-grip, tightening to the point of pain before he lifted off and sank back down with a resounding thud. Stars burst before my eyes, and I groaned, back arching as he fucked himself on my cock. "Yes—fuck—" Jayden babbled, rising and falling with a steep surge that had me close to plunging off the edge.

I splayed my feet on the bed, then snapped my hips forward, forcing Jayden to fall back onto my chest. Wrapping my arms around his back, I felt him tighten and thrust like mad into his tight, hot ass.

"Grayson—" Jayden spat and it bit off into a toe-curling moan that streaked fire down my spine, making my hips stutter.

I fucked him harder at this angle, pulling all the way out to the tip before sinking back in with a force brutal enough to move the bed. The headboard slammed against the wall and the legs screeched in protest, but I was past the point of caring who could hear us fucking. I was so lost to my pleasure. Sanity spilled out of me, and I growled in my throat, biting down on the juncture of his neck, wanting to pierce the skin with my teeth.

"Uh—nugh—I'm gonna come—Grayson—" Jayden's body went limp, and I went off with an explosion of searing come trickling down my stomach, slipping beneath the cracks of my balls and stomach. A wail nearly pierced the air, but I slammed my hand over Jayden's mouth to stop him from screaming his lungs out. Dark spots danced at the edge of my vision. I grunted, losing myself to the insane heat and feel of having Jayden finally in my arms after so long. A fluting and embarrassing broken noise erupted from my throat, and I felt Jayden shiver and another explosion of wetness covered my thighs.

Fuck, he was coming again. It turned me on impossibly harder. I slammed my hips harder, hoping to God I didn't break him in two. *Split him open with my cock.* A scream clawed its way up my throat, and then I was blinded by spangled rays of white lights. I was flung over the edge.

My cock pulsed and twitched, spasming as waves and waves of pleasure tossed and jerked me under with a force strong enough to steal the breath from my lungs. I stilled.

Groaning, I hugged Jayden so tight I thought I might crush him.

Wetness trailed down my cheeks, and it took everything to peel my arms off him. Between the two of us, I didn't know who was shaking more. Jayden's emerald eyes found mine. Wide and brimming with tears, and I realized like a thunderbolt that we made love in Cricket's room. Shit. It was a mistake. I wanted to comfort him, to tell him it was okay, but tears were already brimming in his eyes before spilling over. Jayden collapsed on my chest, fingernails digging into my skin as he choked on a sob.

I was at a loss for words. My chest felt tight. *Did Jayden make love to me because he was missing Cricket? Or because he wanted to be close to someone?* The thought carved through my chest like a knife. I held his shaking frame, not sure what to do or what to say. After several long moments, he calmed. His body went limp in my arms.

"Sorry," he whispered against the crook of my neck. "Not the first time you were expecting."

I chuckled, running a hand through his sodden hair. "No, but it was still amazing."

"God, all we do is fuck and cry," Jayden sighed, wiping his tears

My mouth tugged into a smile. "So? That's the best part of the relationship."

"The fucking or the crying?"

I stared deep into his eyes. "Both." I touched his bottom lip. "Men aren't supposed to cry, but I never cared how it made me look. I never once thought you'd judge me, Jayden."

"And I never would," Jayden replied. "Thanks for... staying here. I really needed a friend."

Friend. The word sloshed around like acid in my stomach. Is that what we were? Bile rose hot and thick in my throat and it took everything to shove it down. Jayden had a lot of friends, it seemed. Friends he took comfort in sexually. *Did I just become one of them? Was I just added to the growing list of friends I had to share Jayden with?* The thought alone made me sick. Curling my arm around his shoulder, a possessiveness took hold of my heart. Then again, he was never really mine to begin with. Jayden made it seem like it all meant nothing. Just a means for comfort when you're feeling sad or low.

But to me, it meant everything. I loved Jayden and still did, no matter what.

No matter how much he hated me.

19

BREAKING THE ICE

JAYDEN TAYLOR

I slowly emerged from the depths of a deep slumber. A gentle warmth caressed my skin, coaxing me into consciousness.

"Fuck," I hissed.

Something wet and gentle lapped at my cock, and a shudder rolled through me. Gray eyes snapped to mine, a bright blaze of silver fire that tore straight through my heart.

"Grayson..." I moaned. Nestled between my legs, working his tongue over my gutted hip bones and down to my aching shaft, swirling his tongue around the slit before taking me back in whole.

"Fuck!" I arched.

My nipples were taut and aching, but Grayson didn't leave them unattended for long. Two fingers came up and pinched them, rolling them hard enough for sparks of pleasure to wrack my entire body. Running a hand through his brown hair, I thrust my hips, watching with rapture as he tilted his head, changing the angle, deepening it so I could see how far he was taking me into his mouth.

Shit. I'm so close to the edge. Grayson teased the bulbous tip, teeth scraping against the thick vein and hollowing his cheeks like a god-damn expert. *Not at all like the virgin I thought him to be.* Fuck, it was just like back then. When he first sucked me off in my bedroom when I turned eighteen, those gray eyes like liquid flames filling my heart and soul with affection. I wanted him inside me.

I wanted him to fuck me again, but I was way too selfish to tell him to stop. The way his tongue worked me over was enough to make me see stars. Grayson's large hands held the base of my cock, stroking long and leisurely as I got lost in a sea of gray.

I love him. Fuck, I love him. My hips bucked down his throat, precome flooding into Grayson's mouth, dribbling down his chin, and my lungs cinched tighter and tighter. Blood roared in my ears as I watched strands of hair fall over his brow and those eyes wrench stinging warmth. A sensuality that burned hot and ripped me apart like silver bullets. My fingers fisted his hair. My mouth fell open in a silent scream as pleasure mounted like a crescendo, sending me almost tumbling over the edge.

The sight of his wet, shiny lips sliding along my cock was mesmerizing. A light flush bloomed on his cheeks as he yanked off, spit and come dripping from his mouth. "Do I feel good, baby? Tell me."

I groaned, thrusting my hips in my face. "Bastard. Don't stop halfway through."

"Pay back's a bitch, isn't it?" he laughed, taking me back into his mouth and sucking down to the root. I shouted, scrambling to grab his arms for purchase as he got back to work. His throat was hot and tight around my cock, and I could barely see straight for how badly I wanted to come.

Then I was falling. Flinging myself off the edge as my orgasm came crashing down around me. I choked on a scream, my cock spasmed and jerked, an opal flooding out of my cock and straight down Grayson's throat. "Fuck!"

Weightless. Flying. The ground vanished beneath my feet and I drifted up to the clouds. Grayson gave a throaty laugh, crawling up my body and settling between my thick thighs. I felt his hands grip my hips, spreading my legs apart, and then the blunt edge of his cock worked inside my already gaping hole. "Ready for me?"

Slipping my eyes closed, I nodded. My limbs felt like jelly, I touched his firm ass, guiding his cock into my asshole. "Yeah," I croaked, not sure when he found the time to lube me up and put on a condom.

Grayson claimed my lips, slow and sweet, licking along the seams of my mouth, tasting every inch of me. Then he inched his cock in, the tip hitting that good spot with ruthless intensity.

I grunted, biting down on my lower lip, trying not to push back into the promise of ecstasy. It fucking burned. I groaned as my ass swallowed down the bulbous tip, and I shuddered as it stretched to accommodate the engorged swell of Grayson's cock.

It gave way and my vision whited out.

"Shit," I hissed as my ass finally surrendered to Grayson's cock, locking our bodies together. I could feel the rapid beat of his pulse against mine, the thundering in my ears as Grayson moved. Sharp. Jerking. Almost as if he'd lost control of his hips. Then he snapped hard and deep, so fucking deep I was sure he was carving out a space inside me just for him.

"Jayden," he gasped, grabbing my hips. "Fuck—you feel so good around my cock—"

Take me. I'm yours. I wanted to say, but the words died in my throat.

A deep groan escaped Grayson's parted lips, as if he hadn't realized how desperately he needed this until now. My soft cock twitched and stiffened, swelling with need once again as he fucked into me. Gripping his narrow waist, I wrapped my legs around him, forcing him deeper. Grayson cried out, and the sight of his biceps flexing with every stroke had my shaft harder than a rocket.

"Jayden—fuck—I'm close—"

Taking his bottom lip into mine, I swallowed his moans until he tensed and came with a muffled cry. My lungs shriveled with each stuttered thrust, until Grayson reached out and curled his hand around my cock, pumping—once, twice—then I was gone. Tumbling head first over the edge, cursing loudly and jerking my hips. Black spots erupted across my vision as hot spurts of come landed on my abs and his chest.

Grayson's forehead fell against my shoulder, a laugh bubbling from his mouth. "I see why people become sex addicts," he mumbled, smearing come into my skin. "We just fucked and I feel like I could take you again."

"Please don't," I groaned. "I don't think my asshole could take it."

Grayson's eyes flashed with delight, but I could tell he was too exhausted to move now. Checking the time, I realized it was still in the wee hours of the morning, only five AM. "What the hell are you doing up so early?" I asked, stretching my aching limbs.

Grayson shrugged. "I always wake up at this time. My father—well, you know what he's like. I just always end up waking up at this time."

"Mhmm," I hummed, and snuggled back into the bed. "Go to sleep. It's the holidays. Being awake at this time should be illegal." Sleep was tugging on my consciousness, trying to pull me under.

Grayson laughed and pressed a kiss to my collarbone. "Wait," he said, thumbing the ridged skin on the scar near my hip. "You were supposed to tell me what this is. You said something about juvie—"

I jerked awake. "What?"

"You said you went to juvie and you would tell me about it..." Grayson trailed off, now looking unsure.

"Oh. Yeah." I laughed, but it sounded hollow. "Nothing to tell, really. Some guy made fun of Cricket at school, so I fucked him up. Simple really."

"And they sent you to juvie?"

"Bitch said I broke his arm," I yawned. "And I probably did, but the bastard deserved it."

"And the scar?" Grayson asked, and uneasiness flooded through me. I wasn't used to talking about stuff like this. Few people knew I went to juvie, not even Ian knew where that scar had come from.

"Some guy jumped me," I replied. "Don't worry, he got what he deserved in the end, so I don't have to worry about him coming back to fuck shit up. My friend Kyle kept me safe the two months I was there."

"Only two months?"

I shrugged again. "I had a full ride to Michigan University. The only reason I went there was because of the guy's bastard parents not wanting to let it go. Whatever. I served my time. Anyway, it was years ago. I barely remember it now."

Grayson stared at me, his mouth thinning into a hardline. "Was this because of me? Because of what happened with Cricket? I know what people were saying that I—I tripped him."

My heart slammed against my rib cage. *It was complicated*. I wanted to tell him no, that wasn't the case, and that I was responsible for my own actions, but everything started with that damn video getting leaked and everyone putting their own two cents in. Some people were positive Grayson tripped him, while others weren't so sure. Back then, I should have known better and not let my anger get the best of me. "I don't care about it anymore," I settled on. "It's in the past."

"Then how can you be so sure I didn't trip him?" Grayson asked, his eyes flashing with anger.

I didn't understand what the hell he was trying to say. What happened back then was a misunderstanding. I realized I had misjudged him. "You didn't... so it doesn't matter."

"But how can you be *sure* I didn't?"

"What the fuck are you saying right now?" I demanded, anger flaring in my chest. "You didn't trip him. You fucking paid for all his medical bills and more. I was wrong before. That's all."

"Did you watch the video?"

I choked on my spit. Staring at him, I saw his hand curled into a fist at my side. Rage was roiling within him and I had no fucking clue why. "No, but I—"

"Then what is this, Jayden?" he barked. "Why did you sleep with me? Why are you fucking me? Why did you invite me here? Was it just because you found out I paid for Cricket's medical bills? Was it guilt? Tell me."

Each word felt like a falling brick over my head and I was too fucking tired for this shit. Come was drying on my stomach and it was five in the morning. "For fuck's sakes!" I hissed. "Can we just talk about this tomorrow? I want to be with you. You're my friend. Isn't that enough?"

The words tasted like acid on my tongue, but everything between us was far too new to label. Grayson was my friend and Cricket's friend. Why couldn't we just leave things like that until we figured everything else out?

"*Friend*?" he spat. "I see. You fuck all your friends."

"What? I—what are you doing?" Grayson scrambled off the bed, tearing off the condom and tossing it into the trash bin. Yanking on his jeans and underwear, I watched him get dressed with a sinking feeling in my stomach. "Where are you going? What the fuck Grayson—"

"Home. This was a mistake."

My heart lurched, and I grabbed his arm, hauling him back onto the bed. "Grayson—*fuck, I'm sorry*—I don't know what I did wrong. What did I say? Everything was fine a minute ago—" My hand trembled as I fought through the panic threatening to overwhelm him. He couldn't leave. Not now. Not like this. I needed him. "Don't go. Please. I'll fix it. Please."

"What am I to you?"

Damn it! Why was it always this stupid question? I gaped at him, my mouth opening and closing like a goddamn fish. Several weeks ago, Ian had asked me the same thing and I couldn't answer him. To be honest, I had no clue what Grayson was to me.

Grayson stared at me. His gaze was as unyielding as steel. *Fuck, he wanted an answer, and I had a feeling he'd walk out of my life and never look back if I gave the wrong one.*

Tears pricked at my eyes, and I knew I had to tell the truth. "I loved you." Grayson's breath caught, but I barreled on. "Back then, I thought I'd die with happiness when you finally looked at me. Then the accident with Cricket happened, and then that love turned into hate. That hate was everything to me. It was all I had. The rage. Now I realize I was wrong, but it doesn't make the feelings go away... I want you in my life, Grayson. That's why I said you're my friend. I can't—I don't know what else to call you or what else we can be to each other since we just—*fuck*—" I ran a hand through my hair. "We just started whatever the hell this is between us again. I want you and I don't want it to stop. I won't be fucking anyone else except you. I promise."

It was hard to explain, but I hoped I got my point across. *What am I to you?* Grayson was the space in between, like white and black. Nothing solid yet, but soon he would be.

"I see."

My body sagged in relief, and I dug my palms into my eyelids. "Now come back to bed. Please. It's fucking five AM and if Duke wakes up, we're never getting back to sleep."

Grayson laughed, then peeled off his shirt and jeans, crawling into bed beside me and burying his face against my neck. "Okay. That's okay for now."

His lips found mine, tasting and feeling. I poured everything I couldn't convey with words into the kiss. I didn't know where the future would lead us, but together, we would embrace this challenge.

Two souls gracefully carving our path.

Our blades of glory painting silver streaks upon the ice.

***

As the sun's warm caress grew more persistent with each passing second, it roused me from the depths of sleep, gentle as a lover coaxing me into the embrace of a new day. I groaned, my senses slowly adjusting to the reality around me, but the warmth of Grayson's presence was conspicuously absent. My heart quickened, my sleepy eyes scanning the room. Then, relief washed over me as I spotted his coat hanging casually over my brother's desk chair. I stretched my tired limbs, wincing at the satisfying crackle of my joints, and, yawning, I rubbed the sleep from my eyes.

After a brisk shower and a change of clothes, I still felt the delightful ache in my muscles from our passionate night together. My bare feet padded downstairs, where the inviting aroma of breakfast wafted through the air. I greeted my mom with a warm kiss on the cheek, then took in the sight of my dad and Grayson engrossed in a hockey game on the television.

"Any plans for today?" I inquired, reaching for the remnants of our meal.

My mum responded, "No, sweetie, just a relaxing day. If you and Grayson feel like it, your father set up the rink for you guys. It's been a while since you both played."

The mention of the rink stirred memories of our joyous winter hockey matches—a tradition we'd cherished, one that had been put on hold since Cricket's accident.

"Yeah, sure," I agreed. "I didn't bring my gear, but I'll dig around in the garage. I'm sure I'll find something."

Hurrying, I left to give Grayson a morning kiss and inform him of my garage expedition. His acknowledgment was distracted, his gaze fixed firmly on the television screen. I chuckled, heading out into the brisk air.

The garage welcomed me with a gust of frigid wind. Cricket's belongings, relics of our past hockey adventures, were still neatly packed in boxes—a frozen snapshot of a happier time. I selected a pair of skates that appeared almost brand new, but my excitement waned when I noticed the distressing damage to the front, stained with remnants of dried blood. I dropped the skates as if they were on fire, and panic seized me, my heart pounding wildly in my chest as the memories of that dreadful night flooded back into my consciousness.

Images of Cricket falling, his head bashing against the side boards with a sickening crunch, rang in my ears. Blood raced through my veins, and the world faded in and out of focus as I struggled to breathe past the knot in my throat. The looks on the faces of the two players who had attacked him, their initial shock and then horror as my brother fell and never got up, were etched into my memory.

Gripping the edge of the box, my knees nearly buckled beneath me. To this day, I had no clue why those guys had attacked my brother.

It had been unprovoked, and it felt like they had deliberately targeted him on the ice.

"Hey," Grayson's voice seeped into my ear, grounding me. "Are you all right? Here, sit down." He grabbed my elbow and guided me to one of the wooden chairs. I hadn't even realized I was hyperventilating until I clutched my chest, sucking in air loudly as I fought through the wave of tears threatening to overwhelm me.

"It's all right. I'm here," Grayson reassured me, cupping my face and kissing my jaw. "What happened?"

My eyes darted to the skates, which were now covered in blood, and I watched his face pale.

"Shit," he hissed, hiding them, but I stopped him.

"Don't," I said firmly. "Let me see. Something isn't right." I reached for the skates, and Grayson handed them to me.

As I inspected them, I noticed a thin strip of tape near the front.

"What the hell?" I gasped, showing Grayson the tape-lined skates. "This tape means that if Cricket tried to stop, he couldn't. His trajectory would be off, making it easier for him to slip and crash into the boards."

Someone tried to kill Cricket.

Someone tried to murder my brother.

20

———

RIVALS ON SKATES

JAYDEN TAYLOR

G rayson's mouth curled into a snarl, and he gripped the skates with trembling hands. "What does this mean? Who would do such a thing?"

"I don't know," I replied, shaking my head. Whoever did this wanted Cricket to fall hard on the ice. Maybe it was a stupid practical joke. "Do you know of anyone on the team that would do this?"

"No. I mean—" Grayson ran a hand through his thick brown hair. "Sometimes we do it to the rookies, but that's only during practice and never on game night. After they fall, we laugh it off and they get new skates."

"What about those guys who attacked Cricket?" I pressed. "What did they say before they attacked him?"

"They were chirping the fuck out of us," Grayson snarled. "Normally we didn't give a fuck, but these guys wouldn't quit. It was almost fucking bizarre how much they wanted to get a rise out of us. I—I was too fucked up from what happened with my dad, so I didn't want any part of what they were saying and tuned most of it out. But they wouldn't have been able to get into the locker room without us noticing. These were Cricket's favorite skates. There's no way he'd leave them lying around."

"Okay…" I said, chewing my bottom lip. "So, let's think back to that day. Besides the team, who else would be in the locker rooms? Coach Cornell, assistant coach Jacobs and—"

His gray eyes flashed with realization. "My father."

The words jolted me like a slap. Mr. Hayes. He was there. I saw him there arguing with Grayson, but about what? What provoked him so much he had to slap Grayson across the face? I watched Grayson's throat bob as he took a stuttering breath. "What were you guys arguing about?"

"Nothing." Grayson cleared his throat. "School."

I felt like he wasn't being entirely truthful, but it didn't matter. Mr. Hayes would have no motive to hurt Cricket. He was a businessman and all the trouble Grayson got into after the accident seemed to make things worse for his business, so I couldn't see him doing anything against Cricket. "Oh. Okay."

We lapsed into silence, both of us lost deep in thought. Grayson sighed and then pulled me into his arms. "I'm sorry. I wish I could think back harder to what happened that day."

"It's not your fault," I replied, then pressed a kiss to his lips. "Come on. Let's play hockey while we still can." I placed the skates away and took out another pair Cricket used to play with. "You can use these, and I'll find some other ones."

I moved to step out of his arms, but Grayson held me tighter.

"Jayden, I swear to God I'll sort this out."

His gray eyes blazed like silver-fire, igniting with a fierce intensity that could scorch my soul. All the air felt like it was punched from my lungs, and my stomach somersaulted. There were so many unanswered questions, and we both owed it to Cricket to find out what really happened back then and who tried to hurt him.

"Yes," I said, drawing him into a brutal kiss. "Fuck, yes."

We'd find out who did this.

Even if we had to set fire to the stars.

***

ZIPPING DOWN THE RINK, my lungs heaved as I chased after the puck. The wind slapped against my cheeks, and the world blurred as I intercepted Grayson, stealing the puck and sending it flying into his open net. I celebrated the goal with a triumphant laugh.

"Man, you're way off your game tonight, Grayson!" I teased, circling him on the ice.

Grayson shot me an indignant look. "These skates are too big. It's like playing with two left feet!"

"Excuses! Excuses!" I sang, provoking a snarl from Grayson.

I skated toward him, but he maneuvered around me, faking left and then right before delivering a slapshot into the net. I couldn't believe it.

"Cheater." I accused, but Grayson's laughter drowned out my complaints as we continued to play.

My dad had set up two nets at opposite ends of the rink, and we'd been playing a friendly game earlier. As the sun dipped below the horizon, the winds grew biting, and the night-time lights illuminated the rink. My face was flushed from the cold, and my throat and nose felt like they were on fire, but I didn't want to stop just yet.

"How about one more goal? Winner takes all?" Grayson suggested, his pink nose contrasting with the cold.

"All of what?"

A sly grin crept over Grayson's lips. "All of you."

My breath caught, and I blinked at him, taken aback. "What does that mean?"

Grayson laughed, his breath forming puffs of white in the frigid air. "It means if I win, you become my boyfriend. Officially."

I shook my head, chuckling. "You really don't know the meaning of 'taking it slow,' do you?"

Grayson shrugged, a mischievous glint in his eyes.

"Okay, and if I win?" I raised an eyebrow.

"If you win?" Grayson's gaze narrowed, and he grinned. "You mean, if I *let* you win. You'll see me dance around as the team's Wolverine mascot during the next game."

The mental image of Grayson twerking on the ice was too much, and I nearly fell over with laughter. "Deal!"

We geared up to play. My heart hammered in my throat. The rink seemed to shrink around us, and I could feel the weight of the moment. Grayson and I locked eyes, determination sparking between us. The game was intense; the puck flying back and forth between us. Grayson's skills were undeniable, and he was playing to win. Despite my best efforts, he scored that crucial final goal. I watched the puck glide past me and into the net, realizing that Grayson had emerged victorious.

I skated over to him, my face flushed with exertion, and my breath coming out in visible puffs. Falling into his arms, I couldn't help but smile. I leaned in and kissed him, my lips meeting his with a mixture of exhilaration and affection. The taste of victory was sweet, but the taste of his lips was even sweeter. "I win," he muttered against my lips.

"Yeah," I sighed and nibbled his lower lip. "You do."

***

THE HOLIDAYS WERE filled with love, laughter, and cherished moments. My heart ached as the time came for me to return to campus, leaving Grayson behind. The familiar hustle and bustle of the dormitory's halls provided a comforting backdrop, but it couldn't chase away the tinges of homesickness.

The past two weeks had been an unforgettable whirlwind of joy and togetherness with Grayson. We had built gingerbread houses, cooked delicious meals, watched hockey games, and laughed until our stomachs hurt. The memories of those precious moments made me wish the holidays had lasted longer.

During our stay, Grayson and I had been inseparable, spending quality time together. Our connection had grown stronger, and the chemistry between us had ignited. It became clear when even my mom jokingly hinted at our newfound intimacy, leaving me blushing.

Walking into my dorm room, I threw my duffle bag onto the bed and let out a long sigh. Tomorrow, practice would resume, and I had a list of tasks to complete before the new school year officially began. I reached for my textbook, intending to catch up on some reading, when a knock interrupted my focus.

My heart leaped, hoping it was Grayson at the door. Eagerly, I rushed over, only for my smile to fade as I realized it was Ian who stood there.

"Hi. Can we talk?"

Opening my door wider, I invited him in and sat on the edge of my bed.

"How are you?" I asked, for lack of better words, and winced when I saw his beaten expression. "Sorry."

"No, I'm—" He cleared his throat. "I'm good. Just thought I'd stop by and apologize for my behavior earlier—"

"No. Please don't—fuck—" I said, running a hand through my hair. "I was such an asshole. I wasn't even thinking about what I was doing to you or how triggering it must have been for you."

Ian kept quiet, his brown eyes watching me.

"I'm a shitty friend. I'm sorry," I breathed.

"Friend..." Ian's throat bobbed, and he gave a curt nod, almost as if he understood everything. "So... you and Grayson...?"

"He's ... my boyfriend," I replied, and heat flared across my cheeks. "Sorry. Fuck, I'm sorry, Ian."

"So, all those times you were slamming him into lockers and shoving him on the ice. That was your way of getting his attention? Kind of like an ape on steroids."

"Well—I wouldn't go *that* far," I said, then noticed Ian's mouth twitch as if he were fighting a smile. "More like a baboon on steroids."

"I thought it was juvenile." Ian huffed a laugh. "Sarah said so, but a part of me didn't want to believe it, but now when I think back on it, yeah, you were totally posturing in front of him."

I felt my face burn hotter and looked away. "Fine. I guess I deserve that."

"And more," Ian said. "But it's okay. I forgive you."

"Really?"

"Fuck no," Ian replied, and my heart sank. "It's going to take a lot more than some lame ass apology for my forgiveness."

"Fine. I'll do your laundry for a week, if that's what it'll take for forgiveness."

Ian kinked an eyebrow. "And my jock straps?"

"I'll hand-wash them all."

"Deal."

We fell into fits of laughter and I lay on my bed, my arm resting behind my head. "Thanks for understanding. I mean it."

Ian snuggled up beside me. "Like you said, we're friends. I wish we were more, but the more I think about it, the more I realized we weren't good for each other. The sex was great, but aside from that, I think I need someone a little more on my level in terms of sensitivity."

"What do you mean? I can be sensitive." I shot back.

Ian chuckled. "Sure, says the guy who bullied his boyfriend just to get his attention. Nah, I mean someone who understands me a bit more. I'm a big guy with a big heart, so I need someone like me. That's all."

"So, someone not selfish like me?"

"Not *as* selfish *as* you. There's a difference."

"Bitch where?" I muttered, and Ian took my hand in his.

"I'm glad you found what you were looking for in Grayson," Ian spoke, his voice soft. "Now that you've fucked, it will put everyone else out of their misery."

I shoved him off and whipped my pillow at his head. Ian dodged and grabbed something else to throw at my head. We spent the rest of the evening catching up and laughing, and by the time the sun set I could do nothing but fall into my comforter and sleep.

***

STEPPING INTO THE bustling locker room, the anticipation of the upcoming game next week was palpable. Eagerly, I hurried to change into my gear, catching Grayson's heated gaze as it raked over my body. I couldn't resist winking at him before swiftly getting dressed, making sure my helmet was secure. Afterward, I joined the other guys and headed out onto the ice for practice.

The drills were intense and fast-paced, designed to sharpen our skills for the game. We wove between cones, executed precision passes, and practiced powerful shots, all under the watchful eye of our coach. The cold air filled with the sounds of skates carving the ice, sticks striking pucks, and the occasional cheer of success.

"This is a hockey rink, not a museum of slow motion. Get a move on!"

Coach's loud commands echoed through the rink, urging us to keep moving and maintain our focus. The puck dropped, signaling the start of a scrimmage. Grayson and I found ourselves on opposing sides, and the competitive spirit between us burned intensely. I couldn't resist the urge to get under his skin.

I shot out from the starting line like a rocket, swiftly maneuvering across the ice, passing with lightning speed. Everything was going well until Evans checked Chris hard, sending him flying straight into me. I let out a chuckle, but it quickly turned into a groan as I stumbled and lost my balance.

Suddenly, I was falling. The sensation of free-falling, combined with the shock of the impact, stole the air from my lungs and sent my stomach into my throat. But before I could hit the ice, I was caught in strong arms. Grayson's concerned face loomed over me, his eyes filled with panic and something else that I couldn't quite place.

He helped me back onto my skates, his hands trembling as he tore off my helmet.

"*What the fuck is wrong with you?*" His voice trembled with anger and fear as he yelled at me, drawing the attention of the other players and even our coach. The coach regarded Grayson as if he'd grown a second head. *What the hell?*

"What?"

Grayson shoved my cracked helmet in my face. A jagged line split down the middle. *Shit.* That had been there since I'd cracked it earlier in a fit of frustration. Panic gripped me as I realized that if I'd taken a hard hit to the head, this helmet wouldn't have protected me, and the consequences could have been dire. Grayson was visibly shaken, tears streaming down his cheeks as he turned away from me and stormed toward the locker room exit. I nodded at our coach and rushed after Grayson.

Grayson was a whirlwind of anger, throwing his gloves to the ground once he got inside the locker room and hurriedly working off his skates. It was a side of him I'd never witnessed before. When I tried to reach out to him, he flinched and shouted, "Don't touch me!"

"Grayson—"

"Don't—" he spat, his hands shaking so badly he could barely move them. I sat down on the bench beside him and grabbed his hands, forcing him to stop.

"Grayson, I'm sorry—I didn't notice—"

"You could have died. You could have—" His voice broke, and he covered his face with his hands. Wrapping my arms around him, I held him close, trying to understand what set him off. Maybe seeing me fall triggered him? I didn't even remember what happened. All I remember was Chris and a shove, then I was falling, but Grayson caught me. Shit if I had landed things would have been very bad. I held him for several moments, watching him take several deep breaths before he finally calmed down.

"Fucking Taylors," he muttered, then pulled away. "Keeping you both safe is proving to be more trouble than it's worth."

I chuckled, patting his back and pressing a kiss to his cheek. Coach Cornell walked into the locker room, concern etched on his face. "Everything all right, Hayes?"

We both nodded. Our coach looked between us with a raised eyebrow.

"I see you've made up," he remarked dryly.

"Yeah, also, I'd like to apologize for my behavior toward Grayson earlier. He didn't deserve that, and I'm sorry."

Coach Cornell clicked his tongue and rubbed his shiny scalp. "Good. Now, there's something I wanted to discuss with you both," Coach began. "The guys and I have been talking, and, Jayden, given your recent behavior, this shouldn't come as a surprise, but we're considering appointing a new head captain."

Time seemed to stand still, and the world felt as though it had dropped from beneath my feet.

A new captain? I'd held the position since the beginning of sophomore year, and now they were looking to give it to someone else? Possibly Grayson? My stomach churned with unease, even though I knew deep down that I deserved it. I had tormented Grayson for weeks, and he was the one who truly deserved the role. But as the reality set in, the ache in my chest grew. I had worked tirelessly to become the captain, confident in my ability to lead the team. The pain in my throat flared hot and constricting, making it difficult to swallow.

"I see."

"No." Grayson's voice sliced through my thoughts, and I turned to stare at him. "We'll keep things how they are."

Coach frowned. "The votes are unanimous—"

"I don't want to be captain," Grayson said. "Jayden is doing just fine. Let's leave things as is."

Coach Cornell's jaw worked, but he nodded. I wanted to say something else, but I stopped myself. Grayson wasn't in the right frame of mind to argue with. "Hurry up in here. I want your asses back on the ice in ten minutes." He turned and left.

Brushing a few strands of hair away from Grayson's face, I sighed. "You didn't have to do that for me. If the guys want you as captain—"

"I don't want to be captain," Grayson snarled.

"Why not? You'd be the better captain," I said and deep down. There was a lot of stress that came with leading the team, and maybe if I stopped this semester, I could focus on my schoolwork and doing better in my classes, and then next year try again for the position. "Why don't you think about it before saying no?"

Grayson shook his head. "No. It reeks of my father. I'm sure he had something to do with it."

My brows pulled. "How? Do you think he said something to Coach?"

"Maybe not to coach, but to someone else for sure..." He sighed and slumped. "Fuck, I don't care anymore. Just don't scare me like that ever again. I thought for sure—when you went down—it was like Cricket all over again and I lost it."

"Okay. I won't, I promised."

Grayson kissed me, slow and deep, before he put on his gear again. I watched him get dressed, feeling like something was off. How could his father have so much influence in the game? What did Grayson mean when he said he talked to someone? Things weren't making sense, and I had the shrinking feeling that Grayson was lying to me about it.

21

LOVE IN THE PENALTY BOX

GRAYSON HAYES

O pening my eyes, my vision filled with a mass of black curls, freckles and moles. Jayden was sitting there with his legs spread wide at his desk, jutting his chin out and waiting for me to say something, a dare in his green eyes. I tried to ignore the fact that he was a fucking wet dream come true and raised my left eyebrow at him. He was not even pretending to study anymore.

"You still have two more chapters to go," I warned, noticing his tongue darting out to lick his pink lips. Laughing, I turned back to my textbook, pointedly ignoring his heated gaze.

"Do I have to?" he groaned, his head thumping on the desk. "This shit is like gibberish."

"If you want to keep your scholarships," I replied, losing myself to my own notes. "Just finish up that chapter, then you'll be done. I think you're more than prepared for the exams. I'll inform Professor Wilson about your progress."

Jayden muttered something underneath his breath and went back to studying. Time flew by. Then Jayden crawled onto the bed, shoving my books away and pressing a demanding kiss to my lips. I chuckled into it, allowing myself to be maneuvered onto my back while he spread out on top of me.

"Next time we're going to my apartment," I said breathlessly between kisses. "Your dorm is way too fucking small."

"Yeah, well, tell that to my eleven-thousand-dollar tuition fee a year. I also wonder where the fuck all that money goes if it isn't to improve my shoe-box-sized dorm room," Jayden responded, and I opened my mouth, eager for more as he slipped his tongue inside, tasting me. Bristling dark hair scraped against my chin, and I shuddered as the kiss sparked pleasure through my veins. I was hard in seconds, my cock swelling with need and pressing against the confines of my jeans.

"Fuck, Grayson," he whispered, claiming my lips once more before he finally let go of me. Jayden's chest rose and fell rapidly, his green eyes swirling like the foliage in the woods, his lips so wet and pink. "You're like a fucking wet dream."

I laughed at that, because funnily enough, I was thinking the same thing about him. Then his mouth was on mine again, swift and urgent, pulling me apart with his tongue and teeth. I felt raging fire licking inside my veins. That he wanted me as badly as I wanted him was so dizzying that I almost came right there and then. I might still be new at this, but sex between us was as easy as breathing and I knew I would never want to give it up.

"Boyfriend," I chuckled, and Jayden growled.

"Fuck yeah," he grunted. The tip of his nose touched mine, and his eyes were half-lidded as he breathed in my air and kissed me on the lips so slowly that I felt every cell of my body singing to him. Then one more time, heat rising quickly. My fingers moved, as if they had a life of their own, twitching against the soft fabric of his t-shirt, scrunching it up while I tried to remember to breathe when the kiss deepened. His lips were so soft, the slow drag of his tongue absolutely divine as he pulled a desperate whimper from me and pressed even closer.

God, he smells so fucking nice I want to drown in his scent. My cock throbbed, filled to bursting. "Hmm," I moaned against his mouth, his tongue licking inside me and stealing another very embarrassing sound from me.

Jayden rutted against me, his lithe body slotting perfectly between my thighs.

"I love how you feel beneath me," he said, sucking my bottom lip into his mouth and pushing me further against the bed with a grunt.

He took my fluttering hands and placed them on his narrow hips, and I rucked up his shirt, thumbing his jutted hip bones, moaning at how sharp and angular they were. My mouth stung from where he'd been nibbling on it.

We pulled apart, gasping for breath, and his warm hand cradled my cheek, his fingers sliding through my hair. "My heart's beating so fucking fast."

Mine too, I wanted to say, but I couldn't speak past the lump in my throat.

"I don't know what this feeling is, but I—I'm falling for you, Grayson, and I—" Jayden's gaze pierced mine. "I don't want to stop. You won't leave me again, right? No matter what?"

"I won't. I promise."

"Fuck—the things you do to me," he murmured, his voice hoarse and so hot that I felt like I was melting. My brain short-circuited when he kissed me again, to savor the kiss—to savor me. Fuck, Jayden was so sweet and delicate, his fingers featherlight on my skin and in my hair, his eyes like the evergreens so crisp and clear. "Stay the night?"

I nodded and wrapped my arms around his broad shoulders. At some point, I'd need to head back to my apartment to pick up some stuff for class tomorrow, but all that could wait. Jayden lay on my chest, pressing a kiss to my neck, resting there for a moment as if he wanted me to absorb his burning heat. *I'm falling for you*. His words rang in my ear. We stayed like that for a while, sharing soft kisses next to the soft humming of students walking in the hallways, while my pulse slowed down and his smile became tender and intimate. Something melted inside my chest like liquid gold.

Everything was a beautiful muddle, and I felt like nothing else mattered as long as Jayden kept me in his arms and continued looking at me like that. Thumbing his jaw, I lost myself to his fairyland-green eyes that were gentle and hypnotic, like the swish of the grass blades, swaying back and forth in an autumn's dreamscape. *I love you too*.

***

WITH EXAMS LOOMING, the university campus buzzed with students hustling to cram before the big tests. The library and the Academic Resource Center were both packed to the brim, leaving me with nowhere to wait for Jayden after his class with Professor Wilson. Fortunately, my confidence in Jayden's academic prowess was high. He had been acing his recent quizzes, and we had been diligently preparing for the final exam.

I took a break and got some fresh air. Although it wasn't bone-chillingly cold, a light dusting of snow covered the ground, and the occasional biting gust reminded me that winter was here. I walked outside, wrapped tightly in my winter jacket, and made my way to the school's bleachers.

As I approached, a smile tugged at my lips when I noticed Evans sitting there, engrossed in something. But the smile quickly faded when I realized what was in his hands—a crack pipe. My breath caught in my throat, and Evans looked up, his red-rimmed eyes locking onto mine.

"Grayson," he said with a forced laugh, but it sounded wrong, almost fake. My mind raced. Getting caught with drugs was a serious offense, one that could get him expelled from school and thrown off the team.

"What the hell are you doing?" I hissed.

Evans stood up, wiping away the tears that had welled up in his eyes. "Nothing. It's not mine."

I stared at him incredulously. "Then get rid of it! Why are you holding it?"

Evans went eerily quiet, his mouth forming a tight line, and his eyes narrowing into dark slits. "I just... wanted to see what all the hype was about."

It was the most bizarre thing anyone had ever said to me. Evans was typically a happy-go-lucky guy, known for his jovial nature. He was a big fellow with dirty blond hair and sea-blue eyes.

"Forget it," he laughed again, tossing the crack pipe into the trash can. "It's gone. See."

I eyed him warily. "If Coach catches you with anything—"

"He won't," Evans gritted out. "It's fine. Like I said earlier, it wasn't mine. I promise. I was just holding it for a friend."

I couldn't help but wonder what kind of friend would put him in such a situation.

"Come on," he finally said, deciding to change the subject. "I found a secluded spot in the library where we can study in peace."

"That place is packed like sardines," I asked, brow raised.

Evans laughed. "Trust me, Hayes, I found it last year when me and my girlfriend Zara were trying to figure out where to fuck."

Zara? Was she the girl I saw him kissing at the party?

"Oh." That surprised me. I didn't know why I thought Evans leaned more on the guy side, but I shrugged, wondering if maybe I was wrong about him. "Sure..." I cleared my throat as we walked. "Look, if you ever need anyone to talk to someone, about anything, I'm here for you, man. Don't resort to other means."

Evans' brows rose, and he chuckled, slapping his hand on my back. "Don't worry, man. I won't. Like I said, I was just holding it for a friend. Trust me." His jaw tightened, and I had no clue what type of friends Evans seemed to have, but having drugs was wrong and he shouldn't keep those types of people in his life.

"Sure," I replied. Then a thought occurred to me that Evans was there that night everything happened with Cricket, maybe he saw or heard something that I didn't. "Do you remember that night Cricket got hurt? Did you see anything suspicious?"

"Nah, bro... just well, your dad was crawling all over the locker room," Evans responded. "That shit was weird."

I clenched my teeth, remembering the bastard's sense of entitlement as he inspected my equipment. As the university's major donor, he felt he had the right to be there before the game started. I didn't remember much from what happened before then. I was too busy trying to do damage control with him and the press around. "Yeah."

"He said something a little fucked up," Evans said, looking down. "Look man, I don't care about that gay-shit. My aunt is gay, and who you fuck on your own time is none of my business, but... before you came into the locker room, he was already waiting in there. And ah—he seemed to imply that you and Cricket were... more than friends? I don't know. All I remember was that Cricket was pissed, and then you came back right before the half-time, and then he was gone after that."

My heart skipped a beat, leaving me stunned and breathless, like I'd just been hit by lightning. "Why didn't you tell Jayden sooner? Why are we just finding this shit out now?"

Evans put his hands up in mock surrender. "Look, the police went by the video footage and until you started asking about it, I didn't think those two incidents were connected."

"Did they fight?"

"Uh—not really. They just kind of glared at each other? I don't know, but Cricket wasn't having it, from what I remember. Your dad seemed pissed too, but it ended pretty fast and then he was gone and Cricket was falling on the ice..." Evans trailed off, then realization dawned on him. "Do you think he had something to do with that?"

I pressed my lips together, refusing to respond. I couldn't be sure. However, if my father thought I was gay and sleeping with Cricket, maybe he hurt him. "Listen, I've got to go. I'll talk to you later—"

"Wait." Evans grabbed my arm. "If you really want to look into this, you should talk to Devon from Northgate University."

"Devon?" I asked. "Why?"

"Because the bastards that were chirping Cricket on the ice, one of them was his fucking cousin. I don't know what they said, but I was at a party a few weeks ago and that dumbass was there. Devon knocked him flat on his ass because, apparently, he was bragging about some payday or something after Cricket got hurt."

I recoiled, as if I'd stumbled upon something putrid, unable to stomach the reality of my father's actions. *He paid them to hurt Cricket.* No wonder everything came out of the fucking blue and those bastards attacked him on the ice. If Jayden ever found out, he'd kill my father. Not to mention what the Taylor family would do. A wave of revulsion washed over me, twisting my stomach into knots. *Jayden would hate me.* The same cruelty ran through my veins.

Yet, I knew I couldn't keep this from him. It would be worse if he found out from someone else. "Thanks man," I said, shaking his head. "Listen, I gotta go."

"Sure," Evans replied. "Let me know how it goes, bro."

I sprinted to my car, knowing it was a drive to get to Northgate University, but I had to find Devon and the truth. Deep down, I knew it was true. All of this because my father thought I was in a relationship with Cricket. Disgust churned within me, like a vile taste in my mouth that I couldn't spit out, making me want to retch. My father was a sick man.

And it was time I brought him to justice.

***

I FOUND A PARKING SPACE towards the back of the university, close to the arena. The thought of calling my old coach crossed my mind, but the idea of speaking to that terrible man made my stomach twist into knots. As I surveyed the area, a man with dark hair stood beside a worn-down white Honda minivan, his voice sounding clipped and agitated in the wind.

"Get in the car, Marcy!"

"No!" a young voice screamed, reminiscent of a toddler's tantrum. Frowning, I got out of my car and headed towards them. Devon's hair was disheveled, his face covered in a deep five o'clock shadow, while a little girl dressed in all pink stood with her arms crossed, glaring up at him.

"If you don't get in the car this instant, I'll—"

"How about a candy?" I interrupted, reaching into my pocket to pull out a swirly mint candy cane. The little girl's cheeks puffed, and her dark eyes lit up as I approached.

"Please, can I have one?"

Devon's jaw worked. "Only if you get into the car." The little girl climbed into the back seat, sitting down properly, as if she hadn't been screaming moments ago in broad daylight. I chuckled and handed her the candy.

"Thank you!" she said, unwrapping it with enthusiasm.

Devon slid the van door shut and sighed through his nose. "Thanks, man. I thought for sure we'd be here all day, again."

"No worries," I replied. A few other guys on the team also had young children and siblings, so it wasn't unusual to see them bring the kids along during practices. "I actually came to talk to you about something," I continued. "Do you remember that night when everything happened to Cricket?"

Devon nodded, running a hand through his dark hair. "Yeah, that was crazy. Sorry about your friend."

"Evans mentioned you have a cousin? The one who attacked Cricket? He was bragging about a payday?"

Disgust wrinkled Devon's nose. "Yeah. Apparently, he got involved with some real estate tycoon who promised him a bunch of investment properties, only to realize it was all a scam. What an idiot. They have banned him from hockey, so I don't think he'll come anywhere near you."

Shock hit me like an icy wave, as if I'd suddenly plunged into freezing waters, sending shivers down my spine. *A real estate tycoon.* That confirmed it. My father had orchestrated the attack on Cricket.

"Are you okay, man? You look a little green."

I swallowed the bile that was rising in my throat. "I'm fine. Just... I'll see you later." I fled before he could respond, my mind racing, as I needed to find hard evidence against my father. Beyond everything else, I needed Jayden.

Hey, baby. Meet me at my apartment later on today. I have something I need to discuss. I texted him while I got to my car.

Sure thing. Cya then. Jayden replied, and I reread the message several times, trying to savor it in my mind. I had no clue how he would react to the news, but I wanted him to understand that I had nothing to do with this. It was as if I could feel the weight of my father's deceit pressing down on me, suffocating me with a nauseating sense of filth. I'd do everything in my power to make this right.

For Jayden.

For us.

For Cricket.

***

ARRIVING AT THE SPRAWLING downtown apartment building, I parked in the garage and took the elevator up to the first floor. A smile crossed my face when I spotted Jayden waiting in the lobby, exuding a mix of sexiness and ruggedness. His tattoos snaked up his neck and disappeared beneath his open crew neck t-shirt. His winter jacket hung unbuttoned, revealing slivers of his pale skin, and his low-slung jeans completed the effortlessly cool look.

"Hey," he greeted me with a smile, and I leaned in to kiss him on the lips.

"Let's head up," I suggested, paying no mind to the curious gazes of onlookers. Unlocking the door to my apartment, Jayden whistled appreciatively, taking in the floor-to-ceiling bay windows, the panoramic city view, white granite countertops, and sleek chrome appliances.

"Damn, why don't we hang out here instead of my crappy dorm room?" he mused.

I chuckled. "Because your place is closer."

Jayden dropped his belongings near the entrance and kicked off his shoes. "Still, this place looks amazing. Did your dad give it to you?"

I couldn't help but cringe at the mention of my father. "No. When my mother passed away, she left me a trust fund. I don't really need his money, to be honest. I mostly use it for school, but once I'm done, I won't need him anymore."

"Sweet," Jayden said, then shoved his hands deep into his pockets. "So, what did you want to talk about? Your text made it sound urgent."

My hands shook as I guided him over to the couch and sat down. Holding my phone in my hands, I braced myself for what was to come next. "I found out something... about Cricket and what happened to him."

The smile on Jayden's face waned.

22

—·—

THE PUCK STOPS HERE

GRAYSON HAYES

"What did you find out?" Jayden demanded.

"First," I said, looking at my phone. "I think we should watch the video of what happened that night. Together."

"Fuck no!" Jayden sprung to his feet, his hand curled into a fist. "There's no fucking way I'm watching that video—"

"Jayden—" I stood, my throat working. "Please. I think—there's information we're missing. Something horrible happened and only by looking at the surveillance video can we confirm it—"

"Watch it yourself," Jayden spat. "I'm not watching it with you. I'm not reliving what happened to my brother."

My tongue felt cleaved to the roof of my mouth. Of course, I would never force him to watch the video, but Jayden never really knew what happened. If we could confront this together, then maybe things would be different. I stared into his eyes, hoping to convey all of that, and finally he relented.

Sinking back onto the couch like a deflated balloon, he sighed. "Fine. Fuck—fine!"

"Are you sure? I won't force you."

"I need to know," he hissed through gritted teeth. "I need to know. Once and for all."

"Okay," I answered, sitting beside him. I found the video online and pressed play. The video unfolded like a malevolent nightmare. It started with the footage of my father entering the locker room. The grainy images captured him moving with an eerie purpose, his presence shrouded in shadows. He remained in the locker room for a brief, sinister interval before emerging. As he exited, my father's lips moved in hushed conversation with two men who would later reveal themselves as the assailants.

In the surveillance video, my father handed them two jet-black event cards, exclusive passes reserved for the highest investors and the most influential tycoons in the city. The cards were like golden tickets to clandestine dealings, granting access to properties that were never even on the market. The men accepted the cards with calculated nonchalance, and the world seemed to slow to a crawl.

As the camera shifted focus, the horror played out on the screen. The heartbreaking sequence showed Cricket's fall, his face slamming into the unforgiving boards, a spray of blood like macabre confetti. Shock rippled through the crowd, mirroring the chills that ran down my spine. It was not a mere trip, and no stray stick had caused his fall.

It was the tape on his skates—tape placed there by my father.

A nauseating surge of bile clawed at my throat as the grim truth unraveled on my phone screen. Cricket had been targeted, not because of his skills or the game, but because my father knew I was gay. The sickening realization hung heavy in the room, choking us with its brutal significance.

Jayden snatched the phone from my hands and flung it across the room. The device ricocheted off the wall, narrowly escaping shattering into pieces. We were left in a heavy silence, haunted by the monstrous revelation. My father had tried to kill Cricket because he thought he was gay.

And my lover.

"This is—" Jayden's chest heaved, he clutched at his throat as if he were choking. "This is fucking insane—your dad—Cricket—"

I grabbed onto him and held him in my arms, feeling like I was breaking apart too.

"Grayson—this isn't real right? Tell me it's all a fucking dream," Jayden sobbed, holding onto me tight. "Cricket will wake up. None of this happened."

God, I wished it were true. Bitter tears streamed from my eyes, and I could do nothing but keep him close to me. We'd have to go to the authorities with this information. My father would be prosecuted. He'd spend the rest of his life in jail for manslaughter, but what about Cricket? His life had been taken away so callously because of one man's prejudice. One man's disgust.

"I'm so sorry, Jayden," I rasped. "Please. I'm so fucking sorry."

"Your father is a fucking monster," Jayden whispered, vengeance within every breath. "And I'll fucking gut him for what he did."

I nodded and pulled back, looking into his eyes. They were lit with fire, but along with that, a deep and unfathomable sadness. No matter what, this wouldn't bring Cricket back. He was already gone.

"Start from the top. How did you come to the information and what the fuck can we do about it?"

***

I TOLD HIM. EVERYTHING FROM start to finish. The horrors I'd faced over the years at the hands of my father. What Evans and Devon shared with me a few hours earlier. How I knew it was all fucking true. I spent all my time with Cricket, so my father must have thought we were sleeping together. Or maybe he got wind of the crush I had on Jayden and mistakenly thought it was Cricket.

Who knew? And at this point, it didn't matter. My father had acted and left a swathe of destruction in his wake. By the time we were finished, the sun was sinking down below the horizon, drenching Jayden's face in the orange, fiery glow of the heavens. Pacing the room, my throat felt like sandpaper and my voice was raw from crying and talking. A part of me wanted to destroy something. Take one of my sticks and smash this place to pieces. *I would never be like him.*

I would never hate so much that it took over my life. Disgust welled up in my throat, making it hard to swallow, like a bitter taste that lingered long after the initial shock.

"We can go to the police station tomorrow," Jayden said, wringing his hands. "I won't tell my parents just yet. They've been through enough."

I nodded and then Jayden stood, falling into my arms as if he didn't have the strength to keep himself upright. "I'm so fucking tired, Grayson," he sighed into my neck. "Things were so much easier when I was a child." He turned to look up at me, his eyes rimmed red. "Take me to bed."

I knew what he meant, and I claimed his mouth in a bruising kiss. I love you, I thought breathlessly as I tore off his belt buckle, walking him backward to my king-sized bed. Jayden fell onto the mattress, bouncing several times, while I crawled over him. Closing my eyes, I lost myself to the rustling sound of the buckle sliding free, and the metallic noise of the zipper going down and the swoosh of fabric as I tugged his pants from his legs. My eyes snapped open when Jayden spread out in front of me, his calloused fingers working off my shirt and tugging the elastic band of my pants. My lips parted, taking him all in, and more tears burned my eyes. *Cricket should have known about us.*

He should have seen how happy we are. Fuck, it was all gone now.

Thumbing my tears away, Jayden cupped my face and kissed me, slow and sweet. "I—" I swallowed around the dagger in my throat. "Make love to me. Please. Fuck me."

Desire flashed in Jayden's eyes and he flipped us over, pressing me down into the bed. Rummaging through his bag, he tossed a condom and lube on the bed. He gazed at me, staring down at my naked body, and I shuddered beneath the prickling bristles of those harsh evergreens.

Tracing the taut lines of his abs and stomach, I reach down to grip his swollen cock, which jutted against his stomach.

"Fuck, baby—" he hissed.

Jayden's lips collided with my mouth as his naked body pressed to mine. I moaned, loud and indecent, because it felt so fucking good. His skin was unbelievably smooth and his cock so hard as it slid deliciously alongside mine.

"Fuck, I love you, Grayson," Jayden grunted the words, threading his fingers through my hair, his palm burning into the side of my hip as he shoved a pillow beneath my ass. "Lift," he said, and I pushed up so he could place it, angling my body up toward him. Running my hands through the soft, dark hair on his thighs, I groaned again. "I've never..." Jayden laughed. "I've always bottomed, but I'm glad you'll be my first for this."

I hummed my agreement. Then his finger found my pulsating hole. Jayden stroked my cock for several minutes, and I writhed on the bed, a sob working its way up my throat. My hands became my eyes while he kept on kissing me and made the most amazing sounds while he jerked me off. Jayden splayed my legs wider, so he had full access, and then I felt something warm and wet tickle my puckered entrance. "Fuck you're beautiful, Grayson," he muttered, working his finger in to the knuckle.

Hovering over me, he captured my lips once again, stroking my cock in time with his thrusts. I groaned, back arching with needy sounds that threatened to undo me while I just focused on feeling him.

"Grayson..." he mumbled, reaching for my mouth and whimpering against it when I took us both in my hand and started working us together. Wet, slippery strokes caused stardust to erupt across my vision and I grabbed his wrist, silently telling him not to continue or else I'd be done for. Reaching down, I stroked his cock from root to tip and Jayden's back bowed.

"Fuck—" he whined, a shudder shaking him when I tightened my grip and kissed his neck, sucking on that sensitive spot under his ear that always made him lose control.

"Can I leave my marks?" I asked, and he whimpered, low in his throat.

"Please..." Jayden demanded, his breath hitching in his throat when my teeth skidded across his hot skin. I didn't want him to beg, but he was so beautiful when he was like this, loose and pliant in my arms, desperate to be touched and kissed and loved. I wanted to give him everything.

I wanted to make him feel good, like he'd never had before.

"I'm going to leave my marks on you, so that everyone will see that you're mine," I muttered after giving his neck a hard suck, and I thought I'd said too much, that it was too unhinged and possessive, but Jayden made a choked-up sound and then came hard in my hand. He gasped loudly, as if the pleasure had taken him by surprise.

"Grayson..." he said, his voice cracked as he rested his forehead against mine and caught his breath, shaking. "God..."

Angry bite marks lined the side of his neck. And I ran shaky fingers along them, my touch featherlight and reverent, and I felt a thrill at the thought of what they would look like tomorrow. He could cover up most of them with a shirt, but there's one under his ear that would be visible. I felt something thick and hot coil in my belly, tightening at the realization that Jayden would have my marks on him for everyone to see.

Fuck if that wasn't the hottest thing.

A pathetic whimper left my mouth. I wanted more; I was desperate for more, and I didn't care if I looked pathetic to him right now. Jayden wrapped those cool fingers around my searing flesh and pumped slowly. He was taunting me. I bucked my hips up and tried to urge him to jerk me off faster. He gripped our dicks together and started to grind and rub us together.

Jayden grabbed the lube and poured the liquid over my twitching hole. My legs were spread wide, and I felt exposed and vulnerable in a way I never thought possible. Entering two more fingers, he stretched me open, working his way to a slow and teasing rhythm that had me seeing stars. Pleasure thunderbolted through me when he struck a bundle of nerves deep inside my core, and I yelped.

"Fuck baby!" I almost came right then and there. Jayden's mouth curled into a smirk, and then he pulled back, grabbing the base of his flushed cock and rolling on the condom. I watched with hooded eyes when he pressed it against my entrance, swollen and thick against the puckered hole.

A hot steel rod nudged my cheeks, and I braced myself, breath hitching when green eyes met mine. "Tell me when to stop."

I grunted when he breached the rim. It stung hot and fierce, making me grit my teeth against the pain of being speared open. Jayden hushed my moans, stroking my now flagging cock as he shoved all the way in and bottomed out.

"Relax, darling," he purred into my ear and then thrust his dick to the hilt, before pulling back out. I panted and felt my body crumble into the soft bed. *Yes, fuck yes.*

Jayden started slow, plunging his hips leisurely into me, building a light shallow pace before getting deeper and deeper. "Fuck, you feel good wrapped around my cock," he groaned, grabbing two full handfuls of my ass cheeks.

It felt so good. With each thrust, I bucked into him and encouraged him to fuck me harder.

Jayden gripped my hard hips. Then set a brutal pace, driving his hips forward with enough force to slam the headboard against the wall. The sound of our sweaty flesh slapping into each other brought a whole new wave of arousal to me. I moaned and rocked into Jayden's thrusts more. My mind begged for more from him. His thrusts were perfect. The sounds of our panting and smacking were exquisite. His fingernails digging into my skin were bringing me to the edge once again.

"God!" I heard him curse. Then his dick twitched, his hips still pressed against my ass.

Jayden collapsed on top of me and panted heavily in my ear as his cock pumped and spasmed inside of me. There was a moment of nothing but panting between us. We basked in the enjoyment of our mutual orgasms.

However, it got uncomfortable. I moved away from Jayden and glanced at the mess we had become. Taking my swollen cock, Jayden kissed me slow and deep, stroking me to completion. Heat unlocked my spine, spreading warm electric sparks through me, and I came with a shout against his lips. White ropes of come erupted all over my abs and his hand, and he chuckled softly, nibbling my lower lip.

"Fuck, that was amazing."

It was. I nuzzled against him and closed my eyes, feeling the waves of my orgasm pulsing through my skin. Jayden cleaned us up, and came back to the bed and lay down beside me. Green eyes found mine in the fading light. "I love you."

My heart tightened, and I pulled him close. "I love you too."

"I don't know why I never—I was such a jackass to you before, but Grayson, I think you should take the captain's position on the team. You deserve it."

My brows rose. "What about you?"

Jayden shrugged. "I'll give it to you for now, but I didn't mean for good."

I laughed, shaking my head. "So, you intend to take it back next year?"

"100%," he promised.

Kissing him, I bit into his bottom lip. "I'd love to see you try."

Jayden nudged my arm and then snuggled down to sleep. At last, the quiet of night enveloped us. I lay with Jayden nestled in my arms, his rhythmic breathing like a soothing lullaby. The weight of the world seemed to dissolve in that tranquil moment. The darkness cradled us like a protective cocoon, insulating us from the chaos of the outside world. The events of the past were mere echoes, fading into insignificance. The video. Evans. Devon. All of it meant nothing, with Jayden in my arms.

This was our paradise, a haven in the stillness of the night.

Despite the turmoil my father had unleashed, I couldn't help but feel that we had found a way to overcome it. With Jayden by my side, I knew we were invincible. It was a comforting notion, one that chased away the shadows of doubt. Tomorrow we'd set things right. Bring Cricket the justice he deserved.

I sighed, thinking about him. His memory was both painful and precious, but now it could finally rest in peace. Closing my eyes, I relaxed and fell into a deep sleep.

My eyes snapped open, and my mind was slow to register the shrill noise in the background. The sound sent a shockwave through my body, making me jerk upright in bed.

There, standing in the doorway, was my father, his face etched with horror as he took in our naked forms. Time seemed to slow to a crawl, and my mind raced with disbelief. *When had he returned?* I felt the scream clawing its way up my throat, but all I could manage was a gaping mouth, a silent gasp, as I locked eyes with the man I had come to loathe.

My father's hair was windswept, and his dark eyes narrowed into sinister slits. His lips rippled over bared teeth, and his booming voice shattered the eerie stillness of the room.

"What the fuck are you fags doing?"

Panic surged through me, and I finally sprang into action, clumsily pulling the blankets to cover Jayden and me. He was already wide awake, his face bearing a fierce and defiant expression, a clear contrast to my shock and dread. I knew this confrontation would not end well. The oppressive atmosphere in the room threatened to engulf us, and I braced myself for the impending storm.

Shit. My father was back and now he knew my deepest secret.

23

— · —

HEARTSTRINGS AND HAT TRICKS

GRAYSON HAYES

J ayden was on his feet in seconds, ass naked like a bull ready to charge at him Scrambling off the bed, I followed, yanking on a pair of sweats and tossing Jayden his t-shirt. He hurried to get dressed, but his face remained defiant.

"Let me handle this—"

"Handle what?" my father spat. "Get him the fuck out of here, Grayson!"

"No."

My father's brow ticked. "What did you say to me, boy?"

"I said no," I replied, my voice stern. "He isn't the one who's leaving. You are."

My dad barked a laugh. "Me? Who the fuck do you think is paying for this place?"

"This is my mother's apartment, and it's in my name," I said, my voice low. "Or did you think I wouldn't know? All the greasy credit cards you've given me, I've never used any of them. My mother has a trust fund set up and once I graduate, I will inherit all of it."

His jaw dropped.

"Now, kindly get the fuck out of my apartment," I said, my pulse throbbing in my skin. This was it. I would finally stand up to my dad and he would leave. Jayden would see it. I'm not a coward. In thirty seconds, my dad was striding towards me, his long legs eating up the distance between us and his hand snapped out to wrap around my throat. "Fuck—!"

"You little shit!" he raged, his eyes flaming with hatred. "Just who the fuck do you think you're talking to?"

Turning to Jayden, I saw the shrinking horror skittering over his face. "Call the police!"

Pain exploded at the side of my temple, and I went sprawling over the edge of the bed and straight onto the floor. In all my years, I never raised a hand to my father. Despite how much of a bastard he was and how I could've fought back, I promised myself I never would. Let the bastard do what he wanted. I'd just take it and escape. But now that Jayden was here seeing everything unfold, acid surged up my throat. I didn't want him to see me like this. Weak and pathetic at my father's mercy, which I had been most of my life. There was a strange shuffling noise, and my dad grabbed my shirt, hauling me up.

"You think because you got your ass fucked, you're a man now?" he spat with disgust. "Well, newsflash, you're the exact opposite. Fuck, all the years I had my suspicious. You could never take a fucking punch and now everything has been confirmed!"

Blood spilled from my lips, the metallic taste flooding my mouth. "And what are you going to do about it? Kill me?"

"I should have. It would have been better if you were dead!" he roared, his fist slamming the side of my cheek.

A white blistering haze filled my vision, and my head snapped back, only to be brought forward again for another blow. I knew this time he wasn't going to stop.

If he had anything to do with Cricket's death, my father would try to kill me now.

Jayden slipped stealthily behind my father. In his swift and silent movement, he grasped a nearby vase and brought it crashing down upon my father's unsuspecting head. The vase shattered with a violent cacophony, and my father crumpled to the ground, unconscious. I lay there stunned by Jayden's quick response; the shattered vase scattered like debris around us.

"Fuck," Jayden said, grabbing my arm and pulling me up. "Are you okay? Shit, you're bleeding a lot." He guided me to the kitchen with his hand on my elbow. "Sit here." He ran to the sink and wet a cloth before dabbing it at my lip and temple. Blood soaked through the cloth and I smiled mirthlessly. "The police are on their way. One second." Jayden walked to the other room and dragged my father into the bathroom, locking the door in case he tried to get out. "Shit. That was scary and fucked up. How long has he been like this?"

"For as long as I can remember," I replied, and felt a pang in my heart.

"I'm so sorry, baby," Jayden said, kissing my cheek. "Don't worry. We'll figure it out. I promise."

There was a knock on the door, and Jayden went to answer it. Four massive police officers walked into my apartment, their hands on their badges. "Grayson Hayes?" one of them said, their hands on their belts. "Are you okay, son?"

"I'm fine," I said, managing to get to my feet. "He's locked in the bathroom."

Jayden told them everything that had happened from start to finish, including my father's homophobic rant and slurs. He even showed them the video and his suspicious that my father was involved in hurting his brother. The officers nodded, and two of them went to get my father out of the bathroom and arrest him. Leading him through the corridor, we locked eyes and a rage I had never seen before gleamed inside his as they led him out in handcuffs.

Good riddance, I thought, and Jayden's hand slipped into mine, entwining our fingers. My heart was hammering, but when he finally left I relaxed. "Do you want to come back to my dorm room or stay here?" Jayden asked while the EMS bandaged my temple and chin.

"Anywhere is better than here," I breathed.

"Okay. I'll pack your stuff and we can go."

I allowed Jayden to grab my stuff, including my hockey gear and anything else I would need for the next few days. The police took our statements and asked if I wanted to press charges or not, and I couldn't give them an answer right there and then. I knew Jayden wanted me to, but that meant a court case and having everyone find out my father had beaten the shit out of me since I was young. Licking my dry lips, I told them I'd think about it and then Jayden and I set off to the dorm rooms.

***

LYING IN BED WITH JAYDEN, my chest felt heavy. Thoughts of my father stirred up disgust deep within me. He despised me because I was gay. I had carried that secret for years, not knowing the reason behind his hatred, but now I did.

Jayden gently caressed my unbruised cheek and let out a sigh. "I'm so sorry you had to go through that. I should've been there for you."

"Please," I replied, my voice trembling. "It's in the past. I never told anyone because I didn't want them to know."

Jayden exhaled. "Still, that monster hurt you and Cricket. I want him to face the consequences of his actions."

I felt the same way, but he was still my father, the only family I had left. "You know," I began, tears streaming down my face, "For a while, I believed I deserved it. I thought it was a punishment for what happened with Cricket. I felt like I deserved the pain."

Jayden shook his head. "No, my love, never think that. Who you love is who you love. Disagreements should never turn into violence."

Burying my face in his warm sweater, I allowed myself to cry, finding solace in Jayden's comforting embrace.

"Thank you for loving me," Jayden said, stealing a kiss from my lips.

"Love, the final frontier."

We both laughed, thinking of the classic Star Trek quote.

"Do you think Evans and Devon will testify?" I asked, wiping my tears away.

Jayden nodded. "I believe so. When I reopen the case against your father, I think it'll blow everything wide open."

Jayden's phone rang, and he quickly answered it. "Woah, Mom, slow down! What do you mean? So fast?" He jumped out of bed and grabbed his coat. "Okay, we'll be there soon."

I rose from the bed, staring at him with concern. "What's wrong?"

He looked at me with a serious expression. "It's Cricket. Things have taken a turn for the worse."

***

WE RACED THROUGH the sterile, harshly lit hospital corridors, panic gnawing at the edges of our minds. Jayden's footsteps echoed loudly against the tile floor, our hurried breaths filling the otherwise silent atmosphere.

When we arrived at Cricket's room, Doctor Mohmad was already there, waiting for us. My parents stood nearby, their faces etched with worry and grief.

"What is it? What's wrong?" Jayden asked.

"I'm so sorry," Doctor Mohmad sighed heavily, his gaze filled with empathy. "Cricket is in the first stage of lung failure. Because he's brain- dead, his body has deteriorated at a rapid pace."

Being brain dead had set off a chain reaction within his body, causing his organs to shut down, with the lungs being the first to fail.

Tears welled up in my eyes, and Jayden clenched his fists, his face contorted with anguish. We were on the precipice of losing someone we both loved dearly and there was nothing we could do to stop it. Tears streamed down Jayden's face as he clung to the last vestiges of hope.

"What can we do? How do we stop it?" he demanded of the doctor.

"I'm truly sorry, but there's nothing more we can do. We've reached a point where we have to let nature take its course. The best choice at this stage would be to euthanize Cricket, to remove him from life support."

Jayden's eyes flashed with anger. "No! He'll wake up! He has to wake up!"

"I understand your pain, but I'm truly sorry, son. Cricket is gone. There's nothing we can do to bring him back."

The room filled with unbearable sorrow, and we clung to each other, trying to find comfort in our shared grief. Cricket was slipping away, and the realization was a crushing weight on our hearts.

"I'll leave you to discuss your next steps." The doctor left and Jayden turned to his mother.

"He's alive. He'll wake up. He has to see my final game. He has to stay alive. I found something else about the case. Something that will help. Mom, please. Don't do this. Dad—" Jayden begged and I could do nothing but watch, my eyes burning with tears.

Mrs. Taylor looked at him. "I'm sorry. I think we should let him go. Let him rest in peace."

Jayden crumpled to his knees as if he were a doll with his strings cut. I lurched after him and knelt down, taking him into my arms as he covered his face with his hands and sobbed.

It was over. My rib cage cracked open.

It was all over now.

***

CRICKET DIED A week later.

His soul laid to rest on the hilltop behind the house near the hockey rink where he loved to spend his days. Standing beside Jayden dressed in black, we watched as they lowered his body to the ground.

"From dust to dust... ashes to ashes..." the priest's voice faded into the distance.

Several hundred people had shown up for Cricket's funeral, including the guys on the team who wore their jerseys in support. Coach Cornell's eyes were rimmed red with tears, and I could barely suppress the sobs that wracked through me.

Then it was over.

We headed back to Jayden's house for refreshments. I was speaking to some guys when I noticed Jayden was nowhere to be found. Striding down the corridors and up the stairs to the bedroom, I found him in Cricket's room, sitting on the bed.

"Are you okay?" I spoke, my voice rough. Running my palm over his back, I sat down beside him.

Jayden was holding Cricket's old Michigan Wolverines jersey in his fists. "It can't end like this. It can't."

"It won't," I replied. "I promise."

Green eyes turned to stare at me with such infinite sadness that it nailed my heart to the wall. "I idolized him. For so long. Cricket was everything to me, and now he's gone. What can I do? Who can I turn to to be my rock?"

Taking his hand in mine, I went silent, mulling his words over. *A loving heart is always there to catch the other when they fall, and to lift them higher when they rise.* It was something my mother always taught me growing up. I wanted Jayden to count on me, knowing I could never in this lifetime replace Cricket, but I could be his stepping stone. His bridge to cross rivers and streams. His pathway to victory and beyond.

"I once told you that 'logic is the beginning of wisdom, not the end'..." I whispered. "I can't ease your pain, Jayden, but if you love me and want to be with me, I promise my love will always resemble a tranquil meadow. A calm against the storm of your pain to which it can gradually subside, maybe even cease."

Jayden choked on a sob. "God, you're a sap."

I laughed, then cupped his face. "I am and proud of it."

"I love you so fucking much," Jayden said through tears, kissing me slowly on the lips.

"I love you too," I replied, smiling back at him. "Now, let's head back downstairs. I saw Sarah a few minutes ago, and I think I need to apologize for being the world's biggest asshole to them."

We headed back downstairs. I saw Sarah and Ian talking to the rest of the hockey team. The minute our eyes locked, she ran over to me, her brown eyes wide and full of tears. "I'm so sorry for your loss." I took her into my arms and hugged her tight. "God, I'm such a dick for ignoring you the past few weeks. Shit—I wasn't thinking. I was upset about what Ian told me and I just reacted. Sorry."

"It's fine," I breathed into her hair, inhaling the scent of her peach blossom soap. "I should apologize to Ian as well. What we did—it was wrong."

Sarah pulled away, looking up at me. "Yeah, but don't worry about it right now. Jayden needs you. Probably now more than ever before."

Ian came over, rubbing the base of his neck. "Look man, if you ever need anything—" he held out his hand and I shook it.

"Nah, I should be the one apologizing to you. Sorry for—uh—" I was going to say sleeping with his fuck buddy, but that didn't seem right. "Sorry." I finished feeling utterly lame.

He knew what I was talking about, so he just laughed. "Water under the bridge man, Jayden and I will always be friends."

Good. I thought, watching Jayden across the room, deep in conversation with Coach Cornell and his father, probably discussing the up-and-coming game. I looked around at all the people who supported us and Jayden and I knew this was what real family was like.

This was it.

This was home.

***

BLACK BRANCHES TRACED the blue-black heavens overhead as people said their goodbyes. It ended up turning into a great evening, with laughter and stories. Mr. Taylor brought out an old photo album and everyone could look through the old pictures of Cricket when he was younger. My eyes were raw by the end of that and my stomach ached from laughing at the stories Mr. Taylor told. By the end, all I wanted was to sleep for a hundred years. Jayden followed me up the stairs, his finger hooked into my belt loops of my slacks as we went to his bedroom.

Jayden sighed and flopped down onto the bed and I followed suit. It had been a long day, and we'd have to get ready to head back to campus in a few days for exams. Jayden's hand touched my knee, his fingers grazing my cock, and my heart rate sped up.

"You'll have to do all the work," I muttered, already half hard.

Jayden laughed and rolled onto me, his face inches away from mine. "I don't care. You look so fucking hot in black. I thought I'd burst all night just from staring at you." He ran a hand over my black button up that was stretched taut across my chest, to my black slacks. "Damn, you should always wear black."

I laughed, and Jayden stifled it with a brutish kiss. Moaning into his mouth, I gasped as Jayden rolled his hips. The outline of his bulge was clear through his own slacks, as if it wanted to burst through the dark-colored fabric. Jayden's legs looked thick and muscular as he pulled off his pants and underwear in one go. His pale cock was hard and slapped against his stomach. I grunted, taking in the black hair that dusted his legs and got furrier towards the apex where his cock was.

Jayden peeled off my pants, not caring that I acted like a dead fish. We laughed as he stripped us both naked before crawling back over me until we were chest to chest. I could feel each inch of smooth skin before his hips pressed closer to mine and together, we groaned.

Curling his hand around the base of my cock, he gave it one long stroke. Thumb brushing over the head before he pulled away. Jayden's fingers left my hips, gripping around my chest as he leaned over me, hands pushing to grope my nipples

"Fuck, you look so good. I'm gonna fuck you so hard, baby," he whispered as he ground his cock into my hole.

Jayden's shaft was so swollen it looked red and veiny like a maple leaf and felt like an entire fist trying to squeeze into me. For a moment, he fumbled with the lube, far too eager to get inside me while I sat back and relaxed into his touch.

"I'm clean, baby, don't worry."

I never did, I thought.

Lining himself up, I felt the blunt edge of his cock push against my entrance.

I tried to twist and work my hips back as he gripped and squeezed my chest, my achingly hard nipples dripping wet as I felt my sensitive asshole stretching open, puckered hole scraping over his cock before it slipped into me. I hadn't even realized I was holding my breath until it came out in a loud moan, but I didn't care as hips slapped my ass and Jayden was already pulling back.

The cock popped free of my entrance with a soft wet pop and I could feel a slurry of fluids oozing from my now gaping hole before the cock pushed back in squeezing back into my warm canal. Each tug free made me quiver in pleasure and each time I was stretched open, I groaned as the heat of his cock filled me repeatedly.

"Fuck—Jayden—" I hissed, sucking in air through my teeth.

Jayden grunted, fisting my hair. His eyes were nearly black with desire and his thrusts so hard the bed legs screeched in protest. My heart hammered in time with his, I could feel myself reaching an apex of desire. His dick pounded into my ass, sending me soaring into the heavens. My shaft pulsed and squirted my precum under me, making a wet mess as I felt my climax quickly rushing to meet the cock buried to the hilt. Jayden. I wanted to cry out.

"Fuck!" I cursed, bright lights blinding my vision as each hot gush of precoma squirted into my ass. It was just enough leverage to push myself back, eagerly swallowing up his entire cock inside me as my body squeezed and milked him for his seed.

I arched my back and pressed into his thrusts hungrily, groaning as I felt his shaft squelch wetly into my hole. Fuck, this felt so good. So right. Jayden. The only thing that filled my vision was Jayden.

Jayden plunged his hips frantically. The curve of his stomach pressed into my lower back as he slid inside me with a moan, tugging just the bulging flesh of his cock in and out of my spent ass as I could feel him getting closer to orgasm.

"Yes—Grayson—I'm close!"

Jayden's moans reached a crescendo as he slammed his hips forward into my ass with a noisy clap. Shouting through his release, Jayden soaked my body with his seed.

Fuck. A burst of bright lights flashed before my eyes. I let out a long, deep moan while below me, my shaft visibly pulsed and rocketed through me. I was flung over the edge. My cock exploded all over our stomachs in searing hot spurts.

Loud wet splats punctuated our combined sounds as his hips rocked and ground into my ass. Even as we settled down, I could still feel his dick throbbing, and warm seed oozed from my hole as we both caught our breaths. As we quickly regained our breaths, Jayden and I straightened up a little. Jayden politely helped me clean up, as come dribbled down my thighs.

"Wait," I said, grabbing his arm as he went to get a cloth. "Leave it. I like it there."

Jayden's mouth curled at the edges. "Cockslut now?"

"For you," I laughed, and he snuggled back down with me. "Only for you."

Jayden buried his face in my neck, his breath evening out into the stillness of the night. "Thank you for being here. I couldn't have done it without you."

"Same here," I replied, stroking his arm. "I'll always be there for you, Jayden. No matter what."

As Jayden's breaths evened out in sleep, I gazed at the Star Trek posters on the wall, holding back a chuckle. Finally, it felt like life had given me what I deserved. *A boyfriend. A family. A home.*

To boldly go where no man has gone before.

Yeah, that sounded about right.

24

— • —

TWO-MINUTE PENALTY

JAYDEN TAYLOR

The deafening roar of the crowd enveloped me as I skated onto the rink, donning my brother's hockey jersey. The energy in the arena was electric, and I spotted Coach Cornell standing nearby, his pride evident in his nod of approval. Gliding down the ice, I scanned the surroundings, catching sight of my parents in the stands, both proudly sporting the Michigan Wolverines colors. Their smiles warmed my heart as I waved to them and the enthusiastic crowd. Even Professor Wilson, although less enthused, had made the effort to be there.

I had recently passed my chemistry class with flying colors, vowing never to revisit the subject again, even though it was likely required for my degree. The memory brought a grimace to my face.

A nudge from Evans brought me back to the present, and I turned to see what had caught his attention. Scouts—four of them, it seemed—were seated in the stands. My heart raced, and I knew this game would be a turning point in our lives.

Grayson's skates sliced across the ice as he came toward me, a smile dancing on his pale pink lips. His gray eyes locked onto mine, and my stomach fluttered as it always did when our gazes met.

After Cricket's accident, I'd always hated gray.

It was dark. Drab. Listless.

Now I realized I was wrong. There was strength there. A resilience in being stuck in between black and white. Grayson taught me that. His gray eyes were like smoldering embers in a blacksmith's fire, a powerful presence that sheltered the storm. I cherished him for that and for everything else he was.

The crowd's cheers intensified, and everyone fell into formation, ready for the game.

We lined up, preparing to face off against the formidable rival university team, the Frostbite Falcons. The world's eyes were on us as I took my position at center forward, feeling the rapid thumping of my heart against my rib cage. Thoughts of the case and how Cricket had finally received justice occupied my mind.

Mr. Hayes had been sentenced to life in prison for first-degree manslaughter, with no possibility of parole. The truth had emerged—he had paid those hockey players to harm Cricket on the ice and had tampered with his skates, all with the sinister intent of causing severe harm. I was convinced he had aimed to end my brother's life.

The referee stepped forward, holding the puck with a stern expression. I locked eyes with the gorilla in front of me, his face set with rage, and I smirked. This game was going to be a walk in the park.

I nodded to Grayson, who came up on my right side. He mouthed the words 'I love you' and my heart soared.

Spock's voice entered my mind *'Death is that state in which one exists only in the memory of others. Which is why it is not an end. No goodbyes, just good memories.'*

Just good memories. I looked up, knowing Cricket was above, watching over me. *This one's for you, bro.*

Then the puck dropped.

THE END

—·—

OTHER WORKS

Cross Blades (Book #2)

O nce inseparable, my best friend and I were torn apart after a
night of fiery passion—a memory forever etched in my mind,
its details lost in a hazy fog. Now, Alex May is my bitter rival, his
indifference cutting deeper than any blade. The looming national state
championships intensify the stakes, fueling the fire of that unforgettable night.

In the arena's dim light, tension crackles. Each stride, each thud
of the puck, echoes unspoken words. The remnants of our once un-
breakable bond intertwine with a burning desire for vindication.

I yearn to reach out to Alex, hoping he'll give me a second chance.
But his walls are high, his heart guarded. Will he ever forgive me for the
mistakes of our past and allow love to mend our broken connection?

Heated Rivalry (Book #3)

With graduation looming, I'm forced to take an extra credit athletic course in hockey—a sport I despise. The ice, the cold, and the game itself are everything I detest. But when a bone-shattering shove on the ice threatens to fracture my knee, I must confront my fears and learn to play.

In a shocking revelation, I discovered it was Devon who had shoved me hard on the ice.

Devon Black.

A demon. A force to be reckoned with, notorious for his bullying tactics on and off the ice.

I hate Devon with every fiber of my being, yet beneath the surface of my hatred lies an undeniable and confusing attraction. It's as if the very essence of him is both repulsive and magnetic, drawing me in against my will.

Graduation approaches and the choices we make will determine our fate—whether bitter separation or a love that transcends the icy battleground we call home. Can Devon and I bridge the divide, or will life's forces tear us apart?

Eternal Ice (Book #4)

Coach Casey. A real piece of work. Rude, uptight—a complete jerk. It felt like nothing I did could ever please him. I was there to play hockey, not jump through hoops like a circus monkey in a suit. The way his mouth curled over his lips when he smiled? Hated it. The way he pushed me harder than ever before? Hated that too.

Then there was that one night we spent together, and suddenly my whole world was upside down. Hated it. Hated him. Yup, Coach Casey was a jerk, but weirdly, I think I might have just liked it. But let's be real, there was no way we could be anything more than enemies. He was my coach, after all, and I was so deep in the closet that I didn't even know where the door was.

Things took a turn for the worse when I found out Coach Casey wasn't exactly who he said he was. Our relationship was forbidden, and Casey's past threatened to unravel all of it. Would we survive? Or would we remain enemies, stuck between love and hatred on the eternal ice?

— • —

About the Author

J.M. Jackie is a writer who specializes in crafting dark and twisted novels, exploring complex human relationships and the darker side of love and desire. She enjoys drinking black coffee and taking long walks with her two large dogs for inspiration. While her writing can be intense, she aims to create stories that challenge readers to confront their own assumptions and beliefs while providing an escape into a richly imagined world of adventure, magic, and occasionally martial arts!